D0095283

# Pel and the Party Spirit

*Also by Mark Hebden*

Death set to music
Pel and the faceless corpse
Pel under pressure
Pel is puzzled
Pel and the staghound
Pel and the bombers
Pel and the predators
Pel and the pirates
Pel and the prowler
Pel and the Paris mob
Pel among the pueblos
Pel and the touch of pitch
Pel and the picture of innocence

# PEL AND THE PARTY SPIRIT

Mark Hebden

St. Martin's Press
New York

 For information, address St. Martin's Press, 175 Fifth Avenue, New York, N.Y. 10010.

Library of Congress Cataloging-in-Publication Data

Hebden, Mark.
Pel and the party spirit / Mark Hebden.
p. cm.
"A Thomas Dunne book."
ISBN 0-312-05491-2
I. Title.
PR6058.A6886P453 1991
823'.914—dc20 90-49303
CIP

First published in Great Britain by Constable & Company Ltd.

First U.S. Edition: January 1991
10 9 8 7 6 5 4 3 2 1

# Pel and the Party Spirit

# 1

The French summer holiday period, Evariste Clovis Désiré Pel decided, was a pain in the neck.

It started in effect on Bastille Day, that riotous celebration of the beginning of the French Revolution when the Paris mob had stormed the royal prison only to find, to their vast annoyance, that it was virtually empty. From the anniversary of that day, it went on, gradually gathering impetus, until the end of August when the nation came to its senses and felt in its pockets to realise with a shock just how much it had spent.

August was the month when you could get nothing done. It was the time of the party spirit, when shops, businesses and factories closed. Paris emptied into the countryside and on to the beaches. Families left the cities in dozens and for a few weeks took up residence in country retreats, beside the sea, in the forests, on the hills, by the lakes. It was the season when the country was invaded by British, Germans, Italians, Americans, Japanese, everybody under the sun, and when traditionally the police were hardest pressed.

Policemen had to have holidays like anybody else but, since they could hardly shut up shop like factories and businesses, half the time in August they were working at half-strength, half-throttle and half-enthusiasm, because it was invariably hot and policemen's feet ached like anybody else's.

The summer holiday was supposed to be a good time to be alive, a time when the sun was supposed to stream down like the glory of the Lord, lifting all hearts, blowing the mind and filling the soul with joy. This year it was different. Something had gone wrong and the winds weren't coming from the south as they should have done, but solidly from the east, bringing all the joy and warmth of the Russian steppes and thoughts of Napoleon's campaign of 1812. There were flurries of rain and clouds so low they looked as if you could reach up and grab a handful.

Not at all, Pel decided, what an ageing chief inspector of the Brigade Criminelle of the Police Judiciaire of the Republic of France ought to have to put up with. Especially when, as was the case at the moment, he was certain he was about to go down with a cold. Going down with a cold was par for the course for Pel. He *always* felt he was about to go down with a cold and very often did. He was, he thought, the only man in France who could go down with a cold in the middle of summer.

Life, he considered, was hard. Particularly just now. The wife he adored had disappeared into the blue. Not for good, thank God – just vanished to clear up the affairs of an elderly aunt in Provence. Madame Pel had relatives all over France – all apparently with bank accounts stuffed with gold, and all of them, since Madame Pel seemed to be the only member of the family not on the point of death, eager to leave her their money.

It was all part of a pattern, of course. Time and time again, during his courtship, Pel had found it difficult to get Madame Pel – the Widow Faivre-Perret as she had been then – to himself. When he wasn't being dragged away by police duties, she was being dragged away to attend sick beds, deaths and funerals, or to attend the reading of some will which invariably left her considerably richer than she had been. This, of course, was no end of an advantage to Pel because a policeman's salary never made for a life of sybaritic luxury.

Her wealth had relieved him of a lot of his worries, because she not only acquired money with ease – with the relatives she had, even without trying – she also knew what to do with it. She ran Nanette's, the most expensive hairdressing salon and boutique in the city, a place where they charged fees not prices yet which was so good clients burst into tears when they had to be refused an appointment. Pel had happily turned over to her his entire fortune – never something to rock her back on her heels, he had to admit – and allowed her to do what she thought best with it. She had already increased it considerably

– enough in fact for Pel's fears of a poverty-stricken old age to fly out of the window.

Although his bachelor days were over, however, at times they returned with a bang. And what a bang! Madame Pel occasionally had to attend conferences where people in her profession talked about how to acquire even more money, and she had to visit Paris, even London, once – for Pel a period of horror – New York. And when she did, Pel was left to the tender mercies once more of Madame Routy who had been his housekeeper in the days when they had shared a house in the Rue Martin-de-Noinville in the city. It had been a perfect battleground for the dislike that had always existed between them because Madame Routy, Pel considered, was the only bad cook in a nation of superb cooks. Her casseroles were usually so disgusting he had indulged in the practice of discovering at the last moment that he had to eat in the city so that she had been obliged to polish off her burnt offerings herself. Her chief joy had been the television, with the volume turned up from 'Loud' to 'Unbelievable', and she had sat regularly watching it while the kitchen filled with smoke.

Madame Pel had taken her on with Pel and, to his surprise, had made her a reformed character. When Madame Pel wasn't there to keep her under control, however, she returned at once to all her bad habits, as if she were trying to recoup some of the ill will she had wasted in being polite to Pel when his wife was around. It was something that bothered Pel because at that particular moment in the contest he felt he was behind on points.

He sniffed and looked across at his deputy, Inspector Daniel Darcy, who sat at the opposite side of his desk, casually smoking as he read through a report. Pel could never smoke casually. While Darcy was totally indifferent to the consequences, Pel suffered from a guilt complex and a certainty that he would drop dead any day with lung cancer, be riddled with asthma or at the very least drive his wife to divorce him because she could no longer stand him smelling like an old ashtray. He tried hard to stop the habit but he never managed it. He had once given up for at least five minutes, then the telephone had gone to announce that he was wanted at the scene of a particularly gory murder and that had been that.

At the moment he was discussing drugs with Sergeant de Troquereau who had been on the track of a drugs dealer for weeks. Information had arrived some time before from Marseilles, which, a major crossroads for all traffic into France, was also one of its major crime spots. They had learned that a large delivery was due, and De Troq' and Debray, one of the other sergeants, were watching every known pusher.

'There are no drugs on the streets at the moment, Patron,' De Troq' was saying. 'There have been. A lot more than for a long time, which seems to indicate that somebody's set up his stall in the area again. It's not glue sniffing or amphetamines. It's plain honest-to-God hard drugs.'

Pel eyed De Troq'. Like Pel, he was small for a policeman, which naturally made him one of Pel's favourites. He was also, in spite of being a cop, a baron. His family was supposed to be poverty-stricken but it didn't seem to make a lot of difference to De Troq'. He was always well dressed and drove a big car with a belt over the bonnet and headlights the size of a lighthouse. Pel liked having him on the team. Not only was his title enough to squash the snobbish people who looked down on an honest cop trying to make a living, it also made Pel feel he was running Interpol or something.

Furthermore, De Troq' was intelligent and had a great ability to fit his private life into the few gaps his work as a policeman left.

'Any leads?' Pel asked.

'There's a kid I'm watching. Name of Marceau. He's a painter at the Théâtre des Beaux Arts. He calls himself a stage manager but he's still only a painter. I think if I lean on him a little I can find out when the delivery's due.'

'You might get the local boys,' Pel warned. 'But, remember, it's the big boys we want. They're different. They drive Cadillacs, Rolls Royces and Mercs and have a screen of small fry in front of them – several, I expect – so nobody knows them. Then, if the little types are pulled in, they can say it was nothing to do with them. Stay with it. Use Brochard as well as Debray if you need to.'

As De Troq' left, Pel sat back, satisfied that he hadn't lit a cigarette for at least two hours. He didn't realise it but he was going to at any minute because at a place called Puyceldome, an ancient fortified town perched high on a hill to the north of where he was sitting, an English writer and his wife who had bought a property there for a summer residence had just discovered it contained a body which, it seemed, had been there for years.

'Perhaps', the writer's wife said, remembering that Puyceldome dated back to the Middle Ages, 'it's been there for centuries. That *would* be exciting.'

At about the time when this discovery was being made, another one was made just off the Route Nationale 6 in an area of thick woodland. It was another body and this time there was no question of it dating back several centuries because the car belonging to the dead man was standing there beside it.

Pel was just coming to the conclusion that, considering that France, indeed the whole world, was involved in a wave of crime with murders two a penny, rapes run-of-the-mill affairs, and muggings, beatings up and other anti-social events daily – even hourly – occurrences, perhaps things in their diocese were remarkably quiet. He didn't know it, but they weren't going to remain quiet for long.

The four events – the discovery of the body at Puyceldome, the murder (for murder it certainly was) in the wood alongside the N6, De Troq's interest in drugs, and the discussion he and Darcy were having – were in no way connected.

Not at first, anyway.

Puyceldome was an ancient town, one of the fortified *bastides* built across France in the days when the English, the Dukes of Burgundy and a variety of other predators were disputing with the king the right to rule his own country. It was four hundred odd metres above the plain, and in dull weather grim to look upon. It came into its own in the heat of the summer when its height turned the icy high altitude blasts that existed throughout the winter into breaths of cooling air across the heat-sodden plain, and the orange-brown stone glowed in the sunshine.

It contained one square and a whole labyrinth of narrow alley-like streets. Its buildings and houses were crooked, many of them built into what had once been the fortified walls. It had one hotel, situated in the only square, a place where the small boys of the little town liked to hold sessions of *le foot* on their way home from school because the arches round the square made splendid goalposts. In recent years the area had become popular with foreigners from more northern countries who fancied living where it was warm and the surroundings were quaint.

Such a pair were George and Ellen Briddon. When George Briddon had suddenly begun to make money his wife had decided to do something she had always wanted to do – live in the warm South where the moon was huge and the stars filled the sky. It was a romantic notion but she was of a romantic turn of mind and she had persuaded her husband to buy the property in Puyceldome. As they struggled to become part of the local scene, she fought to make the house more to her taste.

Because of the large stone head of a cat set above the door, the place was known to the locals as La Maison du Chat – The Cat House – a name that raised much laughter among visiting Americans. No one knew where the name came from but on the steep road up to Puyceldome there was a spot alongside a deep drop called Le Saut du Chat – The Cat's Jump – and it was assumed that at some time in the past somebody's cat had featured in the town's history.

The Briddons' house was one of the larger properties in Puyceldome and it had water laid on, with – when it didn't fail, as it often did – electricity. It had three floors, a magnificent view over the valley, a sizeable courtyard and, in the corner of the courtyard and attached to the house, a bricked-off circular turreted tower known as the Cat Tower, which Ellen Briddon liked to believe had once been a look-out tower. Since it looked out only on the square, this was most unlikely and, in fact, it had originally been placed there to contain a wide iron ladder – removed in the last century – which had enabled the third-floor attics to be reached by the maids who inhabited them. It was Ellen Briddon's idea to put in an iron staircase.

Being an author's wife with the same sort of lively imagination as her husband, she had a feeling she was going to look back into the past. She had heard rumours of the hidden treasure of one of the Dukes of Burgundy, of a man called Sauveté de Crespigny, who, it seemed, had been one of his generals and was not against sticking his hand into the Duke's till. There were also rumours of a woman immured for infidelity, even of the remains of a British prince captured during the Hundred Years War and held for ransom. Ellen Briddon wasn't fussy which it was, though a treasure would be nice. She even had an idea she might emulate her husband and write a book about it and she dearly longed for something interesting. She didn't know it but that was exactly what she was going to get – though not in quite the form she hoped.

She had already made a start by employing one Bernard Buffel, a very old man who was a bricklayer, stonemason and carpenter combined, and whose labour, because of his age, came cheaply. As he chipped away at the old stonework at the top of the tower, Bernard Buffel could see into the square. He was tackling the job from the top because he felt that if he tackled it from the bottom the tower would collapse in a heap on him. From his ladder he noticed men putting up flags. At the end of the month the 730th anniversary of the founding of Puyceldome was to be celebrated. Since the 700th anniversary had been celebrated thirty years before, there was no real cause to celebrate again, but with the building of a new road to the south nearby, there had been an influx of tourists in recent years and the Maire and the elders of the town had decided that a fresh celebration might draw attention to Puyceldome as a tourist attraction, put money in the tills of the shops and find work for the few people who had none. It might even sell a couple more of the ancient properties in the area.

There was to be a week of *son et lumière*, fireworks, musical performances by children from the school, folk dancing by young people – a difficult one, this, because folk dancing had long gone out of fashion and few knew how to do it – and a medieval evening in the square. A company of players had been hired but, because Puyceldome was not very big or well endowed with money, it was of necessity a small company, poverty-stricken and on its beam ends, and consisted of no more than seven actors – four young men and three girls; and of these one couple had already departed, the set of their shoulders indicating indignation and high dudgeon.

Bernard Buffel, known in Puyceldome as Le Bernard because of his age, chipped away at the stonework of the tower, none too happy with the job because the wind that came from the east was cold. With the square of Puyceldome four hundred metres above the plain, the cold was colder than anywhere else and the wind was biting, while, on top of the ladder and unprotected by other buildings, Le Bernard felt it piercing his old bones and doing them no good at all.

Nevertheless, he wasn't unhappy. Despite his age, he was no fool and he had persuaded the Briddons that they should take part in the festivities planned for August by hanging out a flag. For this, naturally, they would need a flag-pole at the top of the tower but, of course, for this the tower would need some bracing as the pointing had all fallen out.

Anxious to be part of the town they had made their home, they had agreed and Le Bernard could see himself in a comfortable job for some time to come. He had warned the Briddons that he would have to do what he called 'investigative masonry' and his stay was already costing them far more than they had expected.

He knew exactly what he was doing, of course, because he knew the tower well. He knew every inch of it because he had worked on it at various periods in his career when the owner at the time, alarmed that it was in danger of falling down, had been obliged to have it repaired. He had worked on it originally as an apprentice employed by his father, and thirty years before he had put a patch on a hole which had appeared at the top near the roof. On that occasion he had bricked up the vents which had been let into the tower to allow light inside, because the then owner had complained that the local urchins spent a large part of their spare time trying to throw bricks and cans through them.

By this time, he had opened a hole almost big enough to get through. That done, he could somehow manoeuvre a ladder through and get inside out of the wind. He didn't fancy that particularly, though, because – according to what he had learned from the local librarian – although there had once been a ladder inside the tower, he certainly couldn't imagine much else because it was far too narrow. God alone knew, in fact, what he might find. What he did find certainly wasn't what he expected.

As the hole grew large enough to climb through he descended the ladder to the courtyard and called on his assistant, a boy of seventeen, his grandson also called Bernard Buffel. His father, the old man's son and another Bernard, had been known as Bernard Buffel Bis, but, since he had run off with a woman from Goillac some years before and had never been seen since, his son had inherited the appellation and was now also known as Bernard Buffel Bis, sometimes even as Bernard Buffel Bis Bravo. He was a tall thin boy who worked none too willingly for his grandfather. He now started to climb the ladder.

'Take the torch,' Le Bernard said. 'There are some stones going down inside where the old ladder was attached, so there are plenty of footholds and it's narrow enough to brace yourself with your back against the opposite walls. I expect you'll find all sorts of rubbish in there because when I was a boy there were vents in the wall and people used to chuck things in. Old papers. Lunch wrappings. Bottles. Used French letters. Dead cats.'

Bernard Buffel Bis eyed his grandfather sideways. 'And then what?' he asked. 'When I get inside, I mean.'

'Report on what you see. So we'll know how to tackle it.'

'All I'll see in there will be darkness.' Bernard Buffel Bis was growing too big for his boots.

The boy climbed the ladder and, disappearing from sight through the hole Le Bernard had made, began to descend like a climber descending a natural rock chimney, using his back against one side and his feet against the other. Unfortunately, he was a big boy and strong and the stones of the tower were no longer very secure in their places. A thrusting foot dislodged one of them. Le Bernard saw it move.

'Come out!' he screamed. 'It's going to fall down!'

His eyes wild, the boy's head emerged and he started to climb through the hole just as the stone he had moved fell out. As it fell, it allowed another stone, which it had supported, to move also. As that one fell, so did another. Almost with a sigh, the side of the tower began to crumble. Le Bernard and the boy managed to scramble clear just in time, knocking Ellen Briddon, who had come to see what the shouting was about, flying as they did so. They had just got clear when one side of the tower subsided gracefully – gently almost – into the courtyard. The stones stopped rolling and the tiles stopped crashing, the last timbers of the turreted roof fell and the dust began to settle. By the grace of God nobody had been hurt but what had been a round slim tower was now only half a round slim tower. All down one side it was open to the elements and it was obvious to Le Bernard and to Ellen Briddon that what was left would need shoring up or that would fall too.

Then Bernard Buffel Bis noticed something lying under the wreckage that had fallen inside the tower. It was a boot – an old boot, dry, grey and dusty, the nails in the sole red with rust. Then he noticed the end of a trouser leg. It was faded but was still blue enough to be identified as part of a workman's overall. And inside the leg of the overall progressing into the boot, he could see what looked like an old brown bone. But it wasn't bone. It was ancient dried skin, dark with age.

'That's a man,' he whispered, awed.

Le Bernard picked himself up, stared at the dusty object lying among the wreckage, studied it for a moment or two, then directed an angry glare at his grandson.

'Now look what you've done,' he said.

# 2

At just about the time Le Bernard was clambering among the wreckage of the Cat Tower for a better look at what they had unearthed, about a hundred and fifty kilometres away at the southern border of the province, a car pulled off the route Nationale 6 on to a side road that led to a stretch of woodland which the driver decided would make a good spot to have a picnic.

His name was Alexandre Méline and he was manager of a private estate well to the north, in Alsace.

He was heading south to see his mother who lived in the Auvergne and, since he hadn't seen his family for several years, he was in high spirits. His car was a small Renault but, despite its size, he had made very good time. Méline was a happy man. He worked for a man who owned several thousand hectares of forestland which it was Méline's job to control. The trees were cut down in two and three-hectare areas at a time and used for telegraph poles and pit props, and the ground replanted so that, by the time they had worked through the whole estate, the newly-planted trees had grown to their full height again and were once more ready for cutting.

It was a profitable business but Méline had a feeling that the man who followed him as manager would find things very different when he took over. Already in France telegraph poles were being made of reinforced concrete, which lasted better, and pit props were no longer of wood but of steel and could be jacked up so there was no need for wedges to give stability. The telegraph poles and pit props that Alexandre Méline tended were already being sold chiefly to Third World countries whose telephone systems were cruder than in Europe and whose mining techniques had not yet caught up with those of the West.

At that moment, though, Méline was untroubled by such pessimistic thoughts. By the time it began to affect French forests, he felt, he would be retired to some tidy little bungalow near his mother in the Auvergne with nothing to do but cultivate a garden and play boules and dominoes with his friends in the bronze-yellow sunshine of the evening.

On the way south he had passed several groups of hitch-hikers. With the holiday period in full swing, half France was on the road. Most of the hitch-hikers were youngsters, mostly male, of university age. Like all university students, they were always going somewhere. To Alexandre Méline it seemed to be a very restless age. Some of the hitch-hikers were girls and some of them, he noticed, were very pretty, bronzed, and attractive. Méline didn't stop for them. He was unmarried and might have been tempted, but a friend of his had once had a bad fright when a girl he had picked up had accused him of rape. Fortunately for Méline's friend, she was known to the police and her racket was to accuse people who picked her up and threaten blackmail unless they paid for her silence. From that day, however, Méline had kept well clear of hitch-hikers, especially as things had changed a lot since then and some of the girls these days were making it quite plain that they would not be unapproachable to suggestions. Méline knew of men who had picked up girls and had sex with them, but he preferred to keep clear of them.

Picking a little side road, he turned in among the trees and began to prepare for his picnic. Méline's picnic didn't consist merely of sandwiches. He had provided himself with food from the delicatessen in the village where he lived – sausage, cold meats, salads, hard-boiled eggs, pickled herrings. He was a big man and liked solid meals. There was no wine, however. The police were strict since President Pompidou had tried to cut down on French drinking habits, and he preferred just a small bottle of beer. Wine could be dangerous stuff to drink at lunch time when you were driving, especially when you were heading south. The sun through the windscreen could be a great soporific and Méline had had a friend who had fallen asleep under its influence and hit a lorry. Méline had a lot of friends and he liked to regulate his life by their errors.

The area was heavily forested and he approved of the way it was kept. He had driven down what appeared to be a working road used by Burgundian foresters as they thinned, cut down and replanted. The road continued for two or three hundred metres, turning first one way then the other, then debouched into an open glade around fifty to eighty metres across.

The glade was covered with crisp green grass dotted with anemones and young foxgloves and around him were acacia, oaks and ash very different from the tall pines of Alsace where he worked. The early afternoon sun was streaming down and he could see the bright rays coming through the trees in golden shafts, like the light entering a cathedral.

'Perfect,' he said. It was just what he wanted. Since he did it every day of his life, he was used to eating his lunch in the open air among the trees. Eating his lunch with someone else was something he wasn't used to.

He was just settling back to enjoy himself when he realised he wasn't alone after all. Beyond a clump of bushes he could see another car. It was a large and expensive Japanese Honda – a car that was becoming increasingly popular in France – but he couldn't see the owner and decided that perhaps he was with a girl and had disappeared into the undergrowth with her for a short session of fun and games. Then he saw him. He was just beyond the car, lying on his back. There was no one else visible and Méline decided his guess was wrong and, instead, the driver of the other car was having his afternoon nap. Perhaps he had had a drink or two and had wisely decided to sleep it off before proceeding.

Preferring to take his lunch alone, Méline pushed his folding chair and his lunch and his bottle of beer back into his car and prepared to drive off and find somewhere else. As he turned the car, however, a bird appeared through the trees, sweeping across the open space in a long glide. He recognised it at once as a carrion crow. Noted as an egg thief, it had always been on the black lists of gamekeepers and foresters and he distinguished it at once by its broad wings and slow wing beat.

What happened next startled him, however. To his surprise, it headed directly for the man lying on the ground. That in itself puzzled him. He knew the habits of most birds and forest animals and he knew the crow to be a timid creature. Then, again to his surprise, he saw the bird land on the prostrate man's chest and take two or three lurching steps forward until it was staring straight into his face. The man didn't move. To Méline's horror, the crow started pecking and he realised it was pecking at the man's eye.

Immediately it dawned on him that something was wrong and, taking a more careful look, he noticed that as the bird had landed a loud humming noise had started. He knew at once what it was because he had heard it before in the forests of Alsace near the decomposing bodies of dead deer. It was made by flies and it was there, like the carrion crow, because the man lying on the ground beyond the bushes was dead.

For a moment Méline considered going to see if there were anything he could do. But even as he did so another crow landed on the figure beyond the bushes and he guessed he would be wasting his energy because, judging by the crows and the number of blowflies, the man must have been dead for some time and it was his job to inform the authorities.

As Alexandre Méline was swinging his car round and shooting off to find a policeman, Chief Inspector Pel and Inspector Darcy were still considering the state of play in the continuing contest between the Brigade Criminelle of the Police Judiciaire and the criminal fraternity in their area.

Pel had been fishing the day before. His wife encouraged him to go fishing as a means of relaxation. Occasionally, she even accompanied him. He didn't for a moment imagine she enjoyed it but it was an indication of her loyalty that she was prepared to endure the boredom, the midges and the hot sun so that Pel could have his relaxation in his little paradise by the River Orche. No French paradise was complete without a stream and fish.

'I wish I hadn't needed to smoke, though,' he said to Darcy. 'But Geneviève's in Marseilles and it runs away with me.'

Darcy looked up. 'Holiday?' he asked.

'No. An aunt dropped dead. She was playing tennis. She was seventy.'

'She deserved to drop dead, playing tennis at that age.'

'Geneviève'll come into money.'

'She always does, Patron. And very nice, too.' There was no envy in Darcy's words because he had a great admiration for Madame Pel.

'It reduces the necessity of not going home smelling like an ashtray,' Pel said gloomily. 'When I know she's not around, I'm tempted to light another.' He sighed. 'I'm easily tempted.'

'You should take fresh air,' Darcy suggested. 'How about jogging?'

Pel gave him a shocked look. All he conceded in the way of exercise was a quiet afternoon's fishing or a stiff game of boules. 'All the same,' he admitted, 'I ought to do something to make me stop.'

'You could have your lungs filled with concrete. That ought to do it. Mind you, it wouldn't be very good for your breathing.'

Pel scowled, his fragile good temper gone with the wind. There was only one person allowed to use sarcasm in his department, only one wit, and that was Pel. Seeing he wasn't going to get much sympathy, he hurriedly changed the subject and decided to go through the members of his department to make sure they were all toeing the line, keeping their noses to the grindstone and their eyes on the ball.

'What have we on the books?' he asked.

'Sheep stealing. Up on the hills in the north. The farmers are getting worried.'

'Put Brochard on to it.'

'He's on holiday.'

'He'll come back. He's a farmer's son. He ought to know what to do.'

'He'll certainly be better than Misset,' Darcy said. 'Misset wouldn't know the difference between a sheep and an orang-utan.'

Misset was the problem in Pel's team. Blessed with fading good looks and eyes that didn't see as well as they had, he tried to hide his dwindling attraction with dark spectacles so that he could look like a danger to crooks and a threat to women.

'Anything else?'

'A break-in at the supermarket at Talant.'

'There are always break-ins at the supermarket at Talant,' Pel complained. 'We ought to have it sealed with plastic. Don't they do it with ships? Moth-balling, they call it, don't they?'

'It would reduce business a bit,' Darcy grinned. 'I've given it to Lecocq. There was also a break-in at the warehouse of the Wine Co-operative at Vauors. Bardolle got the guy who did it.'

'Escaping?'

'No, drunk. He's been up before the beaks before.'

'That the lot?'

'Nosjean's working on another suspected art fraud. He thinks this time the picture's genuine. He's becoming quite an expert. It's that girl, Mijo Lehmann, he's living with. She works at the Galeries Lafayette. She's a useful ex-officio member of the department.'

'That the lot?'

Darcy paused. 'Not quite,' he said. 'Cadet Darras.'

Pel looked up. Cadet Darras was one of his personal recruits. Like the British admiral in the last century who had gone round with his pockets full of acorns to plant for oak trees for the future wooden walls of the Navy, Pel worked assiduously for the police force. Didier Darras was the nephew of Madame Routy, Pel's housekeeper. With his grandfather failing in health, his mother had been permanently occupied and Didier Darras had often found himself calling on his aunt for meals. Being a bit on the mean side, Pel might have been indignant at feeding waifs and strays but, as it happened, he got on well with small boys and Didier Darras, like Pel, enjoyed boules and fishing and had been a good ally for Pel in his constant warfare with Madame Routy.

It had been Pel who had recruited him for the police and he now worked as a cadet in the Hôtel de Police, running the errands and fetching the beer and sandwiches.

'What about Didier Darras?' he asked.

'He's got something on his mind.'

'Well, I know his mother often had to leave him on his own

resources. But his grandfather died recently, so life's surely a bit easier. He used to visit us occasionally, as you know. He seemed to like to talk to me.' Pel looked puzzled, as if he couldn't understand why anyone would want to talk to him. 'But he's not been round lately. It must be Madame Routy's cooking that puts him off.'

'It's not that,' Darcy said.

'What then?'

'It's his love life.'

Pel sniffed. He didn't think much of love lives. Though everything was now happily in order, up to his marriage his own love life had been very simple. There hadn't been one. As a young man he had begun to think he would grow old with stringy buttocks before he experienced the pleasures of the flesh. It was his name, he felt. Individually, Evariste was all right. Clovis was acceptable. Désiré was just about bearable. Together, however, they were enough to make a man worry rats. His wife had solved the problem by addressing him simply as 'Pel'.

He looked at Darcy. 'What's the trouble?' he asked.

'Officer Martin,' Darcy said with a grin. 'The cadet whose place he took. He's on the street now. He's a good-looking type too. I gather he's just got engaged to that girl, Louise Bray, Didier went around with.'

Pel sighed. He knew all about Didier Darras's love life. He had listened to it from the days when Didier Darras was thirteen years old. He had regarded Louise Bray as *his* girl from the time when she had been in the habit of hitting him over the head with her dolls.

'What's happened to him?' he asked.

'He's gone sour.'

'With the police?'

'He's lost interest.'

'He was pretty keen.'

'Well, he isn't any longer.'

'I'll have a word with him.'

Pel was just wondering if he could slip out for a beer, when Claudie Darel, the only female member of his squad, appeared. Pel smiled. Or at least his face changed gear to what *passed* as a smile. He didn't smile easily and it made him feel strange, but everybody smiled when Claudie appeared. She looked like a rejuvenated Mireille Mathieu and, despite the fact that she was practically engaged to a barrister from the Palais de Justice, half the department was still in love with her.

'What's the trouble?' Pel asked, on his best behaviour immediately.

'A body's the trouble, Patron,' Claudie said. 'At Puyceldome.'

'What sort of body? Accident? Murder? Manslaughter?'

'Nobody seems very sure, Patron. It was found walled up in a tower.'

'Walled up in a what?'

'A tower, Patron.'

'I thought people stopped doing things like that in the seventeenth century.'

Claudie smiled. 'Perhaps they did, Patron,' she said. 'It certainly seems to have been there a long time. It seems to be a skeleton.'

# 3

Jean-Pierre Marceau, the painter, De Troq's contact at the Théâtre des Beaux Arts, was surprised when De Troq' sat down opposite him in the shabby little restaurant where he ate his meals. He looked at De Troq' uneasily, guessing why he was there but uncertain what was going to happen.

De Troq' said nothing. He ordered an omelette and a carafe of wine and simply sat there. With his neat frame, his air of arrogance, his well-cut clothes, his silence, he posed a threat without doing anything.

After a while he lifted his head. 'Hello,' he said. 'It's Jean-Pierre Marceau, isn't it?'

The painter nodded, keeping his eyes on his plate. 'Yes,' he said.

'We met in the theatre, didn't we? That time when I was asking about hard drugs.'

'Yes.'

'You were on them. You're still on them, I reckon. Am I right?'

'Yes.'

'You know – ' De Troq' was friendly and bland. ' – I think we need a talk.'

The boy from the theatre looked nervous. 'I know nothing,' he said.

'I bet you do. I want names.'

'I can't give you names.'

'Who do you get it from?'

'I can't tell you.'

'You prefer to go to prison?'

'It's the pushers you're after,' Marceau bleated. 'You can't send me to prison for using the stuff.'

'No, but you can always go to prison under Section 63 of the Penal Code. Non-assistance to a person in danger. Withholding information from the police means that all those kids who're on drugs are put at risk – persons in danger. Thought about that?'

Marceau looked worried. 'I can't tell you. You know what that lot do to informers.'

'I know what the magistrates do to people who withhold information. Where does it come from?'

'The south. North Africa, I suppose.'

'How?'

'In a lorry, I heard. One end's blocked off. It's in there.'

'Whose lorry?'

'I don't know.'

'Who runs the operation?'

'I can't tell you. I don't know.'

'How did you get into it?'

The boy scowled then the scowl faded and he sighed. 'I was at art school,' he said. 'But I wanted to be an actor. I always did. But they said I was no good. I even offered to work for nothing, I was so keen, but they still turned me down. In the end, I got a job as an assistant stage manager. Looking after props. Handing out the bouquet to the hero when he went on stage, to give to the heroine. Making sure Cyrano's nose was on straight and his sword wasn't stuck in the scabbard. Then I got a job as a scene painter. But no acting. I got depressed and then I was offered this dope.'

'Who by?'

'His name's Sammy le Rapide. Speedy Sam.'

'Why?'

'He wears running pumps for a quick getaway.'

'Sounds sense. What's his real name?'

'I don't know.'

'Where do I find him?'

'I can't tell you.'

'Where do you pick up your fixes?'

'I can't tell you that either. It's always different.'

'So how do you know where to be?'

'The word gets around.'

'And when is it to be?'

'I heard tonight. But I'm not certain. I expect I'll hear.'

De Troq' shrugged and became silent. Finishing his omelette, he placed money under his plate to pay for the meal, smiled at Marceau, rose and left. Marceau sat in baffled, frustrated silence for a while, furiously smoking a cigarette, then, flinging down a note, he rose, too, and strode out of the restaurant.

Just as De Troq' was stationing himself in a doorway across the road to watch Marceau leave the restaurant, Pel was arriving with Darcy in Puyceldome.

As they approached, the sun came out unexpectedly, picking up the colours of the ancient stone so that the old fortress-town stood up out of the plain like a huge pink wedding cake. It was broad-based and tapered to a point, so that the rooftops seemed to stand on other rooftops all the way up to the summit, the very peak, where the tower of the church clawed at the sky.

Turning off the main highway on to the winding road up the hill, Darcy's car crossed a bridge over the river and began to climb so steeply it made Pel feel they were going to topple backwards. More turns followed, then the road ran along a ridge of hillside like the backbone of some giant animal. The turrets of Puyceldome appeared above them as if about to fall on them; there were more turns alongside a deep drop – The Cat's Jump, Darcy said – then it ran up in a steep rise to the walls of the town and between tall narrow buildings, to debouch into the main square of the town, a surprisingly large space with a decorated well in the centre and surrounded by ancient buildings whose ground floors contained small shops tucked under an arcade supported by weathered stone pillars. As Darcy drew the car to a halt, Pel drew a deep breath, grateful to have arrived.

Seen more closely, the illusion of a wedding cake was shattered. The buildings were old and many of them were tumbledown. Here and there were square gaping holes where windows had disappeared. Other windows had been bricked up. A few of the roofs over the ramparts, so positioned that they were too difficult or too expensive to repair, sagged heavily and occasionally a wall was propped up by huge beams. At a distance, Puyceldome was magnificent. Close to, it looked its age.

But, unlike so many *bastides*, it was a living town, far from dependent on its gifte shoppes, restaurants and an odd establishment dedicated to not very skilful weaving or pottery. Puyceldome was a thriving town, on the main road from Dijon to Goillac, and was the centre of a farming community, many of its inhabitants commuting daily to Goillac for work.

The fact that the nation was on holiday was immediately apparent. In August, in every town that might attract holiday-makers – and in a lot of them that certainly would not – the party spirit had taken over. Loudspeakers were braying a day-long broadcast of pop music, while the presenters – usually the nearest supermarket after publicity – paid disc jockeys to keep up a non-stop run of jokes and laughter between the jingles advertising their wares. In the countryside, villages arranged communal get-togethers in the form of vast barbecues, *sardinages*, suppers, dancing, fairs, discos, pig runnings, giant cassoulets.

Puyceldome was no different. The umbrella-shaded tables outside the bar of the hotel were full of people, and men were hanging long red-and-white banners from the old buildings. The notice-board outside the tourist office under the arcades was plastered with notices of dances and pageants in the villages around. Only the cars were tucked out of sight, stuffed with difficulty into small open spaces down the backstreets because the elders of the town had wisely seen the danger of their small, cramped and very beautiful centre becoming invisible behind a barrier of tourists' vehicles.

The owners of the house where Le Bernard had found the body weren't very impressed with Pel. They had expected someone tall and handsome who looked like a young Laurence Olivier or perhaps J.R. from *Dallas*.

'Is he really a policeman?' Ellen Briddon asked Darcy. She was a lot younger than her husband, blonde, shapely and very sexy.

Darcy grinned. 'He is, madame,' he said. 'And one of the best there is.'

'He doesn't look much like one.'

'That's his strength, madame. It gives the criminals a sense of false security. They think he's the man who's come to mend the lavatory.'

She wasn't sure whether Darcy was pulling her leg or not and she took another look at Pel. He certainly didn't seem very impressive with his short stature, hair that looked like seaweed draped across a rock, and spectacles pushed up on his forehead. She had a feeling that Darcy, with his good looks, his smart suit, and the splendid white teeth which shone like the jewels in a Disney cartoon, would be a much better policeman. Especially looking as he did now, with his profile in top gear for her benefit.

At that moment she was low in spirits and a little depressed. Her husband, who was considerably older than she was and had never been as enthusiastic about the house at Puyceldome, was in a bad temper and was complaining that he'd never wanted to live there anyway.

'And now the tower's collapsed,' he had growled. 'It's going to cost a fortune to restore it. We should never have bought the bloody place.'

Doc Minet, the police doctor, had already arrived and was conferring with Dr Mercier, the man who had been called by Le Bernard to inspect his discovery. Dr Mercier was, in fact, a psychiatrist from Goillac who happened to have a weekend residence in Puyceldome, but he was also a qualified medical man, and his conclusions were exactly the same as Doc Minet's. Le Bernard's discovery had been dead so long there was no great hurry.

'Could it be medieval?' Ellen Briddon was asking hopefully. Her husband had stamped off in a temper and she hadn't a lot of friends in the area – it was different from Surbiton where she came from and she was hoping to collect a few more when the news spread.

'I don't think so, madame,' Pel said.

'Older than that? Didn't George II – before he became King of England, of course, when he was Elector of Hanover – wall up his wife's lover? He locked *her* up, too, for the rest of her life, didn't he? They made a film about it.'

'I don't think it's as old as that,' Doc Minet interposed. 'There's a newspaper underneath him – *Le Bien Public*, which is published locally – and I don't think they had newspapers round here as long ago as that. Certainly not *Le Bien Public*.'

'Perhaps there are other bodies,' Mrs Briddon offered. 'They say Puyceldome's honeycombed with passages. They run everywhere into the rock of the hillside. They used them for prisoners, or for keeping stores against a siege. Things like that. I was told there was a ghost.'

Pel looked at Darcy who recognised the sign. Pel wasn't used to attractive foreign ladies getting in the way but he was too polite to shunt her off. Darcy did the necessary.

'I think one of my men ought to have your version of the business, madame,' he said. 'Sergeant Aimedieu here will take a statement if you'll be so kind.'

Mrs Briddon was delighted and allowed herself to be taken in hand. She looked at Aimedieu. He was young and good-looking and had a face as innocent as a choir-boy's.

'Perhaps we ought to go into the house,' she said. 'Would you like a cup of coffee or a beer or something?'

Aimedieu had known Pel long enough now to have recognised the signs as well as Darcy and was willing to stretch the interview as far as possible. 'A coffee would be excellent, madame,' he said.

Pel watched them go and turned thankfully back to Doc Minet. 'Go on,' he said. 'Inform me.'

'Well, we'll need to look more closely at him,' Doc Minet said, 'before I can be certain of anything. But I can say straight away that, judging by his clothes, he died more than twenty years ago.'

Pel scowled. When people were found dead, he reckoned that if they could get on to things within an hour or two they had a reasonable chance of finding out what had happened. Months – even days – later, people forgot what they'd seen and how things had appeared. Most people didn't see things, anyway. Most people could sit next to Brigitte Bardot or a man with a loaded shotgun without noticing. A year later they couldn't even remember being there. Twenty to thirty years was beyond the pale. Half the witnesses would have died themselves by then, anyway.

Doc Minet gestured. 'For what it's worth,' he said, 'since our friend didn't die last night there's no point worrying about rigor mortis. That disappeared years ago. I assume there was air getting into that place and, with the heat here in the summer, he's dried out until he's virtually mummified. Flies have been at work on him, of course, and what's left is just bones with the skin round them. We might find more when we examine him properly, but that's the way it looks.'

'Anything more you can tell us?'

'Big guy,' Doc Minet said. 'Probably a fat one, too. He seems to be wearing overalls so he certainly wasn't put there when the tower was built. Perhaps we can find something on him that might help to identify him.'

Pel stared at the wreckage of the tower. 'So how does he come to be bricked up in there?' he asked. 'He obviously wouldn't brick himself in.'

Minet smiled. 'You're asking something,' he said. 'I'll need a little more time to answer that.'

'Is his neck broken? Is his skull smashed in? That would be murder, wouldn't it?'

Minet smiled at Pel's impatience. He was older and fatter than Pel and inclined to move more slowly. 'There are no obvious wounds,' he said. 'But that doesn't mean there aren't any. After twenty-odd years it would be difficult to spot them at first go. But there appear to be no smashed limbs, no broken neck, no crushed skull. I'll tell you better when I've had him out on the slab.' Minet shrugged. 'On the other hand, I think he must have been *put* in there. He certainly didn't wall himself in because, quite apart from the fact that it's not something that people usually do, there appear to be no tools in there. No trowel. No sign of old cement.'

'Then it *must* have been murder.'

'Unless it was an accident and somebody was frightened enough to prefer to keep quiet about it and walled him up so he wouldn't be found.'

Pel's frown deepened. 'I think', he said slowly, 'that we need to know what was happening round here about that time. Can we find a mason, Daniel, who can tell us something about this place? Perhaps also a historian. There must be one. This sort of place always has some Nosy Parker who knows what happened fifty years ago.'

As it happened, their historian was right there beside them. Nobody knew more about Puyceldome than Le Bernard. At some time or other he had probably worked on every building in the little town. But he was still a little shocked – not by the collapse of the tower, or even by the discovery of the body, but by the fact that here was something he had known nothing about.

'How did they get him in?' he asked. 'There's been no entrance to the tower for around fifty years.'

'*Somebody* got him in,' Darcy pointed out.

Le Bernard had no doubt about that. 'He looks to me as if he's been there a long time,' he agreed.

'When was that tower last opened?' Pel asked.

'Well, thirty-odd years ago,' Le Bernard said, 'Lucie Croissard, who owned the place, fancied putting a staircase in – everybody who buys the shitty place seems to want to put a staircase in. But she didn't. The type she chose to do it told her that if she wasn't careful the tower would collapse.'

'It seems he was right,' Darcy commented drily.

'Thirty years ago,' Pel said. 'Let's say, in fact, 1959. Who had the house then?'

'Lucie Croissard. But about 1959 she bought a smaller house and let this one to a couple of youngsters. But they left and she decided to sell. I reckon she was glad to be shot of it. It was bought by a type from the south. He didn't stay long. Name of Callin or Caillas or something. I forget his name. They got me to block up a hole at the top of the tower. He'd tried to open it. For a staircase, they said. The usual. He didn't want a special job. Just a patch. That's what they got. You can see it. He also got me to fill up the vents at the top of the tower. I did. You can see where I did it. I wondered why, and decided they'd buried all their rubbish in there. The refuse collectors were on strike at the time and people were getting desperate, so I thought that was what it was.'

Le Bernard lit a cigarette. Inevitably it set Pel off and he lit one, too.

'It was a hot summer, that one,' Le Bernard said. 'There was a plague of flies in Puyceldome.'

Well, there would be, wouldn't there, Pel thought. With a body disintegrating in the tower. The blowflies would find it without any trouble – they always did – and they'd breed in their millions. It ought to have drawn attention to the body, in fact. But no one would notice the smell because the tower was tall and narrow and would act like the vent of a drain, carrying the smell high up above everyone's head to where it would be borne away by the breeze that blew almost permanently across the town.

Le Bernard looked at the body under the tarpaulin he had provided. 'I reckon it was *him*,' he said.

Pel reckoned it was, too.

'Go on,' he said. 'Inform me. After the type from the south – who came next?'

Le Bernard drew a deep breath. 'Type called Poulex,' he said. 'But he didn't stay long and it was bought by an American called Keitzer. But he never seemed to be here. He was a film director or something and was always somewhere else. Eventually, he went back to America. After that it was a chap from Paris called Duclose. He wanted a weekend house, but he only came in the summer months and then not often. He died. After him – ' he nodded towards the house. ' – this lot.'

'So about the time our friend was put in there it was owned by this Caillas or this Poulex?'

'I reckon so.'

'Why did Poulex sell?'

'He wanted to do things. One of them was to open the tower. But his bricklayer informed him when he started work that if he went any further it would collapse. He sold the place soon after. He was only here about five years.'

'Who was this bricklayer?'

Sous-Brigadier Lefêvre, the guardian of Puyceldome's morals, a stiff-faced policeman not noted for his sense of humour, answered.

'Type called Lupin, sir. Came from St Valéry-le-Grand.'

'Make a note to see him, Daniel.'

Old Le Bernard grinned. 'You'll have a job,' he said.

'Why?'

'He went to live in America. Did very well for himself, too. His son, who used to chase my daughter, sent a photograph of where they live. It's in California. Swimming pool and everything. Suggested she went out and married him. She didn't fancy it. He was a bit flash. She married an estate agent from Goillac instead. She's got three kids. They're growing up now and she's started work again – as a computer operator – and – '

'Hang on,' Darcy said. 'Hang on! This chap who went to America. What's his full name?'

'Lorick Lupin.'

'Any relations round here?'

'There might still be some in St Valéry.'

'What happened exactly? Why did he emigrate?'

'I dunno. He was working on the tower and when he told Poulex it would collapse if he continued, Poulex told him to brick up the hole he'd made and leave it. He said he'd have one more try – from the bottom – and he took out a few stones and got inside to make an inspection. Then he put them back, told Poulex it wouldn't work and left. He warned Poulex the tower was best left alone. He said he'd made it safe. He even worked late one night, I remember. That was the last we saw of him. He moved from St. Valéry to Arne and soon afterwards he went to America.'

Pel stared at the tarpaulin-covered sheet as if he were trying to see through it.

'This Lucie Croissard,' he said. 'What can you tell us about her?'

'She's from here. Lived across the square for a while. She was Lucie Suley then. She married Henri Croissard – also from here – and they lived in The Cat House. When he died and her family married and left home, she decided the place was too big for her and the winters up here too cold. So she bought a house in the valley and sold this place. In the end it came to these people.' There was a faint contempt in Le Bernard's tone, as if foreigners like the Briddons were beyond the pale. 'Now they've decided to do the same thing. And it *has* collapsed.'

'So who's he? Pel indicated the shape under the tarpaulin. 'Could he be this type, Lupin?'

'Shouldn't think so.' Le Bernard shook his head. 'He's got big feet. In fact, he looks to me like a big man. Loro Lupin was a little guy.'

'So who *is* he? He must have been there when your friend Lupin got inside the tower. It hasn't been opened since until now, has it?'

'No.'

'Perhaps that's why Lupin packed it up so suddenly, Patron,' Darcy suggested. 'Perhaps he found our friend here.'

'So why didn't he report him to the police?' Pel asked, his policeman's nose twitching. 'There's something here that smells a bit, Daniel. Something isn't right. I think we need to see this Madame Croissard.' He turned to Le Bernard. 'Is she still alive?'

'Lives with her daughter in Goillac. Last I heard she was still around. Try the bar. I think they're some relation.'

The owner of the bar in the square had already heard of the discovery in the old tower and was enjoying the notoriety he had acquired as the relation of a previous owner. Half a dozen men were hanging over the zinc listening to him. They moved aside to allow the policemen to approach.

'You're the cops, aren't you?' the man at the bar said.

'We are,' Darcy admitted. 'Chief Inspector Pel. Inspector Darcy.'

'I'm Marc Plessis.' The landlord pushed forward two glasses and a bottle of red wine. 'Better wet your whistles. I expect you're dry from asking questions.'

'We've got a few more,' Pel said, reaching for his glass. 'About Madame Croissard, for instance.'

'My wife's aunt,' the landlord said. 'Lives in Goillac. She's eighty-three.'

'Address?'

'Anny!' Plessis turned and bellowed into the kitchen. His

wife appeared at once, flour on her apron and wiping her hands on a kitchen towel. Her husband gestured at Pel and Darcy.

'Police,' he said by way of introduction. 'They want Aunt Lucie's address.'

'Why?'

'Better ask them.'

'We'd like to ask her a few questions about the tower,' Darcy explained. 'You'll have heard a man was found in there. Dead.'

'She didn't do it,' Madame Plessis said.

'We don't imagine she did. But she was the owner around the time he was put in there.'

'She lives in Goillac.'

'We'd like to know where.'

'It's down by the river. She lives with my cousin these days. She says it's too cold up here in winter for her. She won't even come and visit.'

'Just as well,' Plessis commented. 'She's a disagreeable old trout.'

His wife whirled. 'That's my aunt you're talking about!'

'The address, madame, please,' Darcy interrupted quickly.

She whirled back. 'It's in Goillac. I told you.'

'Where? Exactly.'

'By the river. It's one of those streets that end at the river. He likes fishing.'

'Who does?'

'My cousin's husband.'

'Madame.' Darcy was icily polite. 'The address.'

'Rue Josephe-Magne.' Madame Plessis seemed to think they were stupid not to have realised that by now. 'Number 17.'

'Thank you, madame,' Darcy said sarcastically. 'You've been most helpful.'

When they returned to the heap of collapsed masonry, an ambulance had arrived and Doc Minet was arranging for the removal of the body. It had set in the twisted position it had occupied in the narrow tower, its knees raised to its chest, its head tucked down in a foetal position, and it had been impossible to get it inside one of the plastic bags that were provided for corpses. The people who had invented them hadn't allowed for bodies set in odd shapes, so they'd had to use blankets.

The forensic boys were rooting around among the stones, removing them one by one and laying them carefully aside.

'Anything?' Pel asked.

'So far, nothing,' Leguyader, the head of the Lab, said. 'Old newspaper or two. I'm keeping them. They might give you a date. A few coins. I think they must have fallen from his pocket when the cloth rotted. I'll have them cleaned up. What seems to be the remains of an identity card. I think it must have been nibbled by mice or something and it's black with age.'

The Press had arrived – Fiabon, of *France Dimanche*, Henriot, of *Le Bien Public*, and Sarrazin, the freelance – and they were demanding information. Darcy gave them what he knew. It wasn't much and it was thirty years old, so it didn't matter a lot.

As they talked, a message arrived via the local substation and Sous-Brigadier Lefêvre.

'Call from the Palais de Justice,' he said. 'The *juge d'instruction*'s on his way.'

Pel scowled. He didn't think much of legal interference when he was working.

'Who is it?'

'Judge Brisard, sir.'

Pel looked at Darcy. Judge Brisard was an old enemy of Pel's. The Hôtel de Police, in fact, was full of high-tension cross-currents. Most people managed to cope with them but there were always one or two that were difficult to live with. Judge Brisard was one. He was a tall man, young for his job, flabby, wide-hipped like a woman, and with a nice line in marital fidelity which Pel, who had discovered he had a woman in Beaune, knew to be false. He had disliked Pel from the moment they had met because Brisard was unctuous and pompous and Pel was anything but. The dislike was amply returned and the occupants of the Hôtel de Police had been wondering for years which one of them would be the first to break under the strain and shoot the other. At the moment, Brisard was lagging behind and bets were being taken about when he would be carried off screaming that he couldn't stand it any longer.

'How long is he likely to be?' Pel asked.

Lefêvre glanced at his watch. 'Half an hour, sir.'

Pel looked at Darcy. 'It's time,' he said, 'that we were somewhere else.'

Mrs Briddon was still occupied with Aimedieu. Knowing that Pel wanted her out of the way, now that he had finished asking questions Aimedieu was holding her attention by admiring the huge beams that held up the ceiling.

'They date back to the twelfth century,' she said proudly.

'I bet there's a bit of woodworm there.'

'Don't you believe it,' Mrs Briddon said briskly. 'They're as hard as iron. Any woodworm trying to make inroads into them would soon retire with jaw ache.'

'Nice house all the same,' Aimedieu observed.

George Briddon had vanished outside again to check the latest developments and Ellen Briddon was enjoying talking to someone of her own age.

'We decided to come and live in France,' she said.

'You could speak French, of course?'

'Well, not very well. But you can learn a language simply by living among the people, can't you?'

It was a common fallacy that Aimedieu was inclined to doubt. As a boy he had been sent to a family in Portsmouth to learn English but, possessed of practically no grammar and very little vocabulary, all he learned was 'Cheeky boy' and 'Have it again,' picked up from the teenage daughter with whom he had played tennis. Judging by Mrs Briddon's accent, it seemed she was likely to experience the same difficulty.

'You speak English well,' she said. 'How did you learn it?'

'Night school, and a lot of hard work.'

'Oh!' She looked faintly dismayed and slipped into speaking English rather than the laboured French she had been trying. Aimedieu decided it was a good job his English had improved a lot.

Ellen Briddon eyed him speculatively. Her husband liked to go back to England from time to time. To see his agent or his publisher, he said. She suspected he was bored and had often wondered if there was another woman. Aimedieu was not unaware of her sidelong glances. He was a good-looking young man and was used to them and knew what they meant. He tried to divert her attention.

'Have you ever noticed anyone taking an interest in the tower, madame?' he asked.

'Oh, call me Ellen,' she said. 'My husband's George. He's a writer, and in publishing people get to first names very quickly. It would be nice to have a few friends of that category.'

Aimedieu couldn't see a cop providing much of a social scene but he smiled and repeated the question.

'Only the boys just along the road,' she said. 'They keep asking.'

'Which boys?'

'The actors. The boys who're putting on the show during the celebrations. It's going to be quite a big show. They've already started working up the party spirit.'

'What sort of interest have these boys been showing?'

'They asked how old the tower was and when it was last used. That sort of thing.'

As he finished his coffee and left, it occurred to Aimedieu, who was a bright young man with ambitions, that it might be a good idea to interview the young men in question. He got further directions from two men who were arguing in the middle of the square, apparently over the form the show at the end of the month should take.

'Folk dancing!' one of them was saying contemptuously. 'Singing! Fireworks!'

As Aimedieu asked his way, he swung round, his gnarled face close to Aimedieu's. He wore a paint-daubed jacket and an iron-grey beard and he stared aggressively at the policeman. 'Why do you want to know?' he asked. 'Who're you?'

Aimedieu flashed his identity card. 'Sergeant Aimedieu,' he said. 'Brigade Criminelle. Who're you?'

'Oh!' The old man grinned. 'I'm Serge Vitiello,' he said. He indicated the other man. 'Jean-Jacques Le Pape. We're discussing the show we're putting on for the tourists to finish the month. We're on the committee.'

'There are six others,' Le Pape pointed out. 'But we ignore them.'

'Why?'

'They're not worth listening to.'

'Won't our finding the body in the tower put the tourists off?' Aimedieu asked.

'Never,' Vitiello said. 'Tourists are so dim nothing puts them off. In two days' time your stiff will be forgotten. All they want to do is come and gawk. We've decided to go in for a medieval night. Dinner here in the square. Long tables down each side and across the top.'

'Waitresses in medieval costume.' Le Pape grinned lecherously. 'Low necklines. Lots of tit showing.'

Vitiello snorted. 'We'll never afford that,' he said. 'And the girls at the hotel wouldn't do it. The tourists won't mind, though. We're giving them wild boar stew. Good medieval dinner, wild boar stew. Even sounds medieval. Should please. Easy to arrange. The hotel lays it on twice a week for workmen's lunches, anyway. There are dozens of boar in the Forest of Grasigne. But the tourists won't know that. We've got a good show together – including me. Drawing portraits.'

'You an artist?'

'I'm professor of art at the Lycée in Goillac, so that makes me *not* an artist. But I can draw faces. Quickly. I once worked as a caricaturist. People like to see their own ugly mugs coming to life.'

'We decided originally', Le Pape said, 'on playlets. To show how the town came to be founded.'

'After all – ' Vitiello grinned. ' – there must have been a good reason for someone sticking a town in such a stupid place as this. So we thought we might as well let the tourists know. We found the Molière Players. Seven of them. Just right for what we had in mind. Then two of them vanished, then two more. We said that they'd got to get them back or we'd cancel the booking. In the end we decided on a medieval night, anyway. Much easier.'

He indicated the house Aimedieu was seeking, set in the Rue Nobel, one of the winding alleys off the square. In the street outside was a big shooting brake with 'Molière Players' painted crudely on the side. It was white but plastered with brown mud. On the back door was the deathless message, 'Save food.

Eat Tourists,' and in the dirt on the side someone had written with his finger end 'Also available in white.'

The actors' house turned out to be a dark little building with a rabbit warren of bleak stone-walled rooms, staircases and little in the way of comfort. It looked like the sort of place that would cost very little to rent, but the three young men who occupied it seemed as if they wouldn't be able to pay much, anyway. They were occupied when Aimedieu arrived with checking the few properties they possessed. They looked half-starved, all with straggly beards and long hair, and wore ragged jeans and brightly checked shirts that looked as if they had seen better days. One of them, tall and with pretensions to good looks, appeared to be in charge.

'Jean-Paul Remarque.' He introduced himself as they shook hands. 'He's Pierre Béranger. That's Gus Blivet.'

'Been here long?' Aimedieu asked.

'A month.'

'Early, weren't you? The show isn't for another two weeks.'

Béranger smiled. 'You don't put things on just like that,' he said, snapping his fingers. 'You have to think about things a bit.'

'What about these repertory companies that go around giving a different play every night?'

Remarque gave a nervous little laugh. 'They're different,' he said. 'They put on well-tried plays they've been doing for years. They could do them in their sleep.'

'Can't you?'

'We're only just starting in the game,' Blivet pointed out. 'And we do Racine, Molière, Sartre. In fact, we do everything. They're a bit more difficult than the farces these other people put on. Besides, this will be a medieval show. We've got to find out what people did in those days.'

'Why are you interested in the tower?'

'What tower?'

'The one that's fallen down. You must have heard of it.'

Remarque grinned. 'We actually heard it,' he said. 'I thought it was an earthquake at first. There's a fault in the earth's surface here somewhere, I believe. They found a body, didn't they?'

'Yes. Know him?'

'No.'

'So why are you interested?'

'We're not interested.'

'I was told you were. In the tower. I heard you were sniffing round it asking questions.'

The three young men glanced at each other then Remarque smiled. 'Oh, that!' he said. 'We were wondering if we could use it as a sort of backcloth. Do our stuff in front. It would look good. All that old stone. We thought perhaps we could drape it. A few banners here and there. We thought we could borrow a few from the Mairie. They've got some they used for the 700th anniversary.'

'The tower's not in the square,' Aimedieu pointed out. 'I thought all the celebrations were to be in the square.'

Remarque laughed. 'It'll be a bit crowded in the square,' he said. 'Folk dancing. Kids from the school singing. We thought in front of the tower might give us a bit more elbow room. Not much point now, though. The tower isn't there any more. I expect we'll use the square.'

Aimedieu had always been interested in the theatre and wanted to know more. 'How did you come to be an actor?' he asked.

'Me?' Remarque shrugged. 'We were a large family. There were four of us – two girls and two boys. We used to put on shows for friends. We were all good at it. Then it started to fall apart. One sister married and my brother went to Canada. The other sister – ' He shrugged. ' – she just left home. Had a row with the Old Man and walked out. They were always rowing. People do. She wanted her own way. That left me. I decided to try my luck on the stage. I worked in Marseilles, Lyons, Bordeaux. Even a crummy little place in Royan that had started up. Then I was ill for a bit and when I got better there was nothing doing. So I did a bit of work in Goillac and a bit for a TV film company – make-up work; I was good at it – then I met Pierre and Gus here and the others and we started making a living putting on little shows.'

Aimedieu studied them. 'How do you put on a show with just three of you?'

'Well, actually, there were seven of us originally but two of them – Richard and Eloïse – walked out on us and it just left the five of us.'

'I gather it's not playlets you're doing now.'

'No problem. We do anything.'

'And the girls?'

'Odile Daydé and Mercédes Flichy.'

'Where are they?'

Remarque looked at the other two. 'They went home for a holiday before we start work. They'll be back soon, I expect.'

# 4

Madame Croissard was a sprightly old lady of eighty-odd, not at all the ogre Plessis, her niece's husband, had made her out to be. Sure enough, her son-in-law was at the end of the street with his rod over the river. The sun had become hot suddenly and Pel wished he could join him.

'It's August,' Madame Croissard explained. 'It's his holiday and he works hard. So why not? His wife's out.'

'It's not your son-in-law or your daughter we've come to see,' Pel said. 'It's you.'

'What have I done?'

'Nothing, madame. You just happened to have once been the owner of the Cat Tower in Puyceldome. We want to know something about it.'

She beamed at them, decided they looked half-starved and made them sit down while she provided brandy, coffee and buns. 'Now we can talk,' she said. 'I always say nobody can concentrate when he's hungry. What's the problem?'

'The tower, madame. It's just collapsed.'

She gave a little giggle. 'I always thought it might,' she said. 'In fact, I've been expecting the whole of Puyceldome to collapse into the river for some time. What happened? Did a lorry hit it? Those places weren't made for modern traffic.'

'No, madame. A lorry didn't hit it. The new owner decided to open it up and it didn't work. It fell down.'

'When I sold the house I said it would. That was one of the reasons I sold it.'

'Unfortunately, the man you sold it to sold it again within five years – '

'I thought he wouldn't stay. Too self-important.'

' – and he doesn't seem to have passed on the information about the tower to the next occupant, so that it also doesn't appear to have reached the present owner.'

'They should have come and seen me.'

'I expect they're wishing they had. How long did you live there?'

'We took over the property in 1945. My husband was alive then and my children were still at home. They've all disappeared now. Two in the south, one in Paris. When my husband died it was too big for me, so I let it.'

'A shrewd move, madame.'

She smiled. 'I thought so, too.'

She had all her records and account books and all the letters that had been exchanged. She had also known everybody who had lived in the house and they all seemed to have been straightforward enough. Only the man Caillas looked doubtful; and that simply because he had taken the place on a mortgage but had suddenly disappeared and never returned. Since it had proved impossible to find out who he was or why he had disappeared so abruptly, and because only a deposit and one monthly payment had been made to the loan company, the house had reverted to the company.

'What was he like, this Caillas?'

Madame Croissard gestured, wagging a limp hand to and fro. 'Just a man. Bit odd-looking. Big forehead. Lot of bounce. He started tinkering with the tower straight away. I told him it would collapse but he persisted in making what he called an "exploratory opening". At the top, just under the slates of the turret. But within a fortnight or so the scaffolding disappeared and the hole was filled in and he vanished. Monsieur Poulex bought it after him. He wanted to put a staircase in. I told *him* it would collapse, too. He must have decided I was right because he never finished it and in the end he sold to an American – a Monsieur Keitzer. He was in films and had a lot of money. He opened up the salon with a big window that provided a view right across the valley, and had the place replumbed. But then he got bored and sold it and went back to America. A man called Duclose from Paris bought it. He wanted a weekend place but he died two years ago and his widow sold to some Rosbifs.'

'Monsieur and Madame Briddon.'

'That's right. He's a writer.'

'You know the history of the place well?'

'I ought to. I was born in Puyceldome and lived all my life there until I sold out and went to live in the valley. I still know what goes on because I have a niece who runs the hotel and bar.'

'We've met her.'

'She keeps me in touch. She's always coming to see me.' Madame Croissard chuckled. 'I think she's after my money.'

'Did you attempt to have the tower opened?'

'No. My husband was advised not to. But I believe the people who had it before us tried. They didn't get far either. Puyceldome's old and the buildings are ancient and if you start tinkering with them they start falling down. When Monsieur Poulex started on the tower, I believe the man who was doing the job warned him it wasn't safe and he soon bricked up the hole he made.'

'This Monsieur Poulex? Do you happen to know where he lives?'

'Jouissy. He has a business there. Supermarket. He fancied living in the country, I think, so he went to Puyceldome. But it was too cold for him. He now has a flat over his shop.'

Poulex was an overweight man with a moustache. His shop was certainly called a supermarket but, in fact, it was nothing but a large general store run on supermarket lines, with plastic baskets for the customers and a check-out desk. It seemed to be prosperous and well run, however, and Poulex was so occupied with it they had to accept his apology that he was too busy and return an hour later when the rush had ceased. He turned out to be a self-important man who liked the sound of his own voice and was convinced that everybody in the world was out to do him down.

'It wasn't worth what was asked for it,' he said. 'They told me there had been an iron staircase inside the tower, but when

I started to open it up to put one back in, the bricklayer told me it was dangerous. So I got someone else.'

'Name of Lupin?'

'That's right. He quoted me a price that was far too high, but when I tried to find somebody else they all wanted the same. I think they get together, these country people, and think they can force us town-dwellers to pay what they ask. We had words.'

'Perhaps it was just a fair price,' Pel said mildly.

'Never.'

'What happened?'

'I agreed in the end. But I had to be nasty about it. He started work and managed to get inside the tower through the top. He was in there for some time and then he came out and said it wasn't possible, that the stone was too worn or something, and the cement crumbling, and that if he touched it, the whole thing would come down.'

'It seems he was right. It did. This morning.'

Poulex looked startled. 'It did?'

It took some time to get him going again because he seemed to feel the collapse of the tower justified the words he'd had with his string of bricklayers, but they quietened down the complaints in the end and nudged him onwards.

'Go on about Lupin.'

Poulex drew a deep breath. 'He finally said he'd have another go from the bottom. We had more words but in the end he opened up a hole. Not a very big one. Just big enough for him to wriggle inside. He was only a little type. Same result. He said it was too dangerous. He filled the holes – put back the stones – both at the top and bottom. Said it looked distinctly shaky. Even worked late into the night to finish it. In case it fell, he said. The next day he asked me to pay him. But you don't usually pay on the dot, do you? You expect a month at least. He turned nasty and insisted. So I paid. That was the last I heard of him. The next I heard he'd gone to America.'

'And you never heard from him again?'

'Not a word. It was a very unpleasant business. He simply disappeared. I didn't even get a receipt. When I tried to contact him by phone there was no reply. I even went to see him. But the house was empty and the neighbours didn't know where he'd gone to.' A thought occurred suddenly to Poulex, breaking through his feelings of martyrdom. 'Why? What's all this about? Have you found him? Because if you have I'd like to insist on that receipt. The money I paid is tax-deductible – preservation of ancient property – and I've never been able to claim.'

Darcy glanced at Pel. 'Well,' he said, 'we've certainly found someone.'

'I could soon recognise him,' Poulex said. 'I'd like to see him. Where is he?'

'Well,' Darcy said cheerfully. 'At the moment he's in the morgue. But he *was* in the tower.'

'In the tower. What was he doing in the tower?'

Darcy shrugged. 'He wasn't doing anything,' he said. 'He was dead.'

They had just reached the car again when the radio started squawking. It was headquarters.

'The Chief thinks you ought to call in,' they were informed. 'There's been another one.'

'Another what?'

'Another body. They've just reported finding it.'

'Where? In the tower?'

'No, Patron. In a wood off the N6 at Garcy-le-Noir. Sergeant Nosjean's on his way. No identification yet. It's a stabbing. Doc Minet's deputy's gone with Nosjean, and the Lab and Fingerprints have also sent someone.'

Pel pondered on his staff. He could trust Nosjean because he had trained him himself. He would never be the policeman Darcy was because he wasn't ruthless enough, but he used his brains. 'Tell De Troq' to join Nosjean for the time being,' he said. 'He'll need help and De Troq's free.'

In fact, De Troq' was anything but free.

Feeling he was going to get nowhere with his informant, Marceau, he had gone home, put on his scruffiest clothes and a hat he'd bought to keep the sun out of his eyes in Tenerife the year before, and had started to follow the boy everywhere he went. It was nothing new. It was something he had been doing on and off for some time until he'd got to know not only the boy's habits but also the habits of quite a few drug addicts. Then he'd noticed they were beginning to grow restless, visiting bars, talking in groups, and he had realised a new supply must be on the way. Marceau had confirmed it.

Following him in his old clothes, he noticed Marceau and the other youngsters were congregating near the bandstand in the Parc de la Colombière, and could only imagine they were waiting for Speedy Sam, their friendly neighbourhood pusher, to turn up, so he had recruited Brochard and Debray to help him, as Pel had instructed. He would need someone handy in case Speedy Sam ran for it.

It had been raining and when he arrived at the bandstand, the paths and pavements were greasy with damp. He noticed at once that there were two or three youngsters hanging around, sitting on benches. They were all trying to look nonchalant and as if they were just enjoying the weather, but they were all nervous and he knew they were waiting for their pusher.

Speedy Sam, when he arrived, was a surprise. He was a thin pale man in his forties, carrying his jacket over his arm. As he stopped by the bandstand to light a cigarette, one of the boys rose and went to meet him. They spoke for a second and something changed hands. De Troq' moved forward, his hat pulled down, his hands in his pockets. Speedy Sam didn't take alarm until he was within twenty metres of him, then he suddenly stared hard at De Troq' and, with the highly-developed instinct of the guilty, guessed what he was and started to run. Out of the corner of his eye, De Troq' saw Brochard stopping the boy who had bought from him, then he was after the pusher at full tilt.

Speedy Sam was well named. He ran like a hare. De Troq' was no mean sprinter, though, and he was fit and slim. Speedy Sam was older and couldn't throw him off. As they reached the entrance to the park, twisting and turning, Speedy Sam dived into the crowd waiting to cross the road.

Snatching people from his path, De Troq' kept after him,

closely followed by Debray. He saw the pusher on the pavement edge trying to halt his headlong rush, but his feet slipped on the damp paving. There was a scream of brakes and a heavy lorry swung violently and mounted the pavement. There were shouts and women's shrieks; when De Troq' arrived a girl was lying on the pavement in a dead faint, and the driver of the lorry, a man in his early twenties, was leaning against the wing of his vehicle, vomiting his heart up. There were a lot of blood splashes and what looked like brains, a pair of legs lying at strange angles under the wheels, and a running shoe in the gutter. The driver looked up as De Troq' appeared, his eyes streaming, a string of bile hanging from his mouth.

'He ran straight into me,' he said.

De Troq' had just seen Speedy Sam off to the mortuary when Pel's message arrived.

It had been a revolting job digging him out from under the truck and, though De Troq' personally hadn't had to do it, he had had to be there to check the contents of his pockets. What he had found had provided clear and conclusive evidence that he had been carrying on a profitable business supplying the youth of the city, but it had taken a long time and De Troq' was looking forward to a beer and a rest.

He soon saw he wasn't going to get either.

In fact it looked like being a long night.

By the time Nosjean reached Garcy-le-Noir it was already late. A constable was waiting to escort him to the scene of the incident but it was beginning to grow dark when they arrived and the trees were already shadowed and a mist was creeping between them. A police brigadier was waiting for them with another man who looked nervous and ill at ease. Other policemen had arranged a screen round the body and were erecting lights.

'When I got here,' the brigadier said, 'there were five carrion crows going at him.'

'I had to wave a blanket from the car to drive away the flies,' the other man said. 'So the brigadier could examine him.'

'This is Alexandre Méline,' the brigadier said, indicating his companion. 'He found him. I'm Brigadier Varin. I've covered him with a plastic sheet. He's been either stabbed or shot. Several times. I haven't touched him. I thought you'd better get a look at him first.'

Within a few minutes three more cars had arrived. They contained Doc Minet's assistant, a young man with spectacles and a long neck with a very active Adam's apple, called Cham; Du Toit, Leguyader's assistant from the Lab; and Minoli, Prélat's deputy from Fingerprints. Nosjean nodded, satisfied. They were all deputies, because the boss men were occupied at Puyceldome – even Nosjean was a deputy – but everything was well under control.

He stared down at the body. It was that of a young man, dressed in trousers and shirt-sleeves. The sleeves were rolled up. The shirt had been saturated with blood which had soaked into the ground beneath him and dried. There were slashes on his cheek and forearms. He was lying on his back, dead ruined eyes staring upwards at the trees, and his possessions were scattered around him with the contents of the car – maps, dusters, registration papers and a few personal things from the glove pocket. The car wheel was in a pothole and the door hung open.

'You'd better get the area staked off,' Nosjean told the brigadier. 'Have you taken a statement from Monsieur Méline?'

'Yes.'

'With his address?'

'Everything. Home address and the address where he's heading. He was on his way to see his mother, I understand. I had the office check with her by telephone. She's expecting him and she vouches for him.'

'Then we'd better let him get on his way, so long as he's prepared to hold himself in readiness to be questioned again.'

'Of course.' Méline was beginning to enjoy himself now and was aware of the sensation that would be caused by his arrival in Clermont Ferrand. Half the family would be there waiting to find out the meaning of his brush with the police.

A constable was assigned to drive him to the police station in Garcy where he had left his car, and Nosjean turned to the brigadier.

'What have you found out so far?' he asked.

'I've been through the car. The registration papers were on the grass. They indicate that the owner – whom I'm assuming is him – ' The brigadier nodded at the dead man. ' – is a Michel Vienne. Aged twenty-nine, Apartment 6, 8 Rue Plivier, Lyons. I think someone had started to drive the car away but it dropped a wheel in the pothole there, and they couldn't get it out so they beat it, leaving the door open.'

As soon as the photographers had finished, Du Toit's Forensic boys started going cautiously through the dead man's belongings.

'Identification card,' one of them said, holding the document out to Nosjean.

There was no mistake. The picture on the identity card was that of the dead man, and the thumb print was identical to one they obtained from his limp thumb, and others which they found on the car.

'Anything else?' Nosjean asked.

'Somebody's been through his pockets,' Du Toit, the Forensic man, said.

Among the things picked up from the grass was a card in the name of a Michel Vienne, representing a firm called Busson and Company, of Marseilles and Lyons, which, judging by the logo in the corner, were manufacturers of kitchen equipment. Michel Vienne appeared to be one of their representatives. There was a photograph of a young woman holding a baby, an empty wallet, a penknife, a handkerchief, and that was about the lot.

Dr Cham was industriously poking about in the best manner of Doc Minet, his boss. 'Stabbed,' he said. 'No sign of shooting.'

'When did he die?'

'Forty-eight hours ago. Around there.'

When De Troq' arrived half an hour later, Nosjean had reached a few conclusions.

'It wasn't done in the car,' he said. 'There's no blood in there. He's lying in it.'

'I reckon he wasn't dead when he was left either,' Cham said. 'I think he died where he's lying now – from loss of blood and nothing else. If he could have got some help he'd probably still be alive. He bled to death.'

'Robbery?' De Troq' asked.

'Looks like it. I reckon he picked up someone in his car – some hitch-hiker probably – and somehow he was persuaded to drive in here and he was stabbed to death.'

'There are fingerprints,' Prélat's deputy said. 'Some of them women's.'

'Wife, do you think?' De Troq' asked.

'Well, there were a lot on the passenger side of the car. They could well be his wife's. But there were one or two different ones.'

'Then he must have a girl friend he sees occasionally.'

'Unless he's in the habit of picking up hitch-hikers.'

'I wouldn't pick up a hitch-hiker,' Dr Cham said firmly. 'Not these days. You never know what you're getting. You might get a pistol shoved up your nose or accused of rape.'

'I think', Nosjean said thoughtfully, 'that perhaps we'd better try to get those women's fingerprints identified. Perhaps they didn't *all* belong to his wife or her friends. In which case, they probably did belong to a girl he picked up. In addition, we'd better look into his background. It could be that robbery wasn't the motive and was only staged to put us off the scent. Lyons and Marseilles are places where a lot of shady characters hang out. He might be one of them, or at least on the fringe of something they were up to. For all we know he might be the right-hand man of some type who wants to rule the world.'

It was a flippant approach to what was a serious crime. Death was never a subject for jest, but a sense of humour was important. If you lost it, you went home and spent your time reflecting what a lot of rotten people the world contained. Pel often thanked God for Darcy. You needed a sense of humour to be a policeman. Those without one usually ended up manic depressives. The humour was usually black, grim and mordant, but what other kind could there be for men who were always picking up stiffs along the motorway, in back alleys, even in glamorous boudoirs? Blood didn't make for laughter, but after a while you grew so you could make a joke about it.

He listened to Nosjean's theories quietly. His own mind was

occupied still with the body they'd found at Puyceldome. The fact that it was thirty or so years old made no difference. It still seemed to be murder.

'Stay with it,' he advised. 'Have you found out anything about him yet?'

Nosjean was puzzled. 'The Lyons police have checked him out for us,' he said. 'He seems to be exactly what his papers say he is: Michel Vienne, Apartment 6, 8 Rue Plivier, Lyons, representative for Busson and Company, of Marseilles and Lyons, manufacturers of kitchen equipment. He was popular and good at his job. He sold things and sometimes collected cash. He'd been away several days and was supposed to be on his way home – that is, he'd be driving south.'

'Family?'

'Married two years. Small child. No known enemies and no reason they know about to have any.'

'You can't always tell,' Pel said. 'Perhaps we'll move ahead a bit with the post mortem. Who's doing it?'

'Doc Cham.'

'How does he seem? Doc Minet's due to retire soon and it'd be nice to know we'd got someone competent to take his place.'

'He's on the ball,' Nosjean said. 'He uses his head. De Troq's out there handling things.'

As Nosjean left, Darcy appeared. 'I've confirmed the name of the people who rented that property at the time our type must have been walled up in the tower,' he said. 'I got it through the Mairie. Property changes have to be registered and they've got them all. It's pretty clear.'

In fact, it had been very clear. The Maire's secretary had made it so.

'This is an ancient town,' he had pointed out. 'A place the Ministry of Arts and Crafts like to keep an eye on. We're always getting builders and speculators trying to buy property for development, but the Ministry likes to know about things like that and we pass on all information. Madame Briddon was given permission to open the tower because nothing was expected to show outwardly and because permission had been given to previous occupants. We couldn't get around that.'

'The type from the south who bought it', Darcy said, 'was

called Caillas – Armande Caillas. He's down there in black and white. Address in Marseilles – 2 Rue de la Mer.'

Pel looked up. Addresses in Marseilles were always viewed with suspicion.

'Genuine?' he asked.

Darcy grinned. 'I checked. The address is genuine but the owner's name isn't. At the time we're interested in, 2 Rue de la Mer was occupied by one Laurence Luzeau.'

Pel frowned, his mind clicking away like mad. 'I've heard of Laurence Luzeau somewhere,' he said. 'Know anything about him?'

'I'm checking, Patron. He might have a record.'

'It's going to be an old one,' Pel observed. 'If Doc Minet thinks that chap was put in the tower thirty years ago, our friend Luzeau – if that's who Caillas is – must be drawing his old age pension by now.'

As they were talking, the door opened and Doc Minet appeared with Leguyader of the Lab.

'The identity card revealed nothing,' Leguyader said at once with a big smile. 'Not even a name.'

Pel glared. He and Leguyader had detested each other for years and Leguyader loved to announce that he had nothing to offer. Doc Minet smiled and tried to lower the temperature with a little encouragement.

'We've managed to straighten him out,' he said. 'And there are a few things that might help. He's around a metre eighty-eight tall. Hefty. Strong. Big bones. He was wearing working men's boots – and big ones at that – and the overall he had on is an outsize. You're looking for a big man.'

'There's another thing,' Leguyader said. 'Something that might be interesting. Among the debris we found a rope with a grappling hook on the end. It must have been in there with him.'

'A grappling hook?' Pel's eyebrows rose. 'Was someone fishing for something?'

'Somebody *must* have been at some time. It was under the body so it was there before he was. I suspect our long-dead friend was using it when something unexpected happened, so that he dropped it and it fell inside and he went in after it.'

'There's one other thing that might help,' Minet said. 'He had red hair. There was still some attached to the skull. It was the dark red hair you find in Normandy.'

'Every area has its own peculiarities,' Leguyader said pompously, as if he knew all about it – which, being Leguyader, he probably did. 'Here in Burgundy we're known for having round faces. They say it's all the wine we drink and all the food we eat.'

Pel frowned. 'Well, it's something,' he said. 'Anything else?'

'The overalls,' Leguyader suggested. 'The label inside is old, faded and worn but it indicates they were bought here in the city. Made by Jaunet and Company. They were overall makers.'

'Were?'

'They disappeared fifteen years ago.'

'Oh, charming.'

'They made overalls, white coats and butchers' aprons, and sold builders' safety helmets, waterproofs and shoes with reinforced toes. Everything for the industrious working man. I used to buy my lab smocks there. Not much help. However – ' Leguyader leaned forward importantly – 'I've found on the trousers of the overalls traces of soil. Not much, but some. Soil containing calcium.'

He sat back, looking like a dog sitting up and expecting a lump of sugar for a trick. Pel wasn't in the sugar-presenting mood. He sat stolidly unspeaking and Leguyader was forced to continue.

'Soil contains five types of constituents,' he said. 'A mineral matrix derived from rocks disintegrated by weathering forces; organic matter from the decomposition of plants and animals; a mixture of micro-organisms; water; and air.'

Leguyader had been at his encyclopaedia again. It was a standing joke in the Hôtel de Police that he spent every evening reading it so that he could blind Pel's conferences with science.

'Calcium,' Pel reminded him coldly.

'Most soils are formed from parent rocks broken to tiny particles by heat and cold which cause fragmentation by expansion and contraction. Water, by freezing, increases in volume to exert tremendous pressure.'

'Calcium,' Pel said again.

'Wind transports soil particles and erodes rock masses. Plants cause mechanical and chemical reactions.'

'Calcium,' Pel snarled.

'No need to shout,' Leguyader said.

'I'm not shouting,' Pel bawled. 'I just want to get on with it! I'm not here to listen to a lecture. You mentioned calcium. Right, let's hear about calcium without a diatribe on the weather.'

Leguyader flushed and glared back. Their enmity was caused as much by the fact that both were good at their jobs as by differences in temperament. Leguyader liked to think Pel's department couldn't function without the Lab – something which was eminently true – but it was also his pride and joy to claim that his discoveries were the only reason people got sent to gaol.

He sat up now, frowning heavily, and delivered his report in precise terms. 'I found traces of soil on his trousers. As far up as the knee. Clay. Clay with calcium in it. Before he got himself sealed up in the tower he must have worked somewhere where the soil was clayey with a calcium content. The soil at Puycel-dome is not clayey.'

'Thank you,' Pel snapped. 'You can leave the rest to us.'

With Leguyader sent away with a flea in his ear, Pel prepared to head for the Chief's office to present his report. But there was to be one more interruption – Judge Brisard.

'Yes?' Pel snapped. 'You wanted to see me?'

'I missed you at Puyceldome,' Brisard said, sitting down at the other side of Pel's desk. 'What progress have we made?'

'None,' Pel snapped.

'Oughtn't we to have made *some*?'

'Progress will be made,' Pel said, 'when we've had time to get the facts straight. When we have decided who the dead man is. When we know how he came to be walled up. When we discover who exactly was the occupant of the property at the time. It was thirty years ago.'

'We must rely on the team.'

Pel glared. 'We always do.'

'Team spirit's essential.'

Pel was too independent-minded to believe that team spirit

was the be-all and end-all of an investigation and could take the place of brains and a determination to regard police work as a crusade against crime.

'We'll get by,' he growled.

'I shall have to question this man, Bernard Buffel.'

'Of course.'

'He seems to know more about this business than anyone.'

'Naturally. He's a bricklayer, he's worked on the building and he's lived in Puyceldome longer than anyone else who's still active. It seems reasonable.'

'You have no reason to suspect him?'

'I've hardly had time to suspect anyone.'

Brisard looked smug. 'The fact that the dead man, whoever he is, died thirty years ago changes nothing.'

'I didn't think it did,' Pel said.

'The investigation will still have to start from scratch – as if he died yesterday.'

'As I imagined.'

'We must examine every avenue, even the most fundamental, without being influenced by the fact that what we have is not a corpse but a mummy.'

Pel gave Brisard a dirty look. There had been a time when examining magistrates – policemen too, he realised – were faceless individuals who got on with their job without fuss. But television had made them ambitious and a few had begun to see themselves as heroic figures, had even seen the possibilities of advancement as television presented them to the public. Brisard was one. These days he liked to give interviews to the Press and he was always available to the television cameras.

'That's exactly what we're doing,' Pel said.

Brisard sat back. 'When can I expect your report?'

'Tomorrow.'

'No earlier?'

Pel gave him a look that indicated he might be about to bite him in the leg. 'Difficulties we can overcome,' he said firmly. 'Miracles take a little longer.'

They managed to discuss the case a little further without going for each other's throat, but it was largely for show. Brisard had no intention of retreating in a hurry that would look like a defeat, and Pel had no intention of unbending, so they kept up the pretence for a few minutes longer.

The Chief was easier. He had walked a beat himself once and knew the strains and the patience a cop needed. He had once been a boxer and was reputed as a young cop to have saved a lot of would-be criminals from gaol by giving them a smart clip over the ear. Though it was frowned on these days, there were a few who were now even grateful to him because it had brought them up sharp as youngsters and stopped them slipping further into bad habits.

He sent for coffee and brought out the brandy bottle. He knew Pel enjoyed his *café fine* and he had long since learned that it was a splendid way to keep him in a good humour, something he had discovered was always essential. Sometimes he found Pel a pain in the backside with his bad temper, his bigotry and his feuds, but he was well aware that Pel was an asset, too, because he never let his personal failings interfere with his work, and his successes always redounded to the credit of the Chief.

'Go on,' he said cheerfully.

'It's thirty years old,' Pel explained. 'But we've got a lead. We've got the name of the occupant of the property at the time it must have happened, and an address in Marseilles. The address is genuine, but the name seems not to be.'

'Have you got an identification yet?'

'No. But we shall. Leguyader found he has a clayey calcium deposit on the legs of his overalls, so obviously he must have worked somewhere there was soil of that kind. We have to find out where and check with anybody else who worked there.'

'You've got a lot on,' the Chief commented.

'People keep records.'

'As long as thirty years?'

'Such is the bureaucratic urge for paperwork and the delight in referring back to it,' Pel said stiffly, 'people keep records until they're virtually swamped by them. Sometimes, even, firms build new headquarters with vast and expansive cellars for no other purpose than the keeping of records. I keep my old cheque stubs for ten years, my income tax receipts for the same time – you never know with that lot; they might try to make you pay twice. I keep my old notebooks and diaries for fifteen years.'

The Chief grinned. You would, he thought.

'You never know,' Pel said. 'We might be lucky.'

# 5

It was late when Pel reached home.

When a weary De Troq' had appeared to make his report on Speedy Sam – real name Samuel Boulay – Pel had sat up, interested at once.

'Have you got him?' he asked.

'No need, Patron,' De Troq' said. 'It's finished.'

'Don't say he's decided to retire.'

'No, Patron. He fell under a truck. He's dead.'

Pel was silent for a while. 'There'll be a deputy,' he said thoughtfully. 'The boys at the top believe in continuity. They'll have someone handy to step into his shoes.'

He had told De Troq' to stick with Nosjean for the time being until things quietened down, but to keep an eye on the drugs scene when he could. He and Nosjean were old friends, for some years rivals for Claudie Darel's affections, and both were intelligent and knew how to use their heads. He felt he could rely on them to handle the case at Garcy while he and Darcy got on with what appeared to be a more complicated affair at Puyceldome.

He was just leaving when Sarrazin, the freelance – hot on his trail from Puyceldome – arrived, demanding to know what was going on at Garcy. Right behind him were Fiabon and Henriot who, knowing Sarrazin could outdo them every time in news-gathering with one hand tied behind his back, had developed the tactic of following him wherever he went.

They had to be satisfied, and it left Pel irritated and tired. As he appeared in his drive a small boy with a dog was just on the point of leaving. The boy was Yves Pasquier, aged eleven, from the house next door. He had a pretty mother, and even faithful husbands – and Pel could never have been anything else – noticed pretty mothers. Daily he and the boy exchanged news through a hole in their communal hedge.

'On a case?' the boy asked.

'Two,' Pel said.

'Robbery?'

'Sort of.'

'Murder?'

'Sort of.'

'Big ones?'

'Sort of.'

The boy didn't question him any further. He recognised that Pel was busy, tired and absorbed, and Pel didn't volunteer information. A small boy's mind couldn't conceive the cruelty and viciousness that went on around the world.

'How about coming in for a piece of cake,' he suggested.

Madame Routy's steely heart, Pel had discovered, was not above leading her to hand out slabs of cake to small neighbours. But the boy shook his head.

'She hasn't made one,' he said.

Pel's eyebrows rose. Madame Routy was a softer touch than he had thought, and he was surprised. 'Why not?'

'She said she wasn't up to it. I'm going home.'

As he wandered off, Pel opened his door. It was like entering a morgue and reminded him that, as he had for the past few days, he would be eating alone and would be breakfasting at the Bar du Palais des Ducs – until apartheid reared its ugly head, the Bar Transvaal – behind the Hôtel de Police. It was a prospect that didn't appeal.

The house was silent and Pel once more became aware what being alone meant. When he had really been alone – alone that was but for Madame Routy – he had *never* realised its meaning. Now, when Madame Pel wasn't in the house, it was silent in a way that he had never noticed before. His wife wasn't arranging flowers or singing one of the quaint little songs she seemed to pick up. She wasn't in the kitchen or moving through the *salon*. There was no sound of her. There was nothing.

There was no sign of Madame Routy either and he assumed

quite naturally she was watching television. Nowadays, she watched in her room in the evenings but, with Madame Pel away, he suspected she had sneaked off and was probably watching wrestling, or *Dallas*, or *Gardeners' Hour* – even, for God's sake, something to do with politics.

Moving through the house, he poured himself a drink, noting at the same time that Madame Routy had been at the whisky. He was just debating what he ought to do about it when Madame Routy herself appeared. He was just about to deliver a blast when he realised she had been crying. Her nose was shiny and her eyes were red-rimmed, and suddenly he found himself being sorry for the old trout. Normally he might have asked her what she had spoiled for dinner and received the reply that it wouldn't matter as he had no idea what good food ought to be like. It was an exchange they had been using for years. Tonight was different.

'It's Didier,' she said, without waiting for him to ask what was wrong.

'What's wrong with Didier?' Pel asked, though he had already learned of the trouble from Darcy.

'His mother's worried.'

She wasn't the first mother to be worried about her son. Pel remembered his own mother being worried about him when he had announced he was going to be a cop. Cops, he had decided long before, tended to be people who kept a low profile and anybody with the names he bore would inevitably prefer to keep a low profile.

How would de Gaulle have felt if he'd been called Evariste Clovis Désiré de Gaulle? Or Bonaparte? Evariste Clovis Désiré Bonaparte! He'd never have made Emperor. It had soured Pel's life as a young man. Girls in a heavy clinch burst out laughing when he told them his name. One had actually laughed so hard she had fallen out of bed. What was more, she hadn't bothered to get back in.

He eyed Madame Routy warily. 'I've heard about him at headquarters,' he said carefully. 'His work hasn't been satisfactory for some time.'

'It's that girl,' Madame Routy sniffed. 'That Louise Bray who lives next door to him. She always went around with him. Now she's going round with someone else.'

'It's a habit girls have,' Pel said.

'His mother wondered if you could have a word with him.'

'He's too old now for me to "have a word with" him. It was all right when he was small. He's a young man now.'

'Can't you do anything? He always thought a lot of you.'

Enough, Pel remembered, to cheat happily with him when they played Scrabble, enough in the days when he was courting Madame Pel to choose for him the right tie to go with the grey suit he kept for the day when the President of the Republic would pin the Légion d'Honneur on his chest; enough to go fishing with him; enough to enjoy bolting with him for the nearest restaurant when Madame Routy, his aunt, announced that it was casserole for dinner. He seemed to deserve a few thoughts.

'All right,' Pel said. 'I'll see what I can do.'

He finally got round to calling Didier into his office late the following afternoon.

The boy stood in front of his desk. He was tall and good-looking in his uniform but he kept his eyes down and seemed sullen and uncooperative.

Pel didn't mention Aunt Routy. That, he felt, was the worst way possible to conduct an enquiry into a young man's behaviour. Any suggestion that aunts were asking the boss to help control him would immediately and inevitably bring on a fit of the vapours. Instead he went straight to the point which concerned him most.

'There have been complaints about your work,' he said.

Didier didn't answer. He didn't deny it. He didn't even raise his eyes to look Pel in the face.

'They say you're not paying attention to it as you should.'

Pel itched to introduce the subject of Louise Bray but that, he felt, would be a disaster, too. Louise Bray was too personal to be brought in and he stuck to work. 'Well,' he said. 'Haven't you anything to say?'

'No.'

'No, sir.'

'No, sir. Sorry, sir.'

'Is there something on your mind? Debts? Anything like that?'

The boy lifted his head at last. 'I've decided I'm not cut out to be a policeman,' he said.

'There was a time when it was your sole ambition.'

'I've changed my mind.'

'What happened? Everybody thought you were doing well.'

'Oh – ' Didier shrugged. 'Things happened.'

It was impossible to get to the heart of the matter. 'You never come to see us at home these days,' Pel said.

'No.'

'You used to come often.'

There was no reply.

'I still enjoy fishing and a game of boules. Your Aunt Routy still cooks.'

Didier's head lifted and there was a ghost of a smile on his face. 'Not very well,' he said.

'She's improved a lot since my wife took her over,' Pel said. 'And when she doesn't come up to scratch I still bolt and have a meal in town.'

'It's different now.'

'So it seems. Are you thinking of leaving us?'

'Yes.'

'When?'

'I don't know. I haven't made up my mind.'

'We'll need a month's notice. I'd have thought that, as part of my team, you'd have learned fast and been on the road to plain clothes work pretty quickly.' Pel lifted one hand in a gesture of frustration. 'Well, under the circumstances, for the time being you'd better stick close to me. We've got a pretty sticky case. Body thirty years old unearthed by repair work in Puyceldome. You'll have heard about it.'

'Yes.'

'Sergeant Nosjean's got a tricky one too. He might need help. We need someone around to write up the logs. Can you do that?'

'Yes, sir.'

'Good. So be ready to leave the office at any time. You'll be working hard and for long hours.' And let's hope, Pel thought, that would take his mind off himself and Louise Bray. 'How's your shorthand and typing? Have you finished the course at night school?'

'Yes. They're all right.'

'Fast?'

'Yes.'

'And accurate?'

'Yes.'

'Then you've got a job. See that you do it well because I shall be there watching. What you do when the case's over is your affair but when we're on a case I expect the best. Afterwards you can become a clown in a circus if that's what you want but until then you're a cop and I'll be expecting you to behave like a cop.'

As Didier left, Darcy pushed past him into the room.

'Caillas, Patron,' he said. 'I've nailed him. Real name Luzeau. Laurence Luzeau. Known as Lulu Grande-Tête, chiefly because he did, in fact, have a particularly large head. He was also a bit of a bighead in the other sense, too. He thought he was a big-time operator when actually he was just a *demi-sel*. No importance at all. Marseilles police knew him well. They didn't think much of him either and it seems they were right because he got himself bumped off with another guy in a Marseilles bar. Thirty years ago, Patron. About the time our friend got himself sealed up in the tower.'

Pel studied his desk top, deep in thought. 'What else do we know of him?' he asked.

'It seems there were four of them who used to work together: Luzeau, and three others – Pierre Pirioux, Georges Pulot and Albert-Jean Sammonix. Luzeau and Pulot were knocked off in the Marseilles bar. Pirioux was killed soon afterwards in what seemed to the Marseilles police to be a fishy car crash on the Corniche. Sammonix went to America and died there of cancer soon afterwards.'

'It *must* be connected with the tower at Puyceldome.'

'Must be, Patron. It's too big a coincidence otherwise.'

'And our friend in the tower? Where does he come in?'

'I've been talking to Le Bernard. He told me he remembers seeing a big chap with red hair working on the tower. That fits with Doc Minet's thinking. He'd built a little platform at the top, Le Bernard said, and appeared to be sealing up a hole just under the roof. Next day he wasn't there. A bit later – a few days, he thinks – he was there again. Then the next day another bricky appeared and finished the job.'

'So who is he?'

'We'll find out, Patron. I've got some names,' Darcy opened his notebook. 'Baulier. Mesquer. Orvault-sur-Seine. Rèze.'

'Who're they?' Pel asked.

'They're not whos,' Darcy said. 'They're whats. Places. Where our friend from the Cat Tower might have worked. Places where the soil consists of clay with a calcium deposit. I got them from the University geological department. It was easier than I expected. This type led me into an office where there was a big map on the wall done in colour. He just looked at the key and pointed. Clay soils are one of their pet subjects. Farmers think of clay as earth which becomes as hard as brick when it's dry. In fact, they use it to *make* bricks. But when it's wet it was once considered sticky enough to resist all efforts to work it with ordinary agricultural implements. They're getting over that problem these days, but a pure clay soil's considered quite infertile unless it contains lime, potash and soda which make it amenable to cultivation.'

'You sound like Leguyader. As if you've been reading an encyclopaedia.'

Darcy grinned. 'The point is this, Patron. Since it's not very suitable for agriculture, it's the sort of land farmers are quick to sell off for development, and that makes it the sort of land on which the government's usually willing to grant permission for building. Baulier, Mesquer, Orvault and Rèze are all part of a long streak parallel with the River Orche.'

'Go on.'

'I did a bit of thinking. Where would a guy get mud up to the knees? The only place I could think of was a building site. And a large project too. A lot of mud didn't indicate a small project.

Not one house. A lot. It's on big building sites where the mud's deep enough to work its way well up the trousers. I decided to see if there were any big developments around thirty years ago in these spots. There were. There was a new supermarket at Rèze. A new housing estate at Orvault. A factory making parts for tractors at Baulier. Houses for young executives at Mesquer. All in recent years.'

'How recent?'

'Some *too* recent. But the housing estate at Orvault was built around thirty years ago. In the late 1950s. The factory for tractor parts was a bit later. 1960. The other two were too late to be of interest to us.'

'That the lot?'

'It'll do for a start. I've got the names of the firms who were involved. Thermine Super run the market at Orvault. Big firm, with a chain of stores. I dare bet they'll have all their records and know who built the place. The tractor parts factory's owned by Locarez. Another big group. I'll get in touch with them both and find out which firms held the contracts for the building work. That should sort things out a bit. The mud wouldn't be there after the walls went up so only a few of the contractors would be involved – those who employed bricklayers, which is what our friend in the tower was. After that, it's a case of getting the names of the men they employed and finding out what they remember.'

'They'll be getting on a bit these days.'

'Certainly over fifty.'

'When I'm over fifty,' Pel observed gloomily, 'I shan't be able to remember my own name.'

Darcy grinned and pushed his cigarette across. 'What you need, Patron,' he said, 'is another nail in your coffin.'

'You don't help me give them up. That's why I shall be senile at fifty.'

'It's going to be a long job, Patron.'

'Who've you got on it?'

'Lagé. He'll go to endless trouble so long as it doesn't involve walking too far.'

'He *is* due for retirement,' Pel pointed out. 'When I'm that close to retirement I shan't fancy walking far. Especially if I'm as fat as Lagé.'

'I shan't find them all,' Darcy admitted. 'Some of them will be retired or dead by this time. But there must be some, and most would remember whom they worked with – even that length of time ago. We'll find him. We have one advantage. He was big and had red hair. Easy to remember. After that it will become easier because his death *has* to be murder. You don't seal a chap in a tower and leave him there for thirty years because he has measles.'

# 6

The post mortems on the two bodies they'd found didn't produce much. Body number one, the body from Puyceldome, had been dead a long time. That they knew.

'And,' Doc Minet said when he arrived with Leguyader for Pel's conference, 'because of the free access of air into the tower and the fact that it's hot there in the summer, a gradual process of drying occurred. He's really just a framework, because putrefaction took place long since. Flies must have deposited their eggs which eventually hatched and devoured most of the soft tissues, just leaving the skin and the bones with the remains of some red hair going grey. He's still a bit twisted because when he died, he fell in a cramped position and he stayed that way for a long time.'

'How did he die?' Pel asked. 'That's what we want to know.'

'You're asking a lot,' Leguyader said. 'After all this time, with the flesh gone and a process of mummification, it's virtually impossible to say how he died. But it seems no attempt was made to cover the body. There was no sack over him. Nothing like that. In parts where his weight rested on them, his clothes became married into the flesh. We had to soak them in glycerine to free them. There also appears to have been a certain amount of digging beneath him. Perhaps an attempt was made to get him out through the hole at the bottom. On the other hand, the digging might have been done by himself in an attempt to escape, though there were no tools in there, and from what we can tell from his finger ends he didn't use his hands to do any digging. But he was a bricklayer by the sound of him and it seems he must have gone in through a hole at the top – we suspect, in fact, from the position he was in that he fell in – and for some reason wasn't able to get back up the tower to the hole.'

'Wouldn't he have had an assistant who could have helped?'

'That might depend on why he was there.'

It might indeed, Pel admitted to himself. It had begun to seem more and more likely that whatever their red-haired friend had been up to, it had probably been none too honest. If he'd been honest, why hadn't he been helped to escape?

'He'd be working from the top of a ladder, wouldn't he?' he asked. 'So let's get this straight: are you by any chance suggesting somebody climbed up after him and pushed him in? Or stabbed him or clubbed him or shot him as he was leaning through the hole, so that he just disappeared inside?'

'We might be able to tell you more about that later,' Doc Minet said. 'When I've examined him properly. But I felt you ought to know how I was thinking. There's one other thing that might help. He was European. Judging by the overalls, a Frenchman, though he might have been an Algerian, but, with red hair, I'd think not.'

'Nothing further towards identifying him?'

'No.'

'Teeth?'

'The teeth are all there but dental records weren't kept as precisely thirty years ago as they are now and we'll have difficulty. It's in hand, though. They're poor teeth, too, so perhaps he didn't bother with dentists much.'

'Injuries?'

'None.'

'None?'

'Nothing at all. At least, nothing we could find. After all this time it isn't easy but there was no damage to the skull or chest. No perforations or crushing. We looked for wounds or injuries. It wasn't easy but we decided he hadn't been shot or stabbed.'

'So if nobody shot him, stabbed him or hit him with a blunt instrument, how did he die?'

'Poison?' Leguyader offered.

'And then stuffed him in there out of the way?'

'He could have died in there of the poison. Taken by accident in food. Or given him deliberately before he got inside. Slow-acting stuff. But lethal enough to work after he was inside.' Leguyader was always one for a bit of melodrama.

Pel gave him a cold look. 'Find any trace of anything?' he asked.

'No,' Doc Minet said firmly. 'Nothing.'

'There is another alternative,' Pel suggested. 'He might have fallen in accidentally and broken his neck.'

'He didn't break his neck.'

'Could he have been strangled?'

'No indication that he was. The upper horn of the thyroid cartilage – the hyoid bone – was undamaged. It's a little bone and it's the best indication there is that someone's been strangled. It only gets broken when there's pressure on the throat. In any case, he'd be a difficult chap to strangle. He was big and there's no indication of a rope round his neck, so it would have to be done by the hands. And if he was strangled it must have been done *inside* the tower.'

'It would be a tight squeeze with two of them in there.'

'It couldn't have been done *outside* and then the body – of a heavy man – hoisted up a ladder and dropped inside the hole.'

'There's yet another alternative,' Minet added gently. 'He could have had a heart attack.'

'Proof?'

'None. But it could well have been something like that. If he'd been walled up alive he'd surely have protested a bit. Somebody would have heard him.'

Pel sat back, scowling. Doc Minet smiled. 'People do have them,' he pointed out. 'He was a big chap and probably carried too much flesh, so it's not unlikely. But after thirty years or so it's impossible to tell if there was any disease of the organs, impossible to take cross-sections of the cardiac arteries to examine under a microscope, impossible to tell if there's any trace of an infarct or embolism. The same applies to signs of petechiae in the lungs or anything that might suggest he was asphyxiated. Our friend's just been too long dead and, in the absence of wounds or marks of assault, all we can do is assume he dropped dead for some reason we can't discover at this distance in time.'

Pel frowned. 'Right,' he said. 'It was a heart attack and he fell inside. So why didn't anybody inform a doctor or the police?'

'Perhaps they were up to something in there,' Doc Minet suggested. 'And when he died they took fright and bolted.'

'They weren't so frightened that they didn't stay long enough to wall him up. Why wall him up anyway? Somebody weighed up the pros and cons. How old was he?'

'He wasn't young,' Minet said. 'But he wasn't old either. He could have been anything between twenty and fifty. Older than twenty, I'd imagine, because he's fully developed in every way. But younger than sixty because after fifty the bones begin to show changes. He was well built and I should say strong. With red hair and probably, judging by the bone structure, with a prominent nose.'

'After thirty years,' Pel said grimly, 'that will be a great help.'

Even as Pel and Darcy were discussing the post mortem on the body at Puyceldome, Nosjean and Dr Cham were just buttoning up again after their own post mortem on the body found at Garcy.

'Thirteen times,' Dr Cham said, offering a cigarette. 'With what I think were butcher's knives. Whatever they were, they were pointed, single-edged and sharp. Five of the stab wounds were in the back, but none of them need have been fatal. If he'd had attention, in fact, he'd probably have recovered. The other wounds were either in the chest, stomach or side. Judging by the wounds on his hands and forearms he put up a fight and collected more wounds as he did so.'

Nosjean said nothing. Cham, in his opinion, was right.

'What is odd, though,' Cham continued, 'is that none of the wounds seems to have been aimed at a vulnerable part of the body. And there were *two* knives. Both the same type but one larger and therefore slightly broader at the base of the blade than the other. Some of the wounds were wider than the others. Both knives were pointed and long – about twenty-odd centimetres. Say the length of a carving knife or the sort of knives butchers use to dress meat. One was used to stab him six times, the other seven, not counting the slashes on his hands and forearms and the one on his cheek, which I reckon were done as he tried to escape.'

'If none of the wounds was so desperate,' Nosjean said thoughtfully, 'why *didn't* he escape? Surely he'd try to run. He was found within reach of his car. The car had been moved, true, but he doesn't seem to have tried to get in.'

'Suppose he couldn't?'

'None of the wounds was on his legs. Why couldn't he?'

Cham gestured. 'Suppose, when he turned away from his attacker, he found himself facing a second attacker. Two knives were used because there are two different kinds of wounds. But I can't imagine him being attacked by someone with a knife and then that they threw it down and tried to finish him off with a different one. And I certainly can't imagine him being attacked by someone with a knife in each hand. I'm wondering if there were *two* attackers.'

'Two?' Nosjean said thoughtfully. 'That seems to indicate he picked up *two* people. But who'd pick up *two* hitch-hikers these days? And nobody's going to drive into those woods away from the main road with a couple of men.'

'If one had a gun, he would,' Cham said. 'There are a lot of things you'd do with a gun stuck up your nose.'

'But he'd never pick up two men in the first place. Nobody's that silly these days.'

'Well, you don't often see two men hitch-hiking together,' Cham agreed. 'They'd never get a ride for that very reason. Suppose one was a girl. He'd be off-guard if a girl stopped him, wouldn't he? He wouldn't be suspicious of a girl. But, having stopped for her and while she's got the door open so he can't drive off, out pops a man from behind the trees. It's an old dodge. A pretty girl does her stuff to get him to stop. A show of leg. That sort of thing. But then he finds she has someone with her. Probably holding a gun.'

Nosjean had already arranged with the radio studio to issue an appeal for anyone who might have seen Michel Vienne picking up a passenger on the N6 on the day he died. It wasn't a busy road but it was popular with hitch-hikers in the way the motorway wasn't. The police watched the motorway and you couldn't stop, and the only way to get a lift there was to ask motorists at one of the petrol or service stations. The N6 was different. It wasn't so often patrolled by police, and hitch-hikers had discovered it was a good route to use for the south.

Cham's theory had changed things considerably. Nosjean and De Troq' had been busy checking and cross-checking on single hitch-hikers known to have been picked up on the day of Vienne's death. Now they began to look for couples, and there was a surprisingly good response to their appeal. There had been a normal amount of traffic along the N6 and a large number of hitch-hikers, all young and mostly alone, though there had been a few boy and girl combinations. Nobody had seen two men seeking lifts.

Cham had been able to fix the hour of Vienne's death by the half-digested lunch in his stomach so they could assume that he'd picked up his passenger or passengers during the afternoon and this helped them to fix a time.

But all the couples who had been reported to have picked up lifts seemed to have behaved themselves. And, since they had all been picked up well to the north of where Vienne had been found and had all been taken all the way to Lyons, they had to be eliminated. Some of them, in fact, seemed to have struck up a good relationship with their drivers, some of whom – older men with children who hitched lifts elsewhere in the country – had even been friendly enough to provide a meal on the way.

The case was becoming complicated with enough enquiries to keep Nosjean and his team busy. They seemed to have established a few possibilities, however, and Dr Cham had been among their most enthusiastic supporters. As Nosjean finished clearing his desk at the end of the day, the doctor was waiting to buy him a beer. As they rose to go, De Troq' joined them. He had been working with the police in Garcy so that nothing was missed. He looked tired but he immediately held out a plastic bag. Inside was a woman's hair-slide.

'It was found where Vienne was lying,' he said. 'A bit lost in the grass. It must have been underneath him so it must have been there when he fell. Leguyader's boys are undecided how long exactly it had been there.'

'A long time,' Nosjean said. 'Women don't go scattering hair-slides and hairpins about these days.'

De Troq' shook his head. 'Not as long as that,' he insisted. 'The Lab boys thought a few days at the most – perhaps the day before Vienne was murdered, perhaps even the same day.'

'So whose is it?'

'Well, whoever it belongs to, it doesn't belong to his wife,' De Troq' said. 'I've asked her. I thought it might have been one of hers and he had had it in his pocket. Something like that. She said immediately it wasn't hers and that she'd never owned a slide like it.'

'It's not much,' Nosjean said. 'It's a cheap slide and there'll be plenty of them about. I bet you can buy them in the Nouvelles Galeries in packets of ten.'

'It doesn't have a manufacturer's name on it. But perhaps we can find out where they were distributed and which shops bought them.'

'Cheap shops,' Nosjean said. 'Not the sort of shops where they have files on their customers.'

'You never know.' De Troq' grinned. 'She might have been a raving beauty, a child of the nobility, a film star, well known to everybody – '

Nosjean grinned back. ' – Who discussed her purchase with the shop assistant because there was a story attaching to it. She was on her way to an assignation with Jean-Paul Belmondo or Robert Redford and lost her slide and had to nip in to get one to replace it because she was running late. And they discussed it long enough for the assistant to have a clear recollection of it.'

'But it wasn't her,' De Troq' said. '*She* wasn't the type. She's beautiful and kind and had just been offered a part in a glamorous new TV soap opera. But she dropped the slide in the studio and another girl picked it up. Some girl who makes the coffee or sweeps the floor – a different type altogether, mean, cruel, grasping – and she picked it up and dropped it again while she was murdering Vienne.'

They grinned at each other. They were good friends and often put on little imaginative dramas. 'It's a nice line,' Nosjean said. 'Perhaps we ought to set up as script writers.'

'Only one thing wrong,' Cham commented drily.

'What's that?'

'You're assuming that mean, cruel, grasping people are all poor. It's wrong. You must have heard of Cinderella.'

'That's it, of course,' Nosjean agreed. 'We've got it now! It was one of the ugly sisters.'

Sometimes it was possible to get some fun out of police work.

They were all inclined to be busy with their own thoughts as they sank their beers.

The heat had come at last. After weeks of indifferent days and cool winds, the weather seemed to be trying to make up for its past failures. It was humid, and elderly men in the bar carried their jackets over their arms and wiped the perspiration from their faces.

Nosjean was thinking of Mijo Lehmann with whom he shared a flat. He couldn't imagine how he had ever managed to live before he met her, and even his family were now beginning to approve. De Troq' was just glad to be on his own base. Garcy was a small town with a small town's comforts and small-town minds and De Troq' was inclined to be arrogant. He had recently met a girl in the Palais de Justice who also had a title of sorts – Second Empire, not Old Régime like De Troq's, but nothing to sneeze at – and he liked to feel he was moving in the right company. Dr Cham was beginning to see himself as a great pathologist and imagined himself moving without any problems into Doc Minet's place when he retired. As he did so, another thought occurred to him.

'Suppose', he said, 'that the girl who encouraged Vienne to stop and pick up her and her companion was involved in the killing, too.'

Nosjean said nothing. Cham was brighter than he looked and he was beginning to think that for deputies they were doing very well. Himself and De Troq' instead of Pel and Darcy; Cham instead of Doc Minet; Minoli from Fingerprints instead of Prélat; Du Toit, Leguyader's deputy from the Lab. A few bright ideas had turned up without any prompting from the big boys and he began to see them cracking the case without any help from their departmental heads. It was team spirit at its best.

'What makes you think that?' he asked.

Cham finished his beer. 'The wounds,' he said. 'The depth of some of the wounds. I've been looking at butchers' knives in Labarres', the hardware people, and though they're all standard sizes, there are none which fit the wounds exactly. They're all a little wider. Which seems to indicate the blades weren't driven into their full length, so that the widest part of the blade never came into contact with the flesh. That would explain why the wounds aren't the right width, wouldn't it?'

It certainly would, and it made Nosjean think.

'That doesn't seem to indicate the attack was made by someone with the muscle power of a man,' he agreed. 'It takes strength to drive a blade into flesh and it isn't something a woman would have.'

'And it doesn't look to me as if they knew much about it,' Cham said. 'The wounds are just stab wounds, but they don't seem to have been aimed at any vital part of the body. Vienne's dead because he bled to death, not because some vital organ was hit. That also seems to indicate a female. I think men know more about these things because a lot of them have done their time in uniform and been trained in killing, and wounds are the sort of thing that crop up in the sort of books men read, the films they watch. Women don't read that sort of book or watch that sort of film.'

He paused. 'Suppose,' he went on, 'suppose he picked up *two* of them.'

'Two of what?'

'Suppose it was two girls.'

'Would two girls go in for this sort of killing?' Nosjean asked. 'Surely not.'

But it was an idea, and the following day they began to look at the all-girl couples they had previously rejected. The thing seemed to be changing all the time and Dr Cham, unprepossessing though he might be in looks, certainly seemed able to use his brains.

Then they learned that the N6 had picked up a bit of a reputation they hadn't so far been aware of. It seemed that men who were anxious to make sexual overtures to passengers they picked up liked to use the route because it was quieter and well wooded. As a result, girls who were prepared to pay in the way the drivers wished to be paid for the lifts they gave had started to use it, too. With this in mind, it didn't take long to learn that Vienne had used the road often and from this that he had had a roving eye.

They didn't go to Vienne's wife to find out his habits, but called at his office and spoke to his colleagues. What they said indicated that Vienne wasn't the saint his wife thought he was.

'He liked the girls,' they said. 'He always did. After he got married, he kept away from them for a while, but it started again, especially when he was on the trot, doing his rounds of calls. He more than once admitted staying at hotels with women he'd picked up *en route*.'

'Hitch-hikers?'

'Wouldn't put it past him.'

# 7

The interview with Vienne's wife was more difficult. Vienne, his wife considered, was a good husband and father but she had a strong suspicion that when he went off on his selling trips he wasn't above picking up a girl wherever he happened to be.

'I don't know,' she insisted. 'It was just a feeling I had.'

'Would he pick up hitch-hikers?' De Troq' asked.

'I think so. He was a bit soft-hearted and didn't like to see anybody stuck.'

'Even these days?'

'He might have done.'

'*Girl* hitch-hikers?'

Vienne's wife suddenly began to cry. 'A girl hitch-hiker more than anybody,' she wailed.

As the questioning went on, it began to appear that Vienne had had more than a roving eye. He had had roving hands, too, and more than one of his wife's friends had complained about his behaviour at parties. His wife had loyally and steadfastly turned a blind eye.

It began to put a different slant on what they knew, because it now began to seem that Vienne had been *in the habit* of picking up young girl hitch-hikers and then demanding payment in kind for the ride.

The hair-slide they'd joked about suddenly took on a new significance. They had assumed at first that it had been dropped by someone in a family who had happened to picnic a day or two before in the spot where Vienne had died, but now it was no longer the joke they'd made of it.

'Let's find out exactly how long it had been there,' Nosjean suggested.

When they got down to it, it didn't take the Lab long.

'Forty-eight hours,' they told De Troq'.

'Which means it was dropped about the time he was done in,' Nosjean decided. 'Even just before or during the scuffle. Let's assume it was done *at the time* he was killed.'

'In which case,' De Troq' said, 'we might reasonably also assume that it belonged to whoever did for him.'

It was the sort of thing that only happened in fiction. A cigarette with the killer's name on it specially made for his fastidious tastes. A perfume used only by one person known to the victim. A special sort of lipstick. A print from a shoe made for the foot of a cripple known to the dead man. A hair-slide – especially a cheap one – didn't quite come into those categories but the chances were that it *had* been dropped by a girl engaged in a life and death struggle with a man trying to escape. It wasn't much but when you hadn't much it was a great leap forward.

'Let's find out where it came from,' Nosjean suggested. 'Is it a girl's slide or a woman's?'

'A girl's,' Leguyader's man, Du Toit, said. 'I think they were young. Young enough to tempt him anyway.'

'But they didn't have sex with him,' Doc Cham insisted. 'There were no signs that he'd indulged. I think they'd just arrived and they went for him almost at once. I think they attacked him when he wasn't looking. Perhaps when he was bending down, because one of the wounds is in a direction that would be difficult – almost impossible – if he were upright. Perhaps one of them dropped that hair-slide deliberately and as he bent to pick it up, he was stabbed in the back. As he turned to defend himself he was stabbed by the other girl and they continued to stab him.'

'With new knives,' Du Toit said.

They turned. 'What's that?'

'New knives,' Du Toit insisted. 'We decided in the Lab that the knives were new. Old ones tend to leave a sign that they're old. Deposit. Rust. A variety of things. We decided these were new.'

'New?'

'They'd been bought just before they were used on Vienne – perhaps especially for the job.'

Well, that was also an idea worth looking into.

'He fell to the ground,' Cham went on. 'But he didn't die at once. No way. I reckon he must have taken an hour and a half to bleed to death. He must have been moaning with pain, begging for help.'

'But there's nothing to indicate they did anything to assist him,' Du Toit said. 'They must have stood watching him die.'

'I think they went through his pockets,' Cham said. 'And took what was in his wallet and emptied the contents of the glove compartment of the car. I think they then tried to start the car to drive it away but it went into the pothole and, as they didn't really know how to drive – something else that indicates young girls – in the end they abandoned it and walked back to the N6 and got their ride to Lyons.'

It was good solid thinking and the next move was to contact the Lyons police and ask them to keep a sharp look-out for two girls, both young, probably both pretty, who were on the move together. It was a slender chance but it was the only one they had. The other thing, the point raised by Du Toit, was to find where the knives that had been used came from. If they were new, they had recently been bought so Nosjean set his men searching round the hardware shops in towns adjoining the N6 for the one which had sold them.

In the meantime De Troq's drug problem hadn't gone away. Criminals, drug addicts and fools weren't in the habit of consulting with the police on when they might put into operation one of their nefarious schemes, and within ten days it was clear that the junkies about the city weren't going short. De Troq', keeping an eye on the situation in between helping Nosjean with the Garcy killing, saw it plainly.

'It's still coming in, Patron,' he told Pel. 'And somebody's pushing it. It seems to be time to see Marceau again.'

But Marceau was no help. His supplier had covered himself

with anonymity and his information about his fixes came in a roundabout way.

'I don't know who's taken the distribution over,' he said.

'Somebody has, though, hasn't he?' De Troq' pointed out.

'Yes. But I don't know who.'

'Who supplies you now?'

'A type called Gorgeous.'

'Who's he? And where do I find him?'

Gorgeous turned out to be a good-looking, almost pretty, boy of about nineteen. He was dressed in pink trousers and a pale green shirt and, like Speedy Sam, he ran. But he wasn't all that fast and when Brochard, who was again waiting in the wings, caught up with him, pushing in front of him the boy who had bought from him, he was lying on his face, with De Troq' sitting on his head while he went through the pockets of his jacket.

De Troq' looked up and held out his hand to Brochard. In it were several small packets containing white powder. 'Got him red-handed,' he said.

Gorgeous didn't look half so sprightly as he sat in the chair by the desk in the interrogation room. The interrogation room was never a place to give confidence to wrongdoers. It was about as comfortable as the inside of a tank, with brown furniture, brown walls, brown linoleum. A policeman stood in the corner, watching.

De Troq' arranged a notebook on the table before him and carefully sharpened his pencil, taking a great deal of time over it. Sitting at the other side of the table, despite his hostile expression, Gorgeous was plainly nervous.

De Troq' studied him for a moment and leaned forward, resting his elbows on the table. Then he changed his mind and began to light a cigarette with the same care he had given to the pencil sharpening so that the boy was able to absorb the bare, brown-painted windowless room, the hard modern table and the lamp fixed to it with a clamp.

'Name?' De Troq' said. 'Better have it for the record.'

Gorgeous stared back at him defiantly. 'I don't have to give a name,' he said.

De Troq' looked at the policeman and gestured at the boy with his pencil. 'Better tell him that he does,' he said.

The policeman spoke to the boy, who looked at De Troq' a little bewildered. '*Why* do I have to?' he demanded.

De Troq' sat back, as if taken aback by the retort, and the boy seemed pleased his defiance had worked, because De Troq' seemed on the defensive suddenly and it made him feel much more at ease.

As he leaned back, confident again, De Troq' fiddled with his notebook once more then he rose from his seat and began to speak quietly with the policeman in the corner, several times indicating the boy. What he said was unimportant because the manoeuvre was designed simply to make the boy nervous.

The room was airless in the heat and the move succeeded. As the whispering went on, the boy's face took on a pinched look. Several times, De Troq' raised his voice deliberately, clearly talking about prison sentences, and he saw the boy shift restlessly in his seat. Smiling, he slapped the policeman's shoulder, as though the boy's fate were the last thing in the world he was interested in, and returned to the table. The boy had lost his defiance by this time and was watching him warily.

De Troq' picked up his pen. 'Name?'

The boy glanced at the policeman and swallowed. His voice emerged as a croak. 'Douanet,' he cleared his throat and his voice became firmer. 'Philippe Douanet.'

'Address?'

'Apartment 6, 15 Rue Coudray.'

'You at the University?'

'No. I'm a carpenter.'

'Employed?'

'Not at the moment.'

'Why not? Too tiring?'

'I'm not *just* a carpenter,' the boy snapped. 'I'm a designer. I've been taking a course at the Technical College. But they don't like people who've got brains.'

'You a Communist?'

'Why?'

'Just a question.'

The boy gestured angrily. 'No, I'm not interested in that lot. They're nothing but political gangsters.'

'Not these days. And they have the same problems in Russia with drugs we have here.'

De Troq' wrote in his notebook, his face expressionless, as though the boy's attitude was as common as measles.

'How long have you been at the Tech?'

'Seven terms.'

'This one looks like being your last. Where did you get it?'

'What?'

'We know you're pushing.'

The boy's face was grey and sweating. 'I can't tell you. I don't know. I was told to meet him in Moncey and I did.'

'Description.'

'It was dark.'

'Name?'

'I was told, but a lorry was passing and I didn't catch it. In any case, I don't find him he finds me.'

'You pass it on to other students at the Tech?'

The boy looked worried. 'I have done.'

'You'd better give us the name.'

'I can't.'

'Where did *he* get it?'

'I don't know.'

'Where does he distribute?'

'I don't know that either. He just said he had several places. He said he got around a lot and his customers were all over the countryside.'

'Where does he operate from?'

'I don't know.'

'Since you know so little I'd better turn you over to the police. They'll get it out of you.'

'No! Never! I daren't.'

'Was he tall?'

'Medium.'

'Dark?'

'Medium.'

De Troq' sat back. 'I hope there are other types at the Tech who've met this type,' he said. 'Because if you're lying we'd have to believe *you* were running the whole show. And a man in Marseilles was sent to prison the other week for twenty years for doing that. Did you know?'

The boy was silent and De Troq' smiled. 'Your intelligence work's not very good, Gorgeous. Surely, you never thought *you* were going to make a killing out of this business.'

The boy writhed and said nothing.

'I wonder if the people who suggested it to you set you up.'

'Set me up?'

'There's a manoeuvre in war that's known as a feint. It's to mislead the opposition and draw his reserves, or provide the enemy with information it's wished he should have. Usually, the poorest troops are used for feints, because then, when they get killed or taken prisoner, nothing's lost. They're considered expendable. I wonder if *you* were considered expendable, Philippe Douanet, known as Gorgeous. Someone to draw us off the big-timers. Because, for your efforts, you're likely to go to prison for a very long time.'

Douanet's face was white but he said nothing. De Troq' continued coldly. 'Because you were considered expendable, *you'll* be the one who goes to jail. Not the man who's running you. We don't know who he is but he won't be the one who suffers. Not the boss. Not the leader. Leaders never get sent to the front when there's a war on, do they? It's always fools like you. Leaders are never the ones who get their heads cracked.' De Troq' gestured at the policeman. 'I'm going to leave you to the tender mercies of this gentleman.' The policeman obligingly supplied a grimace that might have been a smile but looked more like a threat. 'He's good at his job. You'll be taken to 72 Rue d'Auxonne – which is the delightful name we have here for the prison. I hope you'll think about things. Later you might feel disposed to tell me more.'

As De Troq' rose to leave the interrogation room, the boy gave him a despairing betrayed look.

'Never!' he shouted.

'Never's a long time.'

'I defy you!'

De Troq' smiled. 'Cross-examining you's like whipping a puppy.'

'I'll never tell you anything!'

De Troq' smiled again as he closed the door. He wasn't so sure. But he hadn't time to worry. Nosjean would be expecting him and he felt he could safely leave time and the bleak interior of a prison cell to work on Philippe Douanet.

As he waited for De Troq' to return, Nosjean sat staring at the reports on the N6 murder. So far nothing had turned up from their enquiries. The Lyons police had come up with nothing and neither had the men searching for the shop which had sold the knives. Between them, Dr Cham, Du Toit and Labarres', the hardware shop in the Rue de la Liberté, had worked out what they considered a reasonably good description of the knives and Nosjean's squad were wearing their feet out asking. Labarres' had even produced photographs of a set of butchers' knives they sold which fitted the bill and supplied measurements from the manufacturers, but so far nothing had appeared.

In the meantime, their suspects seemed to have vanished off the face of the earth. Where were they? Nobody had yet come forward claiming to have seen them. Then, staring at the list of Vienne's belongings, wondering if there were anything there that might tell him more of the man and consequently more of the people who had killed him, Nosjean noticed a significant absence. There was no watch.

They had accepted that Vienne's wallet had been rifled but no one had worried about the absence of a watch. Yet Vienne must have had a watch. He was a man who was constantly on the move from one firm to another and must have had appointments. Any man who had appointments had to have a watch.

Nosjean picked up the telephone and rang Doc Minet's office. Cham answered. 'Well,' he agreed, 'he must have had one. There was a white mark on his wrist where he'd worn one.'

Slamming down the internal telephone, Nosjean demanded the number of the local radio station and asked them to broadcast an appeal for anyone to come forward who had recently bought a watch from anywhere other than a jeweller's. Once again, it wasn't much. But it might give them a lead.

# 8

The following day there was an unexpected development and the balloon really went up.

A cop was shot.

His name was Jacques Burges and he was found alongside his little Renault van which was standing at the side of the road just outside Montcerf on the edge of the Forest of Grasigne. The engine had been switched off but the door was wide open. Jacques Burges lay alongside and two spent cartridge cases were found beside him. But they weren't from Burges' gun. That was still in his holster unused, so it seemed there hadn't been a fight, and Burges' left hand still gripped his notebook and his right hand his pencil. The notebook was up to date but the last entry was unfinished and told them nothing.

All it gave them was the date, the twelfth, and the time, 7.30 p.m. It seemed that Officer Burges had had cause to stop someone for questioning and had just been on the point of writing down their particulars and their name when he'd been shot. He'd been hit twice, once in the heart and once in the face.

When a cop was killed there was always a lot of indignation in the Hôtel de Police. And it was always worse when the cop in question was young. Officer Burges was twenty-four and he had a wife and a small daughter, and Inspector Nadauld, who ran the Uniformed Branch and was his superior officer, returned from seeing his wife, looking shaken.

'She's expecting another,' he announced. 'And she's an orphan without any family of her own, while Burges was an only child. His family took to the girl because they'd had a daughter who died. They died a year ago – a car accident – and now Burges is dead. God knows what she'll do.'

The hat went round the Hôtel de Police and all the police stations and substations in smaller towns and villages. The response was enormous because every cop in or out of uniform knew that next time it might well be himself and his family would be as dependent on help as Madame Burges was.

The Press came out with their usual headlines. POLICEMAN BUTCHERED. It wasn't hard to work out how they arrived at them. Look at the files. It had happened before and was all there from last time. When the cops did anything wrong they were '*flics*', when they were beaten up or shot they were always 'policemen'. The Press knew how to behave, and their stories brought in more subscriptions from charitably minded citizens for the fund for Madame Burges.

The Chief was tight-mouthed all day after the killing and Judge Polverari, who was handling the case, looked heavily depressed. Judge Brisard made one of his pompous speeches at the Chief's conference. He was an ardent churchgoer and liked to expound at times when he could find anybody to listen.

'We must give him a good funeral,' he said. 'It'll be expected of us. After all, it was for the glory of France. Young Burges did his job and insisted on doing it, come what may. He chose duty.'

'He was shot when he wasn't looking,' Pel snapped.

'He died bravely and nobly nevertheless.'

Pel snorted. A lot of nonsense was talked about dying, and people regularly pontificated about going to Heaven. War memorials went on about the glorious dead and on the televison Indians shot cowboys who died nobly – as if nobility were some sort of consolation for no longer being able to see or hear or feel.

'There's no glory in dying,' he growled at Brisard. 'If you want to know what being dead's like you should wear a blindfold, stuff your ears with ear-plugs, sew up your mouth, then lock yourself in a dark room and throw the key away. That's what being dead's like. Burges would never have chosen that.'

As Pel stamped out of the room, slamming the door behind

him, Judge Brisard went pink and, glancing at the Chief, announced that there were things he had to do and departed hurriedly.

For a while Pel sat in his room fuming, his face red. He smoked two cigarettes in quick succession. Judge Brisard, he decided, had the brains of a parrot, and a mouth full of parroted clichés. Policemen didn't go round thinking of the glory of God – not even much of the conception of duty. Mostly they found themselves trapped by circumstances – facing a gun for no other reason than that they just happened to have been on the spot when the gun was produced. After that they behaved according to their personalities. The bold and the brave sometimes had a go – and ended up dead. The sensible either ducked or tried to talk their way out of it.

Smoke was still coming out of his ears as the first of the black *camions* carrying policemen set off to fan out from the spot where Burges had been found. Within an hour the Forest of Grasigne was full of cops armed with sub-machine guns, their faces tense, their eyes narrow. There had been a prison break at Auxerre and two men had got free, both of them in for robbery with violence, and it was assumed they had acquired a gun and been responsible, and no one was taking any chances. Since the Forest of Grasigne was as big as Paris and wild enough to contain boar, no one really expected to find what they were looking for, but they were all nervous in case they did.

Searching was a job for Uniformed Branch, though, and Pel's men confined themselves to facts in the hope of getting an identity. Everybody was called in and the enquiry at Puycel-dome was dropped for the time being. A dead cop was more important than a thirty-year-old corpse, and Pel deployed his men wherever they might be most useful. The Chief decided to ask for help in the shape of extra men from neighbouring areas.

'We can't allow them to get away with it,' he said. 'Apart from poor Burges, it's a matter of principle. Burges represented the law and we have to show the law can't be defied or defiled.'

A lot of motorists were put to some inconvenience as their vehicles were halted and searched. Road blocks had been set up and everybody who passed through, on foot, on bicycles, or in four-wheeled vehicles, was questioned. There was nobody who resembled the men from Auxerre, however, and, in fact, it was with some surprise that they heard that evening that the two escapees from Auxerre had given themselves up at Avallon. They immediately swore they knew nothing about Burges and they had to be believed because they had been heading in quite the opposite direction.

The revelation took the wind out of police sails at once and the major operation for the apprehension of the murderers was called off as they tried to work out what second thoughts they ought to have. Only hardened criminals normally took pot shots at cops and, now that the men from Auxerre had given themselves up, they seemed to have no one else they could look at. It left a sort of hiatus in procedure as they began to call in the men they'd deployed in the forest and tried to decide how best they could use them instead; because, whichever way you might look at it, a cop was still dead and whoever had killed him was still at large.

While Inspector Nadauld, of Uniformed Branch, drove in frantic circles round the Forest of Grasigne, trying to round up his scattered men and wishing he hadn't been quite so thorough about their deployment as he had, Pel sat in the Chief's office with the experts, listening to Doc Minet's version of Burges' death.

'I think the one that hit him in the chest was fired first,' he was saying. 'The one in the face was fired after he fell backwards. From the angle, it must have been. No one would bend down to shoot upwards. The bullet entered the head at an upward angle so if he'd been standing up whoever held the gun would have to have been holding it low and pointing upwards. Instead, I think they held it pointing down and, because Burges was on the ground it entered his head at the same angle.'

'The gun was a 6.35,' the Ballistics man said. 'Probably an FAS Apex. Eight-shot single-magazine weapon made by Fabrique d'Armes de St Etienne. Cheap and not difficult to get hold of. People buy them for self-protection. Small and not very accurate. Not a hit man's weapon.'

'So it doesn't sound like a professional?' the Chief said.

'No. And it's also probably not new because it has a hammer

that strikes fractionally off-centre. It shouldn't be hard to identify.'

'If we find it,' Leguyader observed cynically.

'What about the road blocks?' the Chief asked.

'They're still manned,' Pomereu, of Traffic, announced. 'Everybody who passes through's being questioned and searched for the gun.'

They were still at it when Nosjean and Doc Cham turned up at the Hôtel de Police. Nosjean's face was grim as they appeared outside Darcy's office. When Pel returned to his room, Darcy followed him in, and for once there wasn't any smile on his face and the flippant attitude he normally adopted towards his work was missing.

'I've been talking to Nosjean and young Cham,' he said. 'Doc Minet's deputy. They've come up with a bright idea. They've decided that killing in the wood at Garcy was probably done by a couple of girls.'

'So?'

'They're wondering now if this new one – Burges – was done by the same two girls.'

'What?' Pel sat up. 'Girls?' he said. 'What makes them wonder that?'

'They've come to the conclusion that that chap at Garcy had picked up two girl hitch-hikers. They worked out that he wouldn't pick up a male hiker or two male hikers, but they're certain from the wounds he received that he was attacked by two people – and they think now it was by two girls because a man might well pick up two girls, thinking he was safe. He might even have been hoping for a little something on the side in return for his kindness. It goes on all the time.'

Pel lit a cigarette and drew several puffs at it. 'I'd better have a word with Nosjean,' he said. 'Where is he?'

'In my office,' Darcy said. 'With Cham.'

'Send them in here.'

When Nosjean and Cham appeared, Pel gestured to chairs while Darcy closed the door and leaned on it.

'Right,' Pel said. 'I've heard your theory. Inform me.'

Nosjean looked at Cham and drew a deep breath. He explained how he and Dr Cham had reached their conclusions about Vienne's death and why they had thought what they had about Burges.

'Go on.'

'When we read the facts on Burges we immediately thought he might have been shot by the same girls – or by one of them. His van wasn't driven away and that's odd, because you'd expect someone who'd shot a cop would want to put as much territory between them and the crime as possible. Even if it meant using a police van for a while. If they'd taken Burges' Renault they could have been a hundred kilometres away within an hour or so. So why didn't they? For the same reason they didn't take Vienne's car from the woods. Because they couldn't drive. And why couldn't they drive, Patron? Because they had no driving licence. Because they weren't old enough to have one.'

'That makes sense.'

'We've been in touch with the radio people,' Nosjean went on, 'and asked for anybody who saw two girl hitch-hikers on the N6 to come forward. I expect Burges knew of the appeal. Perhaps he spotted two girls and wondered if they were the two we were looking for. He stopped them and asked them.'

'If he did, it seems they *were*.'

'That's what it's beginning to look like, Patron. When he started to ask questions, they shot him. He probably asked to see their identity cards and they fished in their handbags or whatever they were carrying. But instead of ID cards, one of them produced a gun. He was probably so busy looking at his notebook he didn't even see it until he was dying. It hangs together, Patron. We've already decided that Vienne was stabbed by two girls and we thought they must be young because none of the wounds was fatal – as if whoever had done it had only a rudimentary idea of where the vital organs in the human body are situated. Vienne died of loss of blood. Not one vital organ was touched. It all seemed to us to suggest youth or at least inexperience and above all, girls. Burges' murder seems to suggest the same thing, so what more likely than that they're the same girls?'

'Why weren't they picked up at a road block?' Pel snapped.

'The whole area was stopped up. They must have passed through one.'

'I expect they did, Patron. But who was looking for a couple of girls?'

'Have you spoken to Nadauld?'

'I've contacted him by radio and asked if any of his men noticed any hitch-hikers. Apparently, they didn't. They spoke to pedestrians who passed through the road blocks but no one noticed two young girls on their own. They were probably careful to pass through with others, of course, and weren't noticed, especially as no one was looking for girls.'

Pel frowned. 'If they stabbed Vienne to death, why didn't they stab Burges? He was looking at his notebook. He was off-guard.'

'It's easier with a gun, Patron,' Nosjean pointed out. 'A knife involves getting blood on your hands. They probably didn't enjoy that part of it. And they must have acquired a gun because we don't think they had one when they met Vienne on the N6.'

'Well, as Burges' was still in its holster, it must have been Vienne's.' Pel rose and gestured. 'I think you'd better find out if he was in the habit of carrying one. And if so, what kind.'

There was one way to find out. There had been no sign of a gun in the glove compartment of Vienne's car but there had been a duster among the objects scattered around his body and, sniffing at it, Nosjean immediately detected the distinctive smell of gun oil. A visit to the police garage where Vienne's car was still being kept under wraps for the attention of the Forensic and Fingerprint boys and a sniff at the glove compartment confirmed that a gun had been kept in there, obviously wrapped in the duster.

From that it didn't take long to learn for a fact that Burges had been shot by Vienne's gun. Madame Vienne, dry-eyed now and trying to face up to the fact that she was suddenly alone in the world, confirmed that her husband had indeed been in the habit of carrying a pistol in his car. She even managed to find the licence.

'He sometimes had to carry money,' she said.

'A lot?'

'Yes.'

'Was he carrying money the day he died?' Nosjean asked.

'Not that day. He had special days for it. But the gun was always kept in the car.'

De Troq', who had been examining the gun licence, looked up. 'Apex 6.35,' he said.

'Pity we haven't a spent bullet that Monsieur Vienne fired,' Nosjean said. 'That would confirm it.'

'But we have,' Madame Vienne said. 'He practised with it a few times when he first got it. He'd been in the army, of course, and knew about guns and he said he had to know whether it kicked up or down. I wasn't sure what he meant. But he brought a few spent cartridge cases home to show me. I used one of them as a pin holder for when I was sewing. You always need somewhere to put the pins you take out and this little brass thing was just the right size. You could put them in point down and they were easy to pick up again if you wanted them.'

The Forensic boys were happy to make a pronouncement on the cartridge case.

'Same gun,' they said. 'The hammer strikes a fraction off centre.'

# 9

They now had two murders but still no description.

Pomereu and his men came in for a tremendous roasting from the Chief for failing to notice two young girls passing through their roadblocks and, while armed to the teeth and paying full attention to car boots, for taking on trust what backpacks and handbags contained.

'We were looking for a couple of escaped convicts,' Pomereu complained in a bleat to Darcy. 'Not a couple of kids. It's not our job to frighten young girls.'

Meanwhile, flushed with success, Nosjean stepped up the search for the shop which had sold the two knives which had done Vienne to death. Du Toit was still insisting the knives were new and that they were bought not long before the murder. 'By a couple of women,' he said. 'They'd be young and wouldn't look like two housewives, so they might be remembered.'

By now, in addition to the main enquiries as to the how, the where and the why, they had several sets of enquiries going – the origin of the hair-slide, the shop that had sold the knives, the people who might have seen their suspects hitch-hiking.

As their men tramped from street to street or hunched over telephones, Nosjean and De Troq' began to look again at the female hitch-hikers who had so far been noticed along the N6. By checking and cross-checking carefully, they were slowly eliminating them when suddenly, unexpectedly, they hit pay dirt. One couple, described as very young, had a pattern about their hitch-hiking which seemed highly suspicious. They had picked up three rides to the north of where Vienne had been stabbed to death and in every case they had asked the driver if he was going to Lyons. Yet, although they had seemed to want to go to Lyons, in every case they had changed their minds and asked to be set down after only a few kilometres. Finally, they had picked up another ride somewhere just to the south of where Vienne had been found dead and this time, instead of asking to be set down, had ridden all the way into Lyons.

'I think we've got them,' Nosjean crowed.

'I don't think we have,' De Troq' pointed out. 'We've found two girls who might be the ones. But we have no names and addresses or descriptions, and they were obviously on their way somewhere. South, by the look of things. By this time, they're probably on the Mediterranean. Probably the Baltic. Perhaps Italy. Perhaps China. Perhaps even Russia. It's easy these days. They've probably picked up an airliner and emigrated to America.'

Nosjean pulled a face. It was a fair summary of the situation.

'I think', he said, 'that we'd better have a word with these drivers and see what they have to say.'

The four drivers who had given lifts to the two girls were brought to the Hôtel de Police. They were a little nervous, unsure of themselves and not enjoying being involved in a murder enquiry. Like most people questioned over a serious crime, they found it hard to accept that they were merely witnesses and not suspects. However, they confirmed Cham's theory that the girls were young and they all told much the same story.

The first was the tough-looking driver of a Nicolas wine lorry who had picked up two young girls south of Beaune. They had asked him if he was going to Lyons but beyond that they had not addressed a word to him except to answer questions he had put to them. After two or three kilometres, without discussing it with each other or with him, they had asked to be put down.

'What were they like?' De Troq' asked.

Though his description was vague, the lorry driver's conception of them indicated youth, long hair and prettiness.

'Except that they didn't look all that clean,' he added.

'How were they dressed?' Nosjean demanded.

The driver hadn't really noticed.

'Provocatively?'

The word seemed to puzzle the lorry driver.

'What sort of dresses?'

'One had a blue skirt. One a red. I remember that. And long sloppy sweaters.'

'These skirts: short or long?'

'Long – I think.'

The girls had made no overtures to him of any kind, he said. 'Some girls do,' he added.

The second driver, a man called Monnier and the owner of a car, had picked them up at roughly the spot where the wine lorry had set them down. Monnier thought they *were* provocatively dressed. They were wearing very short skirts and had allowed them to ride up as they sat down.

'Where were they in your car?' Nosjean asked.

'Rear seat.'

'Both of them?'

'Yes.'

'Couldn't that be dangerous these days?'

'I suppose it could. But it wasn't.'

'And you could see their skirts had ridden up?'

'In the mirror. I looked.'

'Do you make a habit of looking?'

'Yes.' Monnier grinned. 'I don't think they were wearing anything underneath the skirts.'

'You could tell that?'

'Not for certain. But I thought so. I'm sure one of them hadn't anything on underneath.'

His car had been giving trouble and he had had to stop after a kilometre or two to check the fan belt. When he returned to his seat, one of the girls had moved into the front passenger's seat. When he had driven off, she had put her hand on his knee and moved it up to his thigh.

'She said they were heading south but were short of money and anxious to earn some,' he pointed out. 'When I asked her what they intended to do to get it, she said they weren't very worried how. I thought that if I'd suggested it, we could have driven off the road and I could have had a bit of nooky for a few francs.'

'What did you say?'

'What do you think? I told them I wasn't interested. I'm not.'

Nosjean was inclined to doubt him. Any man who studied the rear mirror sufficiently to discover his passengers weren't wearing underwear probably indulged himself on occasion with female hitch-hikers. There must have been some reason this time why he hadn't.

'Why not?'

'I'm not that kind.'

'So,' De Troq' asked, 'why *do* you pick up girls?'

After a while they got him to admit after all that it *was* his habit to pick up girls for what he might get from them. There were no moral reservations, but this time he had been suspicious and had thought the situation dangerous. He hadn't liked the look of the two girls. He had watched them enough in the mirror to be able to give a description.

'Pretty,' he said. 'Good legs. One had blonde hair – dyed, I thought. Thin lips. The other was similar, but dark. In fact, I thought they were sisters. But the second one had plucked eyebrows. Very thin. Like Marlene Dietrich used to wear.'

It was something to go on.

'How old?'

'Sixteen. About that.'

Nosjean and De Troq' exchanged glances. Murderesses! Aged sixteen!

'What happened?'

'I told them I wasn't interested in sex.'

'But normally you were?'

Monnier grinned. 'Who isn't? But I said I'd still give them a ride to Lyons if the one in the front would stop stroking my thigh and the one in the back would close her legs and pull her skirt down. It was distracting. Soon afterwards they asked to be set down.'

'We think these same girls had been picked up by a truck driver just north of where you met them. He said they weren't provocatively dressed.'

'They were when I picked them up. They looked like hippies.'

'They wouldn't change at the roadside, surely?'

'Why not? They could put a mini skirt on under a longer wider skirt, then take off the first skirt.'

'You know this?'

'I've seen it done.'

'Had they any luggage?'

'Just two big cloth shoulder bags. The sort you can get everything in. They probably even just hitched up their skirts by turning the waistband over. A couple of turns and they'd become mini skirts.'

'Could you see if they'd turned the waistbands over?'

'No. They had these big sweaters on. Big and loose and coming down over their behinds.'

The third driver, a man called Rostane in his late fifties, was a spare desiccated man with grey hair and a straggling moustache. He had picked up the two girls in roughly the spot where Monnier had set them down. He was a writer and was working on a book about Rousseau and his thoughts had been far away.

'Why did you pick them up then?'

'I noticed them,' he said. 'My daughter hitch-hikes. I've warned her not to. She's a student. But you know what youngsters are like. She thinks she's safe. She trusts everybody.'

'I hope you tell her not to.'

'Yes, I do. I picked these two up because of what I'd warned my daughter about. I felt that if they were with me, no one else would be picking them up and they'd be safe. I thought they were two children.'

*'Children?'*

'Thirteen. About that.'

Thirteen! Nosjean and De Troq' exchanged startled glances once more.

'Did they make any advances to you?'

'Advances?'

'Sexual advances.'

Rostane hadn't noticed anything, but he was a little naïve and when Nosjean pressed him it seemed the girls *had* made advances but he hadn't noticed.

'Well, they said they needed money and were willing to do anything to get some,' he said.

'Did they say what they would do?'

'No. Not really.' Rostane slapped his forehead. 'My God,' he said. 'They were offering themselves sexually. I didn't realise.' His mouth hung open. 'Me? Holy Mother of God! Me! They suggested we turn off the road and go into the woods. They said they needed a rest. I told them I was in a bit of a hurry but that they could use the back seat to sleep if they wished. Soon afterwards they asked to be set down.'

'Where? Do you remember? Exactly.'

Rostane did. It turned out to be eight kilometres north of the turn-off to the glade where Vienne had been murdered.

The fourth and last driver, who had taken the girls all the way to Lyons from just south of where Vienne had been killed, agreed with the description of the girls as hippy types and that they wore mini skirts. He also confirmed the colour of their hair, and the thin lips of one, the thin eyebrows of the other.

'I think they were up to something,' he said. 'I was glad to get rid of them. I don't know what it was but they were managing to communicate with each other somehow. Not in words. But I noticed they made gestures to each other. I think it was some sort of secret sign language they'd developed.'

It seemed to be time to get all four drivers in together and let them argue it out. The move was very successful and ended in an argument where they swopped impressions that produced details.

'They were big girls,' the van driver said.

'Tall?'

'No. You know.' Monnier made gestures in front of him with his hands. 'Here. Big boobs. One of them, the older one, had blonde hair that looked dyed. The other had straight dark hair. They wore it long. Well below their shoulders. They were wearing mini skirts or skirts hitched up to look like mini skirts. Heavy sweaters. But no stockings, and not much else.'

'They used a lot of bad language,' the lorry driver offered.

'What sort?'

'You know. The sort a lot of youngsters use these days. They think it's the thing to do. It is, I suppose, with smart-arsed kids.'

Nosjean interrupted the discussion. 'Did either of these girls wear a slide in her hair?' he asked.

There was an immediate dead silence then Monnier spoke.

'They both did.'

'You're quite sure?'

'Dead sure.'

What he said was confirmed by the lorry driver and the man who had taken them into Lyons, and Nosjean gestured at De Troq', who fished in a drawer and brought out a plastic bag and laid it on the desk.

'This one?' he asked.

The three men looked at each other then Monnier nodded. 'That one,' he agreed.

Nosjean was thoughtful as De Troq' showed the four men out.

'These are the ones,' he said as De Troq' returned. 'There are just too many descriptions that fit. Now we have to find out if they bought the knives *en route*. If they did we're a step nearer. Young girls don't normally carry butchers' knives around with them so they must have bought them specially for the job, and they did that because they must have planned it some time before and at that time they hadn't a gun and didn't know where to lay their hands on one.'

They had continued to badger Lyons to keep a sharp look-out for their suspects and had been reasonably confident they would turn up, so it was with something of a shock that they learned that, yes, certainly, two girls answering their descriptions *had* been seen, but not in Lyons.

'Where?' Nosjean asked.

'Near Villefranche. At one of the service stations on the northbound carriageway of the motorway.'

It brought a new angle. The girls they were seeking must have moved north again and were probably now back in their own area, so that God alone knew where they'd got to. They would have to start again, questioning motorists to see if they had been picked up, and alert the towns alongside the motorway to the north in case they were there.

'*They* must have caught the radio appeal, too,' De Troq' said. 'I expect they have a radio. Every kid over ten does these days. They doubtless decided they were better off somewhere else than Lyons.'

As they were talking, the telephone went. It was the man on the switchboard. 'There's a type on the line called Claude Fraslin,' he said. 'He says he bought a watch in a bar. He wondered if it was the one you're interested in.'

'Who did he buy it from?'

'He says a girl.'

Nosjean snatched up the telephone, spoke briefly to the man at the other end of the line, then headed for where his car was parked. Two hours later, well to the north, he was sitting in the office of the manager of a brickworks. With them was Claude Fraslin, the brickworks foreman, a small thickset man with arms like the branches of a tree. He indicated the gold watch Nosjean was holding.

'I bought it in a bar in Avallon,' he said.

'Why?'

'What do you mean, why?'

'Well, do you usually buy watches from someone in a bar?'

Fraslin looked indignant. 'If you're suggesting I knew it was stolen, you're wrong. I was out with the wife and kids and I'd just lost my own watch. It had one of those metallic wrist straps and the catch must have come undone. We looked all over for it but it had probably been gone an hour before I noticed. Then we were sitting in this bar. The kids wanted a drink. Come to that, so did I, and this watch was offered to me. It's a good one. You can see that. And it was cheap.'

'Who offered?'

'This girl.'

'What did she look like?'

Fraslin couldn't help – he'd been looking at the watch not the girl.

'Was she on her own?'

'No, there was another girl with her. A bit younger. She said she was her sister.'

'So you bought the watch?'

'I needed a watch.'

'Did the girl give a name?'

'No.'

'You were taking a risk buying a watch from someone you didn't know. It might not have been any good.'

Fraslin snorted. 'I'm not that stupid,' he said. 'I listened to it. I could tell by listening that it was a good watch.'

'It belonged to a murdered man.'

'Holy Mother of God! I didn't know. Does that mean I've lost the watch?'

'I'm afraid so. It's evidence. We shall have to keep it. Perhaps you can get it back later. I don't know. This girl: did she say anything about herself?'

'Did *she* do the murder?'

'Perhaps. We're not sure yet.'

'She didn't look old enough.'

'You don't have to be apprenticed. Did she say why she was selling the watch?'

'She said it was her father's and he'd just died. They needed the money to go to Paris and find work and they hadn't the rail fare. It was my wife really.'

'What was your wife?'

'She persuaded me. She's soft-hearted – especially for someone young who's in trouble. She nudged me and said, "Go on, Claude. Buy it." So I did.'

Madame Vienne identified the watch at once. 'Yes,' she said. 'That's my husband's watch.'

'You're quite certain?'

'I bought it for his birthday last year. He had a lot of appointments and he needed a good watch. Where did you find it?'

'It was offered for sale in a bar in Avallon.'

'Who by? The man who murdered him?'

Nosjean hesitated. 'We think that the person who offered it was the person who killed him,' he said.

Fraslin's description of the two girls could only have been

described as casual. But a visit to his wife brought better results, because, while he had been examining the watch, she had been studying the girls. Her description matched that of the drivers.

'Aged between fifteen and nineteen,' she said. 'Long-haired. One dark. One fair. Artificial, I'd say. The kids all do it these days. The one with the fair hair, the older one, had thin lips; the other had plucked eyebrows. Very plucked. Like Marlene Dietrich. They both wore short skirts and sweaters and carried large cloth shoulder bags.'

Big enough, Nosjean decided, to carry butchers' knives or Vienne's gun.

He was thoughtful as he drove away. They would now have to put out a new appeal, asking if anyone had given their suspects a lift north and, if so, where to? It was quite possible that by this time they were in Paris and, if they were, the chances of finding them were almost nil. Girls who stood out like sore thumbs on a motorway would never be noticed among the teeming thousands on the streets of the capital.

# 10

There was little they could do now about the body they had found at Puyceldome except await developments. Darcy was still pursuing his enquiries into who had built the factories and houses in the developments along the clayey streak beside the River Orche, and when he had sorted that out it was a case then of going through the names of every bricklayer who had ever been employed on them. It was going to take a long time. Meanwhile there was little chance of much forward progress and Pel's place seemed to be in his office co-ordinating the enquiries Nosjean and De Troq' were making about the deaths of Vienne and Burges. Puyceldome for the time being could be safely left to Aimedieu.

He was bright, intelligent and got on well with people, and Darcy, who was on his way there, anyway, to make a little enquiry of his own, was told to pass on orders and instructions on what to look for.

'Talk to everyone over fifty,' he told Aimedieu. 'Preferably without being noticeable. Somebody must know something about what happened thirty years ago. It's up to you.'

With Darcy in the car had been a small grey-haired shrewd-looking man who was now poking round the roped-off area of the Cat Tower. As he worked, Darcy turned to Didier Darras, who had done the driving while Darcy sat in the back in earnest conversation with the grey-haired man. Didier was standing to one side now, listening to Aimedieu's instructions. He was looking a little sick.

'Does it bother you?' Darcy asked him.

'What?'

'Murder. We've had three. Two connected. Both very unpleasant. Does the thought of blood upset you?'

'No.' The boy shook his head. 'It's happened before. I'm sorry about Burges, of course. I knew him. They killed him in cold blood. I don't like that.'

Darcy nodded. He felt the same. Gangsters and common or garden criminals he could handle. It was the viciousness of the arbitrary murders that bothered him.

'You're setting everything down?' he asked.

'Yes, I'm setting everything down.'

'Everything I've just been telling Aimedieu?'

'Well, not that. No.'

'Why not?'

Didier was startled at Darcy's harsh tone.

'My notebook's full,' he said.

'That's a great help,' Darcy snapped. 'Haven't you a spare?'

'I didn't think I'd need one.'

'That's one of the things you learn as a cop, one of the things you have to appreciate. Or perhaps you don't wish to.'

Didier looked stubborn. 'No,' he said. 'I don't.'

'What had you in mind after you leave us?'

'I could always become a clerk at the railway station. That's all I am now.'

Darcy glared. He was as dedicated to police work as Pel was and he disliked indifference in anyone. 'Before moving on from cadet to policeman,' he said, 'one of the things you have to learn is that paperwork's important. That's why we have the Incident Book, why we have records, why we take statements. So that everything's there in black and white. Arresting a criminal takes a minute. Writing it up afterwards takes hours. But it's that writing up that policemen will look at when they wish to make an arrest in the future; and it's there that they'll learn that the man they've got is probably guilty even when he says he's not – because he's done it before and it's there on paper that he has. Go and buy a notebook from the shop across there before the Patron finds out.'

Didier scowled and walked across the ancient square to the shop under the arcades, more determined than ever to resign. As he entered the shop Jean-Paul Remarque, of the Molière

Company of Players, was just leaving. Under his arm he held a thick book entitled *The Middle Ages – Life and Entertainment*.

A girl was stacking boxes of pencils, scholars' notebooks and loose-leaf files. She produced the notebook Didier asked for – a thick affair with a wire spiral hinge.

'You can have it cheap,' she said. 'It's old stock. We want to get rid of them.'

She was pretty and looked a little like Bernard Buffel Bis. Enough, in fact, for Didier to ask. She grinned at him.

'He's my brother,' she said. 'I'm Bernadette Buffel.'

'There must be a bit of confusion in your family from time to time. Do you work here?'

'No. I'm still at school but I help in the holidays. It's in the holidays when the tourists arrive that it's busy. It's my aunt's shop. Everybody in Puyceldome's related.' She laughed. 'Her name's Bernadine. I'm glad you came in.' She gestured at Remarque who was crossing the square. 'He's trying to pick me up.'

Didier hadn't failed to notice her attractiveness. 'Does he do it all the time?' he asked.

'He's always coming in, pretending to buy something. He doesn't spend much because he always asks for things he knows we don't stock. He just wants to talk. To me.'

Despite his decision to resign, Didier became at once the all-protective policeman, keeper of the Republic's Conscience. 'I'm a cop,' he said. 'I'll keep an eye on the place.' He didn't bother to ask himself how, stationed as he was most of the time in the Hôtel de Police miles away. He could always make a point of finding an excuse to see Aimedieu, he decided.

The door of the shop was plastered with notices for pageants, get-togethers, discos and fireworks in the area over the holiday period.

'There's a lot going on round here,' he commented.

'There always is in August.'

'Ever go to any?'

'Sometimes. *He* asked me.'

'Who?'

'That actor. He says he's studying what to do for the medieval night they're putting on. *I* think he'd like to get me in a corner.'

Didier put on his stern policeman's face again. 'I'm all for fireworks,' he said. 'There are some at Gonne. Are you going?'

'Yes.'

'I've got a scooter. With two helmets. Matching ones.'

She went pink, obviously not yet used to being asked for dates. 'I'm going with a party. My brother and some others. But I could meet you there.'

She spoke uncertainly, as if she expected to be turned down, and Didier reacted by becoming even more the custodian of France's good name.

'Fine,' he said. 'I'll see you.'

'There's a disco at Argentre on Friday,' she suggested and Didier smiled, feeling much better, even with a little of his pride restored.

'Fine,' he said again. 'I'll take you.'

Darcy was still occupied with the grey-haired man but he kept glancing round impatiently. 'I'd better go now,' Didier said. 'The Inspector's looking for me.' He studied the telephone on the counter and made a note of the number in his new notebook. 'I'll give you a ring.'

As he left he bumped into Aimedieu. Behind the innocent expression of a cherub, Aimedieu had a shrewd and sympathetic mind and Didier admired him considerably.

'Darcy was rough on you,' Aimedieu said.

'That's nothing,' Didier said. 'You should hear the Old Man.'

'Bad temper?'

'Yes.'

'Nothing odd about that. His wife's left him.'

Didier's eyebrows shot up. He had always admired Madame Pel and he had known her even before she and Pel had married. He was shocked. 'She has?'

'Not for good.' Aimedieu grinned. 'Just on business in the South or somewhere. For a fortnight. He'll be better tempered when she returns.'

The grey-haired man had finished poking round the ruins of the Cat Tower and was heading for the car. As the doors closed and Didier climbed behind the wheel, Aimedieu turned and saw Ellen Briddon watching him.

He had long since decided that the job he'd been given at

Puyceldome was ideal. All he had to do was appear there in the morning and go away again in the evening, after taking coffee with all the golden oldies in the place, often with a glass of *marc* thrown in. And there was always Ellen Briddon to fall back on. She had clearly taken a fancy to him and was more than willing to have him in her *salon* and offer him the drink of his choice.

She was attractive, good-humoured, naïve about France but eager to learn and, younger than her husband, only a little older than Aimedieu and very pleasant to be seen with. Aimedieu felt he was onto a good thing, especially as she seemed a little disillusioned with her husband.

She greeted him with a smile. 'Hello,' she said. 'You again?'

'You'll be seeing me round here a lot,' Aimedieu pointed out. 'I'm in charge.'

'Oh, I'm pleased. Do come and let me give you coffee when you fancy one. There are so few people here to talk to.' She sighed. 'The language barrier.'

'You'd do better if you learned French,' Aimedieu said.

'I suppose I would. I must do something about it this winter. I ought to get you to teach me.'

Aimedieu didn't respond to the invitation. More than one woman had shown interest in him and he preferred not to become entangled.

She had noticed his reluctance and appealed to his sympathy. 'It's such a funny place, this,' she said. 'It's haunted. Did you know?'

'Does it worry you?'

'Oh, no. But it's there.'

Aimedieu's ears had pricked. In the few years he had worked as a policeman he had come across some strange things but this was the first time he had come across a ghost.

'Have you seen it?'

'No. But I've heard it. A sort of high-pitched wail. I first heard it a couple of nights ago.'

'Sure it isn't just the wind? They say this place is undermined by underground passages. If the wind got in, there'd be a sort of wail, wouldn't there?'

Mrs Briddon was not to be denied her ghost. She'd set her

mind on a ghost and she was determined to have one. None of her friends in Surbiton had a ghost.

As they talked the Molière Players passed, heading for the bar. The company seemed to have swollen. In addition to Remarque, Béranger and Blivet, there were now three girls. The two who had disappeared on holiday appeared to have returned, plus one of those who had left earlier to seek her career elsewhere. Aimedieu supposed it hadn't worked out and she'd returned to where she knew there was work.

Two of the girls were not very prepossessing and looked as if they had been dressed from the old clothes basket of a charity organisation, at the very least from unwanted dresses out of the property basket. The third girl looked more organised and seemed quite good-looking. They interested Aimedieu. Having once wanted to be an actor himself, he wondered what made them tick. He excused himself to Mrs Briddon and caught them up.

'Missing players back?' he asked.

Remarque gave him an uneasy look. 'Yes,' he said. 'About time, too. Came a few days ago. This is Odile Daydé and Mercédes Flichy. That one's Henriette Guillard.'

The Daydé girl was tall with thick eyebrows. She had short dark hair and a skirt like a Mother Hubbard down to her ankles, and wore what looked like green property jewellery. Mercédes Flichy had short reddish hair, full lips and glasses. They seemed to be in their middle twenties. The third girl, Henriette Guillard, seemed older, with jetty curls like a gypsy, and somehow seemed to possess a professional air the others didn't have. The Flichy and the Daydé girls didn't look like actresses, or even very sexy, and Aimedieu, who knew about girls, had always thought the one essential for a successful actress was to be sexy.

'Do you wear glasses on stage?' he asked Mercédes Flichy.

It was Remarque who answered. 'Of course not,' he said quickly. 'She'd look fine playing Juliet, or Roxane in *Cyrano*, with specs, wouldn't she?'

'Can she see without them?'

'She doesn't have to. She learns the moves. When actors have rehearsed the moves they can do them instinctively. She could do them in pitch darkness.'

Aimedieu watched the group as they headed for the bar. As they disappeared inside, he followed them. Le Bernard was sitting outside talking to Serge Vitiello, the artist. They were discussing the show they were going to present.

'Stilt walkers,' Vitiello was saying. 'Fire eaters. Medieval songs and dances. The tourists will lap it up.' He gestured about him. 'A few more banners, of course. Torches stuck in the walls. The holes are still there. They've been there for five hundred years so they should be all right.'

'Even a ghost,' Aimedieu said cheerfully.

'A ghost?'

'Madame Briddon says there's a ghost.'

Vitiello snorted.

'She says she's heard it moaning. It would round off your show beautifully if you could induce it to walk round the square clanking its chains.'

'Rubbish!'

Le Bernard was not inclined to dismiss the suggestion so lightly.

'There was some English prisoner brought here during the Hundred Years War,' he said. 'Some English milord.'

'Didn't that happen with one of their kings?' Aimedieu asked. 'They held him at Montrichard on the Loire, didn't they, until they could raise enough in England to bail him out?'

'This wasn't a king. Just a milord. He was kept in one of the underground passages here. This place was riddled with them until they were all blocked up. He's supposed to walk along the Rue Millerand. It used to be part of the battlements. He seems to have moved his area of operations, though, now. He's been heard in the main square.'

'Sure it wasn't the wind?'

'It wasn't the wind.' Le Bernard was indignant.

'Ever see him?'

Le Bernard shrugged. 'I've seen some funny things in my time.'

'Ever see anything funny around *here*?'

'What sort of funny?'

'Well, if you saw Brigitte Bardot standing at the bar there, that would be funny, wouldn't it? In the same way, if you saw a man carrying a bag with a big label on it – "Gold" – you'd consider that a bit funny, too, wouldn't you?'

'Well, that's something I've never seen,' Le Bernard admitted. 'In fact, you don't see half the funny things you used to. In the evening, you don't see anything at all. Everybody's indoors watching *Dallas* on television. We can get it two nights a week here. Once from Paris. Once from Switzerland. The square used to be full of people in the evening – even in the winter. Talking. Arguing. Having fights. Kids playing. Not now. They all get square eyes watching the box. You never see anything. No cars. No dogs. Even *they're* asleep in front of the television. I saw those actors come back the other night with one of their property baskets, and that's about all. They had this basket and some sort of canvas painted to look like a street or something.'

'When was that?'

'Three days ago. They said they'd been putting on a show at St Just. They had that Peugeot brake they run. The one that used to be white. They'd had a bit to drink and they were swearing because the basket was heavy. I expect they'd had a good night and picked up more dough than normal. In places like this people like to see a live show. It makes a change from television.'

'Were the girls with them?'

'Two of them. The other was off somewhere looking up books on medieval entertainment, they said.'

'Do you often see them coming home?'

'Now and again. When I've been to the bar for a game of dominoes. You get sick of television. I nearly *didn't* see them, mind. The Rue Nobel, where they live, is darker than most. The light on the wall was broken by kids kicking a football about and it's never been replaced. Nobody cares, you see, because these days nobody's ever out at night. It's the television.'

Aimedieu grinned. 'I take it you don't like television much,' he said.

# 11

If nobody else had made any headway, Darcy had. Darcy was always the most dogged of Pel's squad, and when he returned from Puyceldome he appeared in Pel's office, as full of excitement as if he'd found the lost city of Atlantis.

'We're on our way, Patron,' he said. 'Lagé's got the names of those firms who built along the clay streak.'

Pel sat up. Darcy had the sort of energy which, if connected to the city's electricity services, would have lit it up for a year. He made Pel tired but he also brightened his day with his enthusiasm.

'Hubard and Company were the firm who did the brickwork for the supermarket at Rèze,' he said. 'Passoni Brothers did the work for the estate at Orvault. Up to half-way, anyway, then their development department was taken over by Hotners. I've asked them all to supply a list of every man who was employed on the building sites.'

'A lot of them would be casual labour. I bet they were pleased.'

Darcy grinned. 'As it happens, their accounts departments have the names. They take them for tax purposes, even casual labour, and they've still got their old ledgers. They'll take some finding but they'll do it.'

'I bet you had to lean on them.'

'A bit. It can be done, Patron. I'll get Claudie to help.'

'Use young Didier, too. It'll occupy his mind. It might even take it off Martin and that girl of his. What's the next step?'

'We sort out the carpenters and electricians from the lists we get,' Darcy said. 'Doc Minet thinks the guy we found at

Puyceldome was either a bricklayer or a common or garden labourer. His hands were big and calloused, he says. In any case, he'd surely not be an electrician or a carpenter or a glazier or anything like that because there's no electricity laid on in the tower and there's no door – it was bricked up a couple of centuries ago, Le Bernard said – and no windows. That ought to narrow the field down a little, because the only thing that's been tampered with is the stonework. So we're looking for a stonemason or a bricky or something of that sort.'

Darcy lit a cigarette and offered the packet. Pel shook his head firmly then weakly changed his mind.

'I had a guy out there today looking at it,' Darcy went on. 'Name of Lourdais. Professor at the University. Faculty of Architecture and Building. He had a sniff round and he agrees with everything Le Bernard said. The place is exactly as it was built except for a bit of repair work here and there over the years. He said it was certainly opened at the top about thirty years ago, which is when our boy found himself inside. He can roughly tell the date of the repair work. Apparently mortar's changed over the years.'

Pel looked in admiration at his deputy as he paused for breath. There wasn't much that Darcy ever missed.

'He confirmed', Darcy went on, 'that the tower was fixed at the top at the time, because any other way would have caused it to collapse. But – ' Darcy paused for dramatic effect. ' – there is certainly proof that somebody did try to open it at the bottom – our friend, Lorick Lupin, the missing bricklayer who vanished to America. Le Bernard had his facts clear enough. One bricklayer worked on the hole at the bottom. Two worked on the hole at the top, perhaps three, one of them the type who worked on the hole at the bottom. Lourdais could recognise different styles. Little touches laymen don't notice. Le Bernard was dead right all along the line. We'll find this guy in the tower, patron. There must be somebody who was employed by Hubards or Passonis or Hotners who can remember a beefy type with red hair and a big nose.'

* * *

Nosjean was always different from Darcy and he was gloomy when he appeared in Pel's office to make his report. The energy, the brains and the enthusiasm were there, but he'd always been a worrier and was inclined to be depressed by failure.

'We seem to have lost them, Patron,' he said. 'They've sunk without trace. Lyons picked up a report that they'd been seen on the motorway near Villefranche but then they seemed to disappear. Some commercial traveller who heard the radio appeal told one of the motor-cycle cops he met at one of the service stations. The cop immediately started a search but they'd vanished. I expect they got a lift and eventually moved away from the motorway. We've put out another all-areas bulletin asking for them to be picked up if seen.'

'How are your enquiries going?'

'Two came up, Patron. We decided the slide belonged to the girls we're after and we found Vienne's watch. They'd sold it, so we've got a description now, but it could fit hundreds of girls. They're said to be hippies – it's a term that's been used by everyone who saw them – but it's a pretty normal comment on anyone who doesn't dress in a conventional manner. There've been several reports of hippies buying knives, but so far they've all turned out to be just ordinary housewives.'

Pel offered condolences and encouragement, which was all part of his job, and Nosjean left, feeling less the failure he thought he was. As he reached the sergeants' room Claudie Darel indicated the telephone.

'Beaune police,' she said. 'They've discovered another knife sale. Only this time there were two, not one.'

Nosjean snatched at the telephone. 'Couple of girls,' the cop in Beaune said. 'Description matches the one you've put out. They bought butchers' knives. Not one – two.'

'Where?'

'Droguerie Pêche Moran. It's in the main square.'

Nosjean and De Troq' shot off in De Troq's big roadster at once. De Troq' was supposed to be poor but, Nosjean decided as he clung to the side while De Troq' flung the vehicle round the corners, poverty was perhaps a comparative thing.

The knives had been sold on the third of the month and it had been a girl called Gabrielle Muchonne who had made the sale. She was a tall girl, with dark hair done up on top of her head, a splendid figure and endless legs which both Nosjean and De Troq', being virile young men in spite of the fact that they were both engaged elsewhere, noticed at once.

She described the two girls again for them. 'Medium height,' she said. 'They came in late. One of them had fair wavy hair and one straight dark hair. Both of them wore it down to the shoulders and down the back. I didn't like them very much.'

'Why not?'

'There was something about them. I don't know what it was. But they scared me somehow. One of them – the fair one – had thin lips and a tight mouth. Perhaps that was it. And the other had those artificial-looking eyebrows, like Marlene Dietrich had.'

Nosjean and De Troq' looked at each other. The girl's words were exactly the same as those used by the drivers.

'They were younger than me and smaller,' she went on. 'But there was something about them.'

'Tell us some more,' De Troq' suggested. 'What exactly was it that frightened you about them? There are plenty of people with thin lips and plucked eyebrows who aren't frightening.'

Gabrielle Muchonne thought for a while. 'I think it was the way they insisted on having the knife points made sharper.' She picked up a knife from a display stand alongside her. 'Try the point. You can't get one much sharper than that. I couldn't think what they wanted them for.'

'No mention of barbecues or anything like that?'

'No. But they said they were camping and didn't use forks so they weren't interested in knives without points. I suppose that was something else that frightened me about them.'

'What did they buy in the end?'

'Butchers' knives.'

'Could you show us? Exactly.'

They moved around the display stand. There were several trays, all containing single-edged, pointed knives in various sizes.

'Which did they buy?'

She picked up two of the knives and laid them down on the counter.

'We'd like to take these away with us,' Nosjean said. 'We'll give you a receipt. We'd like them as evidence.'

The girl looked concerned. 'Were they used for that murder on the N6?'

'We think so.'

The girl looked at them, impressed. They were a handsome couple, Nosjean dark and looking like Napoleon on the bridge at Lodi, De Troq' fair, his hair neatly cut, his features immaculate, and bearing the air of someone who knew he was important, as only a baron – even an impoverished baron – could.

'They asked me to sharpen them,' she said. 'I told them they were already very sharp. But the fair one insisted on them being sharper.'

The knives, she said, had cost ninety francs.

'I got the impression', she went on, 'that ninety francs was about all the money they possessed. They priced them very carefully and rejected the most expensive ones. And when the fair-haired girl took her purse out of her shoulder bag, I didn't see any more money inside it.'

'You didn't think to tell the police?'

'Not at the time.'

'Did you tell your employer? Surely you must have had some ideas about what they intended to do with the knives.'

The girl looked on the verge of tears. 'We've always been told that the customer is always right and that it's not our business to question why people want the things they buy. I read in the papers about the murder – I don't read the papers much – but when I heard the radio appeal it dawned on me that the two girls the police were looking for might be the two girls who bought the knives.'

'They might indeed.'

'And then I noticed one of them called the other Gabrielle. The same name as mine.'

'Gabrielle's a pretty common name,' De Troq' said.

'We'll ask at youth hostels,' Nosjean suggested. 'They always insist on having names. They might have a description.'

'Unless they gave false names and called themselves Catherine Deneuve or Brigitte Bardot. Girls do.'

As De Troq' suggested, the name wasn't much to go on, but the two knives they had brought away from the hardware store were.

'They fit the casts we made of Vienne's wounds perfectly,' Dr Cham said. 'They were knives exactly like these two.'

'Which means that the girls who bought the knives', Nosjean said, 'were *our* girls – the ones we want. They bought them with the express intention of committing murder for money and offered sex as a means of getting drivers off the road. Four of those who stopped got away with it. One because he looked too tough to handle, the others because they said they weren't interested in the offers they made. Vienne was perfect. A man with a good-looking car, a man who might have money on him. He was tempted by the sex they offered and drove off the main road to the secluded spot where he was murdered.'

'Fine,' De Troq' said. 'The only problems now are, Where are they? and Who are they?'

Without knowing where the two girls they were seeking had come from, it was almost impossible to trace them from a Missing Persons report, and so far they had no idea where in France the girls had lived. The only thing they had with certainty were the descriptions, the fact that they had bought two sharp knives in Beaune and that early the following day they had obtained a lift with the driver of the Nicolas truck and then with four other men, one of whom had been Vienne.

'It seems to me,' Nosjean said thoughtfully, 'that if they bought the knives in Beaune late on the afternoon of the third, then they wouldn't leave the town that night. They'd leave next morning.'

'In which case where in Beaune did they spend the night?'

'It wouldn't have had to be expensive. Gabrielle Muchonne said they didn't have any money.'

'Well,' De Troq' said, 'if they were prepared to offer themselves for money the following day, the chances are that they were also willing to do it the night before. Which seems to indicate that they probably tried to find some man who would provide them with a roof and a bed in return for a bit of nooky.'

'If they were minors no man's going to admit to doing that.'

'Perhaps they aren't minors. Perhaps they just *look* like minors.'

'Beaune's not a big town. Thirty thousand? About that. I bet we could find out if they'd been trying it on. The square's where all the prostitutes go. There's a bar they use. The Camion Rouge.'

It didn't take long. The obvious people to ask if a couple of under-age females had been trying to pick up men were the local prostitutes. There were two of them in the Camion Rouge, sitting at one of the tables, drinking coffee and smoking. Their faces lit up at once when Nosjean and De Troq' appeared and eyed them. They broke into smiles as they crossed the bar and sat down opposite.

'Hi, *chéris*,' one of them said. 'I'm Maureen. You looking for a nice time?'

Nosjean grinned and fished out his identity card. 'Police,' he said.

Her face fell. 'Oh, Mother of God! Trust me to pick a *flic* for the first customer of the night.'

'Keep your hair on,' Nosjean said. 'We're not the Vice Squad.'

'What are you into then?'

'Murder. We're looking for a couple of kids – girls. We think they might have been around the square here. We think they're on the game but they're travelling – and we thought you might have noticed them since you have an interest in anything of that sort that goes on.'

The woman frowned. 'You sure you're not going to run us in?'

'We've got better things to do.'

'On the knock, were they?'

'We think so.'

*'Two kids!'*

'Two girls. Both young.'

'Holy Mary, it's amazing what girls get up to these days.'

The other woman leaned forward. 'There were two kids outside one night trying their luck.'

'On the third?'

'About then?'

'Did anyone go with them?'

'They were too young. They didn't look very clean either. As if they were sleeping rough.'

'What happened?'

'We saw them try one or two types, but then they disappeared in the direction of the Ste Marie Youth Hostel.'

'Which is where?'

'Montier-les-Bains.'

'Thanks. You've been very helpful.' Nosjean put some coins on the bar. 'Let's have drinks for the ladies, Patron,' he instructed.

The two women beamed. 'Next time I'm arrested,' Maureen said, 'can I arrange for you to do it, sergeant?'

They could hardly imagine that the two girls they were seeking would have given their correct names at the youth hostel, which, like other youth hostels, would have insisted in its own interest on having names. But perhaps the two girls had been too tired or too tensed up – even too drugged up – to care and had given their correct names for once. The names they got were Fanny Corton and Anne-Marie Sorois and they just had to hope they were genuine.

It turned out that they weren't, because one of the girls had been heard to call the other 'Sonia' and that girl had called the first one 'Gaby'.

'So their names are Gabrielle Something and Sonia Something,' Nosjean said. 'Well, that's another step forward. Let's see if we can find two girls with those names who know each other – at schools, perhaps, in families, in hospitals, in reformatories or prisons.'

De Troq' gave him a sideways glance. 'We've got quite a job on.'

Nosjean shrugged. 'Haven't we always?' he said. 'Isn't that what we're here for?'

# 12

If you weren't Sherlock Holmes – and Pel wasn't and didn't even fancy the idea because he thought Sherlock Holmes a pompous ass – police work, you found, didn't depend on brilliant deductions but attention to detail.

And detail was something he was always pushing at his team.

'Detail,' he claimed. 'The little details that are easily overlooked. Team work. Team spirit.' It was just what Brisard had suggested, but coming from Pel it was different.

On the whole, with the certain exception of Misset, his team tried to remember his advice. Detail, of course, depended also on one's ability to spot it and not everybody possessed that valuable asset. Darcy was one who did.

His first efforts with the lists provided by Hubards, Passonis and Hotners were not very successful. A lot of the men were retired, a lot were even dead. And nobody seemed to remember a large beefy man with red hair and a big nose. Working painstakingly through Hubards' list and Passonis' list, he was beginning to despair of getting anything from Hotners' list when a man called Aloïs Mauff came up trumps.

'I remember a chap like that,' he said. 'Big. Red hair. A beak of a nose. Worked at Orvault.'

'It sounds like him,' Darcy said. 'What was his name?'

'I don't know. I was only about nineteen when I was working for Hotners. I was still an apprentice bricklayer. I didn't know the older people there.'

Charming, Darcy thought bitterly. But, at least, he seemed to be on the right track. There *had* been a big man with red hair and a large nose.

Then Mauff lifted his heart. 'My father would have known him though,' he said. 'He worked there too. He'd be about the same age.'

'I'd like to see him.'

'It'll be a bit difficult.'

'Don't say he's dead?'

Mauff grinned. 'No. He's not dead. He's in Sicily.'

Darcy was eager to get in touch with the older Mauff. 'Got his address?' he said.

'No. He's on a bus tour with a lot of golden oldies. Pensioners. Women mostly. It's some club he belongs to. He's seventy-three and a widower and he likes the ladies. He says that one of these days he'll be back with a new wife and this time, he says, he'll pick one with a lot of money.'

'When will he be back?'

'End of the week.'

'Where does he live?'

'Two doors away from me. Just down the street. Me and my wife are keeping an eye on the house till he comes back. I'll give you a ring.'

It meant containing their souls in patience until Mauff senior returned from his old folks' outing. But there was plenty else they could do in the meantime. Le Bernard, basking in his importance as consultant to the police, kept contacting Aimedieu and the local cops with wild theories, while efforts were also being made to find the address of the bricklayer, Lorick Lupin, who had gone to America and made himself a fortune.

Then Leguyader produced a new angle in the shape of a coin. He appeared in Pel's office, dancing about like a poodle wanting to be let out.

'Well, go on,' Pel said. 'You'd better tell me before you burst.'

Leguyader produced a small plastic bag and emptied its contents on to the desk. 'Coins,' he said mysteriously.

'I can see that,' Pel said. 'I assume there's something special about them or you wouldn't be here with them.'

'Found under the body in the tower,' Leguyader said. 'All normal coins. Cleaned up, of course. All in circulation thirty years ago. No modern coins like the ten-franc piece, for instance. And – ' He fished out another plastic bag. ' – this.'

The second bag contained a single coin which he laid on Pel's desk as reverently as if it were the Holy Grail. It was yellow and wasn't any coin Pel had ever seen before.

'Sorry I took so long.' Leguyader was uncharacteristically friendly and Pel immediately suspected an attempt to score off him. 'It was encrusted with dirt and took a long time to clean. And we've been a little busy lately, of course. Two stiffs in one day and then another – poor Burges – to follow.'

Pel leaned forward, pulling his spectacles down off his forehead so he could see through them.

'What is it?'

'It's not a modern coin. Nor is it thirty years old. Much older. It's not even French.'

'So?'

'It's a Maria Theresa.'

'What's a Maria Theresa?'

'An Austrian coin. It's worth a lot of money.'

'It has some significance?'

'Oh, yes,' Leguyader said cheerfully. 'It has a lot of significance. To you.'

'Why?'

'It came from the Cat Tower. We found it with the others.'

'It was in his pocket?'

Leguyader was enjoying himself. 'Where else would it be? But this one's rather different, isn't it? It's gold. I've checked.'

'Gold?' Pel looked at the coin as if it might leap off the desk and punch him on the nose.

Leguyader smiled. 'It's surely strange for a common or garden labourer or bricklayer to be wandering around with gold coins in his pocket,' he said. 'Especially coins as old as that. It seems to need explaining. It's very valuable.'

As Leguyader marched out, satisfied at having given Pel something difficult to think about, Pel called Darcy in.

As he entered, Pel gestured at the coins Leguyader had left. 'From the Cat Tower,' he said. He pointed to the single coin resting on its own away from the others.

'This one,' he went on. 'It's a Maria Theresa, Leguyader says. Know anything about Maria Theresas?'

Darcy shrugged. 'Nothing, Patron. Austrian, I suppose. Didn't they have an empress of that name?' He peered at the coin. 'But she was a long time ago. Gold, I'd say.'

'Leguyader says it *is* gold. He tested it.'

'Is it important?'

'It might be. It was found with these others where our unidentified friend had been lying. They must have been underneath him and we decided they'd fallen from his pocket as his overalls rotted. Remember? This one seems to be different, though. Leguyader says it's very valuable and I expect he's right. He usually is. If so, what was our friend in the Cat Tower doing with it in his pocket?'

Darcy frowned. 'Perhaps it wasn't in his pocket,' he suggested. 'Perhaps it was in the tower when he was put inside. Or when he climbed inside of his own accord. Perhaps that's *why* he climbed inside.'

'For one coin?' Pel looked very sceptical.

'It would be worth a bit to a collector, I imagine, but on its own it doesn't constitute a fortune. So, if that's the reason our friend was in the tower, perhaps there were more than one. Perhaps some had been hidden there.'

'I wonder if there's something special about it. Think Nosjean's girl friend, Mijo Lehmann, would tell us?'

'She'd certainly know.'

'Give her a ring and ask her if I can call on her.'

Darcy grinned. 'Why don't you take her out to lunch, Patron? She's attractive enough.'

Pel nodded and decided he might.

Mijo Lehmann was small and dainty, with the sort of face that could never be called pretty but had a sort of elfin charm that touched Pel. It had certainly touched Nosjean. She grinned at Pel.

'Come to look me over, Chief Inspector?' she asked as he ordered aperitifs.

'Should I?'

'Jean-Luc Nosjean and I are thinking of getting married.'

'Oh! Congratulations.'

'But not just yet.'

Though she wasn't a numismatist, she knew all about Maria Theresas.

'It's a special sort of coin,' she said. 'The sort governments use to pay other governments with when they want a favour.'

'What sort of favour?'

'Political. Changing sides or defecting. In wartime. There are Maria Theresas, American silver dollars, British sovereigns, Napoleons, Louis-d'or, reis, guineas, and a few others. They're well known for use as bribes when it's an advantage for some rebel colonel to take over and topple an awkward government. The British used them in North Africa during the war there to keep the North African tribes quiet during the desert campaign. The Austrians used them in Italy at the time of Garibaldi to bribe his followers to defect. We used them in Morocco and Algeria at the time of independence. I expect we used them in Indo-China when it belonged to us, to try to get their leaders to support us when the Vietcong were getting organised. I'm surprised you've got hold of it.'

'Why?'

'They're pretty closely guarded on the whole. There are a few in private collections but most of these things – like silver dollars and Napoleons – are in banks, and belong to governments, who keep them for such emergencies as I've described. Where did you get it?'

Pel looked puzzled. 'In a tower in Puyceldome,' he said. 'A tower which was built in the thirteenth century and hadn't been opened for thirty years. It was found under the body of a man we found there.'

Mijo gave him a quizzical look. 'It isn't worth much on its own,' she said, repeating Pel's own words. 'But a lot would be worth a fortune. If somebody found them I reckon they must have asked around to see what they were worth – at museums, numismatists, antique shops. If I were you, Chief Inspector, I'd ask around, too – to see who it was.'

# 13

The holiday period progressed. It was well into its stride now. Indeed, though the party spirit was still going strong, the period was almost past its best. The tourists were beginning to show a jaded look and were belting about with less enthusiasm, especially since it was now very hot indeed. There were even complaints about the loudspeakers planted in towns and villages, and the heat was beginning to get on the nerves. For the young and those unencumbered with responsibilities, however, it was a good period because every resort was working at full blast and in the countryside where, once the cold came, they sealed up everything for the winter and people often didn't see their neighbours for days, they were taking every advantage of the warmth to throw their village parties.

Didier had duly met Bernadette Buffel at the fireworks at Gonne and plucked up courage to ask her to go with him to the disco at Argentre. There, he asked if she'd go to the *sardinage* at St Just. She would.

Ellen Briddon's warmth towards Aimedieu was also beginning to progress beyond mere friendship to something a little deeper – deep enough, in fact, for Aimedieu to start to worry about it and realise that something would have to be done soon about pulling out before George Briddon returned from England.

It rained the day before the *sardinage* at St Just but on the day of the event it miraculously brightened up and the heat came back, but with a fresher feeling brought by the downpour of the previous day.

Tables had been set up under the trees in the valley by the

river. A carousel and swings had been erected for the children, a bar and ice cream stall had been established, and three men with accordions were bashing out romance on a raised dais.

As it grew dark, coloured lights were switched on and the smell of grilling fish began to drift across the valley. Men and women with baskets containing mountains of bread appeared, followed by more with plates of melon and bottles of port wine. To his surprise, Didier found himself sitting opposite Aimedieu who was accompanied by Mrs Briddon. Her husband was still in England attending to the last of his business and she was flattered to have been invited, feeling she was at last being allowed into the closed community of the countryside.

The melon was followed by tuna fish on rice and bottles of local wine.

'"Black" wine,' Aimedieu explained. 'The growers are supposed to send all they make to the co-operative but a few keep a bit back for their friends. That's where this came from. It's cheaper. Le Bernard fixes it. He fixes everything.'

Mrs Briddon was in transports of delight, not only to be there but also because Aimedieu was handsome and the lights and the wine were making her feel romantic. As the plates of smoking sardines appeared she beamed around her.

'Why sardines?' she asked. 'We're hundreds of miles from the sea.'

Aimedieu shrugged. 'Sardines are cheap just now,' he explained. 'That's all.'

A few people began to dance to the accordions and Ellen Briddon looked appealingly at Aimedieu. As they danced she clung to him as if she'd fall down if she let go and he broke off as soon as he could. As they regained their seats, Le Bernard was sitting next to him and, to break the spell, he turned to the old stonemason.

'Heard any more of the ghost?' he asked.

'Last night,' Le Bernard said. 'I expect he was cold. It was chilly after the rain.'

'It's the wind.'

'There wasn't any wind last night.'

'Maybe a cat trapped in one of the underground tunnels.'

Le Bernard obviously didn't agree.

'Has it happened before?'

'Oh, yes. When we were having the 700th anniversary celebrations. Somebody told the Minister who came. He thought it was funny. It turned out to be a lost dog.'

Le Bernard fished in his pocket and produced a battered wallet. 'I've still got a photograph.'

'Of the ghost?'

'No. The celebrations.'

The photograph was an old snapshot and it was cracked and bent but it clearly showed the square at Puyceldome. It was packed with people, all grimacing at the camera beneath banners floating from the walls in the breeze.

'That's the Minister,' Le Bernard said. 'He made a speech. That's me standing next to him.'

Aimedieu peered at the picture. The Minister, fat and pompous-looking, was obvious. A younger Le Bernard was peering round his elbow, obviously determined to be in the picture. In the background, just visible, was the Cat Tower, complete with ladder and, at the top, what looked like scaffolding. Aimedieu passed the picture to Ellen Briddon.

'That's your tower thirty years ago,' he said.

'A lot of people came,' Le Bernard said. 'From all over the place. They'll come again on the twenty-eighth, I reckon. In fact, there'll be more. They put on a play then about how Puyceldome was founded and about the defiance of the Comte de Goillac and his capture and torture by the King.'

'Not exactly the thing to get people into a festive spirit.'

'They were rotten actors, too. That's why this year we decided on a medieval evening. It'll be much better.'

Police enquiries often produce nothing, and a lot of cops do a lot of legwork and get aching feet for nothing. But sometimes they pay off and a major enquiry takes a step forward – usually a very small step, but a step nevertheless.

Darcy had put Claudie Darel on to enquiring about Maria Theresas and she came up with a result.

'There were enquiries at antique shops and numismatists around thirty years ago,' she said. 'Nobody's certain of the exact date but a lot of antique shops remember because it started a scare and pushed up values and collectors started selling what they possessed to get the best price they could. The police at Goillac remember it, too, but their records are in a mess. They put me in touch with a former sergeant, though. He retired ages ago but he made enquiries at the time because it was believed somebody was fixing the market. He found that enquiries *had* been made.'

'Who by?' Darcy asked.

'They identified the enquirer as a type called Lulu Grande-Tête. Real name Laurence Luzeau.'

'We know Laurence Luzeau,' Darcy said. 'That's interesting. He was a *demi-sel* from Marseilles.'

Claudie nodded. 'That's right. I checked. I also made a few more enquiries and found that the same enquiries he made were made again about six years later.'

'Who by?'

'This time it was a type called Lorick Lupin.'

Darcy frowned. 'Lupin? He was the bricky who was employed by Poulex to get into the tower. He went to America. Was he in on it, whatever it was? And whose coins were they?'

As Darcy headed back to his own office, the telephone rang. 'Type called Mauff,' the man on the switchboard said.

'Put him on.'

The message was hardly cataclysmic, but it was important. It was from the younger Mauff and he was short and to the point.

'The old man's back,' he said.

'Married?' Darcy asked.

There was a short laugh. 'He didn't manage it.'

Mauff senior was a bright little man, white-haired but with sharp black eyes that were full of mischief. There was little wonder, Darcy decided, that he expected to pick up a wife with money.

'Sure,' he said. 'Alfred Fouché. He's the type you're looking for. Big chap. Almost two metres tall. Came from Caen in Normandy. Red-haired. That dark red you get up there. Big nose. He was a bricklayer. A good one too, but he used his mouth too much and was always stirring up union trouble. It's always that sort who do. He'd be just the sort people would get in touch with if they wanted anything shady doing.'

'Why?'

'Well, he'd been in prison, hadn't he?'

'Had he? What for?'

'Theft. Pinching petrol. A lot. Over a long period. Later for assault. He beat up the foreman. He gave his wife a hell of a life.'

'Is she still alive?'

'She might be.'

'Where?'

'Same address, I imagine. Rue Trois Croissants, Néris. I haven't heard she's left. I bet you've got him in your records.'

'I'll look him up,' Darcy said. 'Know anything more about him?'

'No. He just disappeared. We heard he'd gone south looking for a better job. He just vanished. About thirty years ago. We just assumed he was another like Lorick Lupin, who went to America.'

'You knew Lupin, too?'

'Oh, yes. We all worked together at one time or another.'

'What was *he* like?'

'Lupin? Why? Was *he* involved?'

'He might have been.'

'Little chap. Sharp as a knife. Brave. Once saved a kid from drowning in the Tarn at Trébas. Nobody could bully him, though a lot tried because he was only little. Built like a jockey. Good at his job though.'

Darcy frowned. Somehow all these people, Le Bernard, Lorick Lupin and Alfred Fouché, all bricklayers or stonemasons according to what they were doing, were all part of the puzzle. He wondered how much.

He took his information back to Pel. 'We've got him, Patron,' he announced. 'His name's Alfred Fouché. Almost two metres tall. Heavily built. Big nose. Red hair.'

'So what was he doing in the tower?' Pel asked.

Darcy shrugged. 'Up to no good, I reckon. He had a record.'

* * *

Fouché's wife *was* still alive. She was in her late seventies now and a little deaf but she had lost none of her bitterness at her husband's disappearance, and was accordingly a little disconcerted to discover she had misjudged him for thirty years.

'I just assumed he'd run off with another woman,' she said. 'Or that he'd died.'

Well, Pel thought, he'd certainly died.

'He went to catch a bus to go to work,' she went on, 'and just never came back. He was like that, mind you. Disappearing for a day or so at a time. He chased girls. He couldn't keep it in his trousers. But *this* – murdered!'

'We don't think he *was* murdered, madame,' Pel said. 'We think he might have had a heart attack. He was a big man. Had he any history of heart trouble?'

'No. But he was fat. Too fat. I was always telling him. What was he doing in that hole?'

'We were wondering if *you* knew?'

'Up to no good, I'll bet.'

'Did he give you any idea what he was doing?'

'He said it was a special job. He was good at his work, I'll admit that, and often did special jobs for people. They said he'd been seen repairing that tower at Puyceldome.'

'That appears to have been the case. Did he mention exactly what he was doing?'

'He said he'd been asked to do a job for someone. He didn't say what it was. He stopped work on the site at Orvault so he'd be free and was lounging about the house for a day or two. He said he had to be free because he'd be called on at any time and that the money he was going to get made it worth while. Then he got a telephone call.'

'Did you hear what was said?'

'No. He spoke very quietly. I thought he was trying to hide it from me. That was why I was certain he'd gone off with a woman. I thought he'd taken time off work to be ready and was waiting for her, whoever she was, to telephone to say her husband had gone out, or was abroad or something and the coast was clear. Not at the time. But afterwards. That's what I thought the telephone call was for. You know – "Okay, Alfred, now's the time."' She frowned. 'The only thing that puzzled me was that he went off in his working clothes with his tools. You don't usually do that if you're going to run off with a woman, do you? You put on your best suit and leave your tools at home. Then I decided that perhaps it was just camouflage so I wouldn't suspect anything. After all, people running away from their wives do that, too, don't they?'

Pel had to admit that they did.

'I never thought he was up to something fishy. But he might well have been. He was as good at that as he was at chasing women.'

When they sat back and thought about it, it began to seem more clear. With his record and character, it seemed obvious that there had been something in the tower that had drawn Fouché there – either for himself or on behalf of someone else. And whatever it was – and it began to look as if it might be a stolen coin collection – it seemed he had been employed by Lulu Grande-Tête to handle it.

He'd been used to remove stones from the top of the Cat Tower and somehow – and it began to look more and more like a simple heart attack – he'd died in there and, because he was so big, they couldn't get him out and had had to leave him there.

'Perhaps they *could* have got him out,' Darcy said. 'But not without drawing the attention of the police to why they were there. So, for some reason, they simply bricked him up and left him.'

'Intending to come back later?'

'That must have been the case. But something prevented them and he remained there and the coins remained there.'

'But they didn't, did they?' Pel said. 'Except for one, they disappeared.'

# 14

That evening when Pel returned home, Madame Routy was watching the television. But for once she seemed to have little interest in it and Pel, assuming she was still worried about her nephew, Didier Darras, didn't demand she turned it off.

He tried to console her a little as he poured them both a drink. 'I'm keeping an eye on him,' he pointed out. 'He's not getting up to mischief.'

'Is he doing his job properly?' she asked. 'His mother's worried. She was proud of him in his uniform.'

'He's not doing anything he shouldn't be doing,' Pel said. He'd better not either, he thought darkly. Not while he's working with me.

The television was going on about a missing girl at Treffort in the Jura. She had gone out riding, it seemed, and her horse had returned without her. It had been carefully examined and, as there had been no sign of injury, it had been assumed that the rider, a girl called Sybille Junot, had been thrown. A major search was now being made along the route she normally took when she went riding.

Switching off the set, Pel drowned his sorrows with a second large whisky and, having downed that, tried another. The result was indigestion and a bad night and he rose the next morning feeling as if he'd mislaid part of himself during the hours of darkness.

When he reached the office, Darcy followed him into his room.

'Type called Dunoisse telephoned,' he said. 'Inspector

Charles Dunoisse from Guinchay. He said he was at school with you and knew you well.'

Pel stared at him blankly. He had no recollection whatsoever of any Charles Dunoisse.

'What did he want?'

'Help.'

'What sort of help?'

'He's handling this business of the missing girl at Treffort. They're thinking now that it wasn't an accident. They've covered every inch of ground she'd have covered and searched the hospitals and they've found no trace of her.'

'Pity the horse can't tell them.'

'They think now that it must be an abduction. He wants advice and help. He remembers we had the Rensselaer abduction here and he's never had to handle one before. He's hoping you can give him some advice. The girl's parents are wealthy and, if it isn't the sort of mindless murder we get these days, he's beginning to be afraid that it's a kidnap job.'

'It's an occupational hazard with the rich these days,' Pel admitted. 'What's happening?'

'At the moment, nothing. They're still searching. If they find her dead they'll handle it their own way. But if he feels it's a kidnap, he's asked if he can come and see you.'

'Why me?'

'Because you're Evariste Clovis Désiré Pel.'

Pel gave Darcy a dirty look. Then he realised Darcy wasn't laughing at him. He was just trying to indicate that Pel had built up quite a reputation for himself.

'I'll do what I can, of course,' he said. 'What else have we?'

'Nosjean's started to make headway again. They've got new descriptions of the girls and they think they've got the first names. They appear to be French, too, so that rules out foreign students travelling round France.'

In fact, Nosjean and De Troq' were searching among the lists of girls missing from home for two from the same area with the names they had, who might have linked up. So far they'd had no luck.

Photofit pictures of the girls had been made from the descriptions they'd received and tried on the four drivers. But the drivers hadn't looked carefully enough to be sure of the details – you don't spend a lot of time looking at your passengers when driving – and they couldn't be sure.

'It'll take years,' Lagé said as the matter was discussed in the sergeants' room. 'Children these days don't seem to enjoy being at home. What's even worse is that not all parents report their disappearance. Some are even happy to see them go.'

'My lot', Misset said, 'can go any time they like. I'm thinking, in fact, of sending them to play on the motorway. My wife, too. Her I'd like to clamp into the nose cone of a rocket and fire her off into outer space.'

They were still arguing when Claudie appeared. Misset tried to engage her in conversation but she brushed him off and headed for Pel's office.

'Patron,' she said. 'Those coins! I've got them! They weren't part of a collection. They were part of a large number that were due to go to Algeria. You'll remember that thirty years ago was the time of that attempted coup by a group of generals against de Gaulle after he offered independence.'

Pel remembered it well. He had been in Paris at the time and the mobs were on the streets led by students yelling their five-syllable slogan – '*Algérie Française*.' Five syllable slogans – 'Ho Ho Ho Chi Minh' had been another – had been very popular with demonstrators at the time. Pel had gone out of his hotel to see what all the noise was about and, caught up in a mob of students fleeing down the Champs Elysées, had had to run like a hare himself to avoid being hit by the lead-lined capes of the pursuing police. Riot police didn't stop to ask questions. They just lashed out.

'There was a lot of dirty business going on at the time,' he agreed.

'Yes, Patron. And a large sum of money in gold coins went missing. Two million francs' worth of it. From the airfield at Goillac. It was stored secretly in a hangar. It had been collected by representatives of the rebel generals and was to have been flown to Algiers to be used to finance their operations and bribe local leaders. The police found out all about it later. Instead, it was snatched. There was no violence. The gang were lucky and they'd got somebody on the inside.'

Pel frowned. 'A bullion robbery? Who did it?'

Finding out involved nothing more than going to Records – those pieces of paper covered with writing Darcy had warned Didier about – and there it was, proof. It had all been written up thirty years before and it was now available for the new generation of cops to study and use.

Darcy was intrigued. 'It was Lulu Grande-Tête. Laurence Luzeau himself. There were four of them. The cops handling the case worked it out. They must have hidden it in the tower at Puyceldome.'

'So if they did, why didn't they come back later and take it out?'

'They couldn't, Patron. They were dead. You'll remember. Lulu and one other, a type called Georges Pulot, were wiped out in a shoot-out in a Marseilles bar soon afterwards.'

'Because of the robbery?'

'It was thought it was a gang feud, but the police couldn't find anyone who wanted them dead so they scrubbed that idea. They never did find out who did it. I expect it was the types who'd raised the money for the generals. They were a ruthless lot if I've read my history correctly.'

Pel nodded. 'Go on. You're doing all right.'

'The police tried to pick up the remaining two members of the gang but one of them, Pierre Pirioux – known as Peter the Painter – was killed in a fishy car crash. They thought he'd been forced off the road at high speed. The last one, name of Sammonix, they pinned down in America six months later but by then he was in hospital in New York, dying of cancer. He was dead within two months. That's why, I suppose, no one ever found out what happened to the loot.'

Darcy smiled. 'Goillac's very interested, by the way, Patron. They're intrigued by all the enquiries we're making. They hastened to point out that if we recover the money, it's theirs.'

'That's where they're wrong,' Pel said sharply. 'If we find it, it's ours! At least, until someone decides what to do with it! And the credit's ours, too. It would look nice in our statistics, and Goillac's done nothing spectacular to include it in theirs.'

Darcy laughed. Pel was never one to let any kudos slip away to anyone else. He was quite indifferent to how it affected him, but he was well aware how much a few trumpets and drums helped the morale of his men, and he never allowed anyone else to snatch what was theirs.

'I reckon', he said, 'that Lulu, or Caillas – the type who bought The Cat House from Madame Croissard – wanted somewhere quiet and safe to hide the loot and lie low for a time. The Cat House was available and was perfect. In those days there weren't many tourists and Puyceldome's way off the main road hidden among the hills. They didn't have to raise much cash either. Just enough for a deposit – and it wasn't a lot for a place in Puyceldome in those days – and then a monthly sum to the loan company. In fact, they only paid one monthly sum because then they disappeared.'

Darcy grinned. 'No wonder they got away with it,' he went on. 'I expect whoever collected the coins and parked them at the airport ready to be flown out thought the thieves would bolt and put a watch on airports and ports, hoping to pick them up there. Instead, they stayed in Puyceldome right under their very noses. And they could hardly call in the police or make much of a fuss because it was illegal money that was to be used against the established government of France, so that any investigations had to be done by themselves. And, not having the facilities we've got, they never found it. The police only learned about it after the generals' rebellion collapsed and the generals were arrested and put on trial. But neither they nor the people who raised the coins ever found out what happened to them. Nobody did. Until now.'

It was possible to obtain photographs from Marseilles of the men who had been shot in the bar. Darcy took them along to Madame Croissard.

'Recognise any of them?' he asked.

'No,' she said.

It wasn't the reply he'd expected and he decided she was now so old she needed a little prompting.

'Could they be the men who bought The Cat House?' he asked.

She was quick to catch on. She looked at Darcy and bent over the pictures again. 'Of course,' she said. 'I thought they looked familiar. Of course they're the men. I remember them well now. I wasn't thinking of people of thirty years ago.' Her finger rested on one of the faces. 'He was the leader, I think. At least he seemed to give the orders. He had a big head.'

'Name of Laurence Luzeau, otherwise known as Lulu Grande-Tête.'

The finger moved. 'This one drove the car.'

'Peter the Painter. Pierre Pirioux. Involved with one or two getaways.'

'And the others.'

'Georges Four-Eyes. The spectacles, of course. Real name Georges Pulot. And Albert-Jean Sammonix. He doesn't seem to have had a nickname.'

She chuckled. 'In the company he kept, he must have felt very deprived.'

The fact that their quarry had all left the land of the living was disappointing, of course, and didn't add to their hopes of recovering the missing coins. Lulu and his friends were clearly beyond their reach but they still had to find what had happened to the money. Somebody had it and it was their job to find out who.

Their chances looked slender until Lagé came up with something. It came from a friend of a friend and he hurried to pass it on to Darcy who immediately took it to Pel, who was rooting in his drawers and stuffing his pockets with packets of cigarettes. Darcy recognised the symptoms. Pel was going somewhere and was taking precautions in case he ran out of cigarettes and the *tabacs* had closed.

'Patron,' he said. 'I think we might be getting somewhere at last. Lagé's found a relation of Lorick Lupin's in Tonnay-Boutonne. She says Lupin went to live in San Francisco. We have an address. I think we should contact the San Francisco police department. According to all those films on TV, they're pretty good. We should get them to find Lupin for us.'

Pel looked up as he stuffed a notebook in his pocket. 'Not now,' he said. 'Later. We're going to be busy.'

'Something else, Patron?'

'Yes. Dunoisse rang up again. That missing girl at Treffort *has* been kidnapped. They've had a communication.'

As they roared down the motorway in Darcy's car, Pel sat in silence. He was in no way pleased to pick up yet another case – a kidnapping into the bargain – because he had plenty on his plate already. But a kidnapped girl couldn't be ignored and the Chief had made the position plain.

'When you were promoted Chief Inspector,' he had pointed out, 'the idea was that your skill and ability were to be available to anyone in the area of the Midi and the West who wanted them. You're not just a detective, you're a consultant. You'd better get on your way.'

Pel was troubled – not because his workload had increased; that was normal enough. It was just that nothing was ever simple. The police were never allowed to complete one job before another turned up. Criminals, he considered bitterly, were an inconsiderate lot.

Missing girls were two a penny, of course. Every cop knew that. They even asked for trouble. Girls these days weren't satisfied with being girls and being pretty. They wanted to be liberated, and the Sixties had made them want to leave home. But this was a kidnap and a kidnap was a different kettle of fish. Nevertheless, he couldn't help wondering if the girl had laid herself open to it.

At Guinchay, they were met by Inspector Dunoisse. He was a large man growing too fat, with a mandarin moustache and spectacles.

'Evariste Pel,' he said, shaking hands warmly. 'I remember you so well.'

To his shame, Pel had no recollection of ever having met Dunoisse before, but he put on a good act of recollecting. 'I remember you,' he said. 'That time when – ' He paused, and Dunoisse inevitably supplied the necessary details.

'When we climbed the headmaster's wall to his daughter's bedroom.'

Did we, by God, Pel thought. I must have been more of a devil than I thought.

'Not that anything happened,' Dunoisse went on. He was a

cop, after all, and cops never admit to funny business. 'We were too young at the time. It was just a dare.'

He looked like going on all day and Pel caught Darcy's eyes. Darcy was quick to catch on.

'This missing girl,' he said, before Dunoisse could enthuse any more. 'No sign of her?'

Dunoisse's face changed. 'None,' he said. 'We'd begun to accept that she was dead. Then we found her riding hat, lying on the grass on the route she took, but there was no sign of her in the area. There was always the possibility that she'd been concussed, of course, and drifted off somewhere, or that someone had found her unconscious and picked her up. We searched all the hospitals and every wood and copse where she might have wandered. But I had my doubts because there were tyre tracks in the dust in the lane a few metres from the bridle-path where she was in the habit of riding. Then this letter arrived, demanding a ransom. It was posted in Goillac. At least it's got a Goillac postmark. They're asking a ransom of five hundred thousand francs.'

'Modest enough,' Pel observed. 'Perhaps they're not very experienced.'

Dunoisse nodded. 'I was obviously right,' he said. 'I decided she must have been stopped where we found her hat, pulled off her horse and shoved into the car that made the tyre marks.' He fished in his brief case and produced a plastic bag. Inside it was a sheet of paper.

He passed it across to Pel. Glued letters cut from a magazine spelled out the message. *Five hundred thousand francs,* it read. *We'll be in touch. Urgent. No police*. The last words were underlined in violet ink.

'It arrived yesterday,' Dunoisse said. 'At her home.'

'Somebody who was in a position to keep an eye on her movements?'

'Could be. We've checked around, but, quite honestly, we've found no one who might want to do the family harm.'

'Five hundred thousand francs could be quite an incentive. What do the parents say?'

'They want to pay up. They want their daughter back.'

'Well, you know the procedure. We don't agree with that but

we accept what they must be going through. We ought to watch them, though, so that if they try to deposit something we can watch who picks it up. What do we know about her?'

'Name Sybille Junot. Eighteen. Good close family. Very ordinary. They came originally from Vonnas, near Orléans, and the girl was born there and went to school at the Lycée there. Then they had a bit of luck. The old boy, who was a builder's merchant in a small way, owned some waste land and the developers wanted it. When he sold it, he found he was pretty wealthy and decided to retire. They did very well out of the deal. They were lucky.'

'Not at the moment,' Pel said grimly.

'No.' Dunoisse shook his head. 'Not now. They took their time and rented a house and the girl finished her education at the Lycée at Guinchay. Then they bought a small farm at Treffort about twenty kilometres away. Just so they could have a couple of fields and a stable, because the girl was nuts about horses. There are quite a few establishments of that sort around here. Stud farms. Training stables. Privately owned places. The family didn't get involved, though. They've lived a quiet life and they seem to be well liked. The girl rode a lot and fancied one day breeding horses. She went to a stable for several years before they got their money to learn about horses. How to look after them. The diseases they get. That sort of thing. She was good on a horse, too, and was a lightweight. Natural rider. The horse she was riding was a big animal but reasonably docile and unlikely to throw her.'

'I think we'd better see the people who knew her and get a bit of confirmation before we see the parents. Someone without bias.'

'The village priest? He knows her.'

The priest, an old man with a deeply-lined, suffering face, confirmed what Dunoisse had said. He had known the family since they had arrived in the district and was prepared to vouch for them.

'A very devout family,' he said. 'Law-abiding, kind. They had no enemies. There was no envy at their good luck. The girl was popular. She's pretty, slight, dainty, but good with horses.'

'Could it be a cruel joke?' Dunoisse asked.

The priest's shoulders moved. 'I doubt it, my son. They were popular and very much liked.'

The Junots were a couple in their fifties, both with the marks of years of hard work in their faces. The farm they had bought was small, as Dunoisse had said, with one or two outbuildings and a couple of large meadows alongside which had been wired off into smaller areas for horses. The tears had finished and they were calm but clearly under strain.

'She was a good girl,' Madame Junot said.

'Boy friends?' Pel asked.

'The only thing she was interested in was horses.'

No girl, Pel felt, was interested only in horses. 'You'd better tell us what happened,' he said.

'She went off for a ride. It's good riding country here. Plenty of space. That's why we bought the place. She insisted she didn't want just to hack about on bridle-paths. She wanted to ride properly. She set off on Arabe, as she did regularly. She has two horses – Arabe and Tunis – and she rode them alternately so they got plenty of exercise. She was usually away for two or three hours but she stuck more or less to the same route in case of accidents.'

'That was for her mother,' Junot said. 'She grew up in the city and doesn't understand horses and she felt that, so long as Sybille stuck to a reasonable route, if there was an accident we'd know where to look.'

'Very wise, madame. Please go on.'

'Arabe – he was her favourite – came home on his own. She'd been gone around five hours. That was a lot longer than normal and we were beginning to grow worried, then we saw Arabe standing at the gate. We went down to him. The reins were hanging loose and he kept getting his foot in them. There was no sign of Sybille.'

'And then?'

'My son saddled up Tunis,' Junot said. 'A neighbour took Arabe. They went over the route she normally took. No sign of her. Then they sort of scouted around, looking in the copses, thinking she might perhaps have dismounted or felt ill and the horse had been frightened and run away.'

'Did she carry money with her when she went out?'

'Only a little. For the telephone in case of accidents. That sort of thing.'

'And the riding hat?'

'We found it near the Chemin des Marguerites,' Dunoisse said. 'It was lying in thick grass and wasn't at first noticeable. We found it as soon as we mounted a proper search.'

'Any sign of a struggle?'

'There might have been. Near where the tyre tracks were. But it's hard to tell. Horses use it a lot. The dust had been stirred up.'

'Could anyone have had any reason to want to harm her?' Pel asked. 'Someone, for instance, who was jealous of your good fortune in coming into money?'

Junot considered carefully then shook his head. 'I don't think so. The people round here seem to get on with us. There's been no sign of unpleasantness.'

'Young men: there *might* have been someone you didn't know about.'

'There might have been. But I doubt it. She wasn't a secretive girl. She was always open.'

'Nevertheless, young girls are sometimes a little shy about a boy they've fallen for.'

'The only one I can think of is Jean-Philippe Chevilland at Haute Campagne, the farm next door. He teased her a bit about horses. I think they got on well together but I don't think it was any more than friendship.'

'Friendships develop.'

'They just joked. He pulled her leg and said tractors did more work than horses these days. But he knew she was good with horses and he thought she'd make a go of breeding them and training them. He even helped her occasionally. Because they'd always had horses at Haute Campagne – farm horses, of course – and he knew a lot about them. I know she liked him but I think that's all it was.'

'I've spoken to the boy,' Dunoisse said. 'He was at the market at Treffort all day. I've spoken to a dozen people who can swear to seeing him. He's pretty upset and helped in the search. It's my impression that, even though she might not have been keen on him, he was certainly keen on her and wouldn't wish to harm her. From what he said, they were growing pretty close.'

Pel turned to Madame Junot. 'Try to think of anything that might help. Anything she might have done or said which will give us a lead.'

Madame Junot looked on the verge of tears suddenly. 'She never did anything much,' she said. 'She was a quiet girl. She usually talked about horses. Occasionally Jean-Philippe came over from Haute Campagne and they talked together.'

'Alone?'

'Yes. Of course.'

'Where?'

'Not in her bedroom, Chief Inspector, if that's what you're thinking. They used to sit in the tack room where she kept her harness and saddles. They couldn't get up to much there. It has a cobbled floor like the rest of the stables, and it contains wooden horses for the saddles to rest on, hooks in the wall, a few cupboards. And two stools. She used to sit in there writing her notes or polishing leather. She took horses seriously. There was nowhere there they could have got up to anything.'

Pel wasn't so sure. While he had no wish to denigrate anyone who was innocent, he had found that young people could get up to things practically anywhere if they wished to.

'There's the spare stall, Mother,' Junot said. 'It's full of straw for her horses.'

Madame Junot had stopped dead, as if the same thought had occurred to her as had occurred to her husband and to Pel, then she nodded.

'Yes,' she admitted. 'There was the spare stall. But surely – ' She shook her head. 'No,' she said firmly. 'I don't believe it.'

'So – ' Pel paused. 'Let's forget that. There's nothing else she did or said that was unusual?'

'No. Only – ' Madame Junot paused. 'She mentioned she'd met an old school friend. Or not exactly a friend. Someone she knew at school. That's what she said. Is it important?'

'It depends on who the school friend was.'

'It was a girl.'

Remembering Nosjean's case of the two murderous girls on the N6 who had also killed a cop, Pel wasn't sure that being a girl made much difference these days. He had learned to deal with perverts, petty thieves, crooks of all shapes and sizes, all the rubbish of human life, but the idea of young girls who could kill arbitrarily was something new to him and had to do with drugs, pornographic videos and the general violence of the age, and was something else entirely.

'I think we ought to try to find this friend of hers,' he said. 'What did she tell you about her?'

'She said she'd met her while riding.'

'When?'

'It was a day or two before she disappeared.'

'And this friend. Was she riding too?'

'She didn't say.'

'Did she say where they met?'

'No. She had various rides. One of an hour. One of two hours. One longer. According to how much she wanted to exercise the horse. We knew them all and I made her stick to them because she liked riding alone and you never know, do you? She always told us which route she was taking.'

'And this Chemin des Marguerites?'

'It isn't far away and she always had to pass or return by it whichever way she went.'

'Did she mention the name of this school friend she met?'

'No.'

'Describe her?'

'No. All she said was that she'd met this friend she'd remembered from school.'

'What school would that be?'

'I think she must have meant the Lycée at Guinchay. But it might not have been, because she was at the Lycée at Vonnas before we came to live here. She said she remembered her because she was older and you always remember the older pupils, don't you, because they're the ones who do things for the school. You never seem to remember the ones younger than you because they're not really noticeable at that age.'

As they left, Junot laid his hand on Pel's arm.

'I feel I ought to warn you, Chief Inspector,' he said. 'If we have to, we shall pay up. We consider our daughter's life more important than catching a few criminals.'

Pel didn't argue. He could see the point. But he had no intention of just leaving the thing alone.

'Get a list of all girls who could have been at those Lycées at the time she was there, Daniel,' he said. 'Particularly those who were ahead of her. They're bound to have the records still. She hasn't left school all that long, and at the very least, this friend she met might have seen someone hanging about.'

# 15

Puyceldome was looking at its best when Didier arrived. The sun on the ancient stones glowed pink and made the place look like an ancient dowager done up for a ball – all its scars and all its wear and tear showing, but, in the sunshine, as if it had all been well glossed over to leave only a general impression of pure beauty.

He had ridden there on his scooter, enjoying the sunshine and the scenery and the breeze, and found himself looking forward to seeing Bernadette Buffel again. His message for Aimedieu was important.

Aimedieu's guardianship of the town had been extended for the time being. He had been on the point of being withdrawn but the discoveries Claudie and Darcy had made had put a different complexion on things. The kidnapping at Treffort was holding the attention of Pel and Darcy, however, and Didier had brought instructions that Aimedieu, who had interviewed everybody he could think of, was to start all over again. This time he was to concentrate not on who had or might have worked on the Cat Tower, but on anyone who had been seen handling or talking about unusual coins, or anyone who had appeared to have come into wealth rather suddenly.

What pleased Didier, however, was the news that, because of the new demands on the team caused by the kidnapping, he was to do what he could to help. After today he would be picked up every morning at the Hôtel de Police by Aimedieu and driven to Puyceldome and then driven back in the evening. It sounded like a doddle.

Parking his scooter and seeing no immediate sign of Aimedieu, he allowed his gaze to fall on the stationery shop under the arcade. Putting his head round the door, he saw Bernadette Buffel behind the counter. She looked up and grinned.

'Has that type been in again?' he asked.

'Which type?'

'The actor type.'

'Once. But Aunt Bernadine was here so he bought a packet of cigarettes and left. They're in the schoolyard down the hill at the moment rehearsing for the medieval night. Come and have a look.'

Passing behind the counter, Didier was led through the living-room behind the shop to a window overlooking the valley beyond the ramparts of the town. He could see into the asphalt space in front of the village school. Gus Blivet had stilts strapped to his legs and was capering about – very skilfully, too, Didier thought.

'He's good,' Bernadette said. 'He's done it before, of course. He told me he once worked in a circus as a clown.'

Didier became aware of her standing immediately behind him. As he turned, he found her face within a inch of his own and it was too much for a strong upright boy. Greatly daring, he gave her a peck on the cheek. She giggled, went pink and gave him a push.

'You'd better be off,' she said. 'Before that chief inspector of yours catches you.'

Didier grinned. It *was* a doddle, he decided.

Aimedieu was inclined to think it was a doddle, too. He liked the idea of working on his own and he knew what the enquiry into the kidnapping could entail. There would be hours of leg work, everybody tense and in a bad temper, and Pel would be impossible. It was much more comfortable in Puyceldome.

He had already talked to everyone in the place over forty years of age and had thought that would be the end of it. Hearing about the kidnapping, he had expected to be withdrawn and sent to the ends of the earth to knock on doors and ask questions. Instead, he had been given a new set of instructions, a new set of enquiries, and told to get on with it.

On the other hand, Mrs Briddon was still alone and Aimedieu was beginning to grow nervous. She seemed to be growing more and more enthusiastic and had even informed him that she wasn't looking forward to her husband's return. She seemed, in fact, to be dropping strong hints that she wouldn't mind setting up house with Aimedieu and he wondered if she'd ever considered how she'd manage on a cop's pay. It was never enough to provide a life of luxury and he couldn't imagine her in the tiny flat he occupied. Romantic France was fine when you were in England, but La Vie Bohème was a different thing when you were practising it in person.

As he walked towards her house, he saw Remarque, the leader of the Molière Players, climbing out of the old brake they used, his arms full of costumes.

Aimedieu nodded at the brake. 'Does it go?' he asked.

Remarque smiled nervously. 'Oh, it goes well. It's only the woodwork that's beginning to look tatty.'

'Does it have a wooden engine too?'

Remarque gave a sickly smile. 'It'll do for us. I'm teaching Daydé to drive.'

'I thought everybody over the age of ten could drive these days.'

'She's been too busy to learn. She can start a car now and steer and change gear.'

'She's practically on the motorway.'

As Remarque went into the house, Aimedieu followed. Like Mrs Briddon's *salon*, the actors' rooms had become a regular calling place. They never seemed to welcome him but, on the other hand, they didn't exactly push him out again either. It was almost as if they felt they ought to play safe and stay on the right side of the *flics*, and he wondered what they'd been up to.

Today they all seemed to be occupied with preparing for the medieval show in the square on the twenty-eighth. There were brightly-coloured costumes everywhere and the book Remarque had been seen carrying, *The Middle Ages – Life and Entertainment*, was lying open on the table, a mug of cold coffee standing on it. It had made a brown stain and was not at all what the library would appreciate, Aimedieu decided. Henriette Guillard was studying what appeared to be a book of medieval drama and was sitting apart. Somehow, Aimedieu had a feeling that she didn't get on with Remarque and he wondered if he'd been trying to get her in a corner as he'd heard was a habit of his. Mercédes Flichy was reading a comic book. Alongside her, her spectacles rested on a copy of *Le Bien Public*. As Aimedieu appeared, she picked up the glasses and put them on. Around the newspaper, the table was full of used mugs, wineglasses full of sediment, and an array of dirty plates, some containing food.

'Got another actor?' Aimedieu asked.

Remarque looked puzzled and Aimedieu indicated the plates piled on the table. 'Seven,' he said.

They stared at him then the expression on the face of the girl called Odile Daydé changed abruptly. She had been strumming expertly on a guitar and she slammed it down and snatched up one of the plates and sent it skidding into a corner of the room.

'You fool,' she snapped at Remarque. 'I've told you before it shouldn't be on the table!' She transferred her angry glance to Aimedieu. 'It's for the dog,' she snapped. 'It's a stray that wanders in.'

For a moment there was silence then she picked up the guitar and started plucking at it again.

Remarque stared at her. 'It'll be a lute on the night,' he said to Aimedieu.

Henriette Guillard, who had been watching the exchange, turned her attention back to the book on the Middle Ages. She seemed to be learning the words of a song and occasionally she hummed part of a tune. It seemed surprisingly modern and her voice was nothing to write home about.

Béranger was filling bottles on a chair in a corner of the room. He appeared to be using paraffin.

'Petrol bombs?' Aimedieu asked cheerfully. 'Going to start a revolution?'

There was another silence, again hostile, but Aimedieu had long since learned to ignore hostility. Béranger answered him.

'For the fire eater.' He spoke sullenly as if it were none of

Aimedieu's business. 'Meths for immediate ignition, paraffin for the flame. It looks good. Bright orange-yellow with black edges and a bit of smoke. Fire eating was always a feature of medieval shows. Among unsophisticated people, it had the look of magic.'

'Who's doing it?'

'I am.'

'So am I,' the Daydé girl said. 'So keep out of the way or I'll singe your eyebrows.'

'It's not a job for a girl,' Remarque said.

'Anything you can do, I can do, too.'

Remarque looked uneasy but he said nothing and Aimedieu decided he wasn't a very powerful personality and that the Daydé girl, as he'd noticed before, invariably seemed to get her own way.

'I hope you're good at it,' he said to Béranger.

'I've done it before.'

'Don't you ever burn yourself?'

'Not if you blow the paraffin out hard enough, keep the light away from your face and wipe your mouth after every go.'

'You seem to be pretty expert.'

'It's a daily occurrence in a circus and Gus and I have both done our stints in circuses.'

Aimedieu looked at Remarque. 'How about you?'

'This is small stuff,' Remarque said coldly. 'I've been entertaining people all my life. Acting's nothing. I told you, we were a big family and used to give shows. They were good shows, too, because we could all do something. Just the sort of stuff we'll need for the show on the twenty-eighth. I can do sleight-of-hand, sing, dance, blow flames. All exactly what medieval strolling players did. I can even walk on my hands, and do handsprings.'

He started pouring white powder out of a chemist's jar.

'Cocaine?' Aimedieu asked cheerfully.

Remarque gave him a sour look and didn't answer.

'Explosive then?'

'It's magnesium powder,' Remarque snarled. 'Gives a bright flash and a lot of white smoke. It's very effective.'

'Where did you get all these ideas?'

'They're in all the old books. You've only to use your head to realise what the magicians used in the Middle Ages.'

'You seem to be very good.'

'We find out. And then we practise. We're practising now.'

'And you're in the way,' the Daydé girl snapped. 'We're going to start juggling.'

Pel was doing a bit of juggling too. Only *he* was juggling with four major cases – a long-dead man found in a tower who ought not to have been there, two brutal killings and now a kidnapping. And so far they hadn't made any firm steps in any of them.

They'd dropped all their other enquiries temporarily. All the enquiries in the world didn't bring back dead men, and a young girl in danger came first. Aimedieu could look after Puyceldome and Nosjean could look after Garcy. Didier's hope of spending his time in Puyceldome near Bernadette Buffel's shop had been blasted immediately and Pel would have liked to pull in De Troq' too. But De Troq' had said that the boy known as Gorgeous had been talking and, though he hadn't any names, he was suddenly nearer to the supplier who had fed Speedy Sam. Knowing De Troq', Pel guessed it wasn't just an excuse to dodge work, so he left him to it and dragged in everybody else he could spare and lent them to Dunoisse to add to his own men. If nothing else, they had more experience than the men in Guinchay.

Lagé, Misset, Claudie, Debray and Brochard were all wearing their feet out making enquiries for Dunoisse while Darcy was permanently on the telephone. The rest of the squad – and it didn't leave many – were looking after the city on their own. Pel knew that the word would soon get around and that there would be a rash of small crimes as petty crooks took advantage of the situation. But it wasn't any use panicking. Panic helped no one. And he had to remember that there were other things to occupy his attention.

There were already three files on his desk, one now labelled Fouché, one Vienne, one Burges. Somehow, Pel had a feeling they were connected but he wasn't sure how.

As he studied them the telephone rang. It was Dunoisse from Guinchay. He sounded tired.

'They paid up,' he said at once.

Pel frowned. 'I suppose you can't blame them. And the girl?'

'She hasn't appeared. They were expecting a message to go to some spot where they'd find her. But none came. Instead, a demand for another five hundred thousand came.'

'Growing greedy, are they?'

'It's a pretty easy way of earning half a million.'

'I'll come to see you.'

Feeling like a man dragged four ways at once by wild horses, Pel yelled for Darcy and they drove down to Guinchay, Didier in the rear seat clutching a notebook.

Dunoisse was looking haggard. In front of him was a tape recorder. 'They also sent a tape,' he said. 'And a photograph.'

The photograph of Sybille Junot showed her holding the newspaper in front of her. The date was clear and was that of the day before. Behind the newspaper they could see the top part of her body and her legs. She looked terrified and her shoulders and legs were uncovered.

'The bastards have taken away her clothes,' Dunoisse snapped. 'She was wearing jodhpurs and a jersey when she disappeared.'

They studied the picture, looking for a clue to the girl's whereabouts, but the background was a draped sheet that gave no indication of where it came from.

The letter setting out the kidnappers' demands had been formed by cutting out letters from a newspaper. They had been stuck on a sheet torn from what appeared to be a notebook. It had holes along the top as if it had had a spiral binding, and the paper was cheap, pulpy and faded along the edge. Dunoisse had put it in a plastic cover.

Pel studied it. 'The usual,' he said. 'But this one's different in that it has a footprint on it. As if the paper was dropped and someone trod on it as they picked it up. Perhaps they were drunk. Or drugged. It's not much, but it might help.' He held it out to Didier. 'See it reaches Leguyader. Tell him we want a report on it. See that Fingerprints see it, too.'

As Didier took the plastic envelope, Dunoisse lifted a finger for silence and, reaching across the desk, switched on the tape recorder. There was a whirring sound, a few clicks, then a thin frightened voice.

'Papa. This is Sybille. I'm being held prisoner and they say you've got to pay a ransom or you'll never see me again. Please help me. I'm frightened, Pappy. They say this is serious and they'll telephone to tell you where to put the money. They say they want another five hundred thousand francs. That's a lot of money, Pappy, but I think they mean what they say. Please help me.'

Pel sat quietly for a while as Dunoisse switched off the tape recorder. 'Room with a high ceiling, the sound experts say,' Dunoisse pointed out. 'There's a bit of an echo, it seems, and no outside sounds such as you might expect to hear from passing traffic. They've analysed it and checked. Somewhere where the air's still – that is without passers-by or anything on wheels around.'

'They're amateurs,' Pel said thoughtfully. 'They allowed her to say too much. Professionals get their prisoners to read a short sentence from a paper. So short, people like your experts have nothing to go on.'

'There isn't anything, anyway,' Dunoisse pointed out.

'There might have been,' Pel said.

# 16

Nothing – not even a kidnapping and two murders – could stop the August party spirit. It had to continue because the whole of France was on holiday and gaiety was rampant. The children had to be amused, the place was flooded with foreigners, and the village parties continued, while the preparations for the medieval night in Puyceldome continued unabated.

It rained several times before the night of the show and there was even a howling thunderstorm the day before. The long faces at Puyceldome were reflected in the long faces of the tourists and campers in the area who had bought seats for the outdoor supper.

But during the morning it brightened up. There was still a cold breeze but the skies cleared and the long tables were erected round the square with confidence. A group from Goillac – guitars, trumpet, electric organ and drums – drove into the square with their van and began to set up their stalls. In the hotel, Madame Plessis was shrieking at the maids, and the barman, a cigarette drooping from his lip with two inches of ash, was polishing glasses as hard as he could go.

As Aimedieu crossed the square, he saw Remarque appear from the Rue Nobel where the actors lived. Aimedieu had long since promised to take Ellen Briddon to the medieval night – not as a guest at one of the long tables, because a cop's pay didn't run to luxuries of that sort, but as a spectator. He was very much aware that the whole of the enquiry into the man found in the tower now rested on his shoulders, but he felt no one would object to him partaking in the roistering. Puyceldome was his patch and, you never knew, he might bump into someone paying for his drinks with a Maria Theresa or a Napoleon.

Remarque looked worried enough to draw Aimedieu's attention.

'What's up?'

'Guillard's left. She's let us down.'

Aimedieu wasn't surprised. He'd always felt that she was a cut above the rest. 'Why did she leave?'

'Slight disagreement. Heard of a better job.'

'What will you do?'

Remarque didn't seem to hear him at first but then he came to life and turned. 'Oh,' he said, 'we've got it all worked out. We'll be all right. Daydé will play the lute and Mercédes will sing the songs and do the dancing. We've found one or two she can manage and she's been practising. Daydé can join in and, when she isn't dancing, she'll do a bit of fire eating.'

'Don't set yourselves on fire.'

The square was hung with long red and yellow banners bearing crosses, wild boars and the local coat of arms. A carpenter was just finishing boarding over the top of the well in the centre of the square so that it could be used as a raised stage. More men were hanging extra flags, pennants and oriflammes about the old buildings, while a flat screen of canvas mounted on a wooden frame and showing a medieval castle that might well have been part of Puyceldome was being shoved into place by a slight young man with a straggly beard in the doorway of the Mairie.

A girl appeared alongside Aimedieu. She was pretty and he couldn't understand why he'd never seen her before because he wasn't one to miss a face or a leg or a nicely curved bosom.

'Are they still putting on the playlets?' she asked.

'They're certainly putting on something.'

'I thought they'd have to give up when we left.'

Aimedieu's eyebrows lifted. 'Were you part of the Molière Company?'

'For my sins.'

'You'll be Eloïse then, who left with Richard.'

'No, I'm Colette and I left with Camille.'

Aimedieu frowned. 'You were the girls who went on holiday?'

'No, we didn't. Camille decided to get married. She's in Lyons. I telephoned her last night. I got a job as a teacher at the drama school in Dijon.'

'Why did you leave?'

'Well, it's obvious, isn't it? Jean-Paul Remarque was too fond of backing me into dark corners. They drink too much. They probably use other things, too.'

'Drugs?'

'You tell me.'

'You with Henriette Guillard?'

'Who's she when she's at home?'

'She's one of them. She's just left.'

'I don't blame her. Did he try to get her in a corner, too?'

Aimedieu grinned. 'Are you going to pay them a call?'

'Not likely. I've just come to collect my belongings. I left them at the hotel.' She looked shrewdly at Aimedieu. 'Anyway, what business is it of yours?'

'Everything's my business. I'm a cop.'

'Ah!' She grinned at him. 'Pity I'm not staying. I always got on well with the fuzz.'

By dusk, Puyceldome was more than ready. The folk dancing and the chorus singing by the children from the school had been going on during the afternoon as a sort of curtain raiser and there were people in the square all day. The folk dancing had been a little confused, and, while the parents of the children had undoubtedly enjoyed hearing their offspring perform, nobody else showed much excitement. The high spot was the medieval evening.

As it grew dark the kitchen of the hotel became red-hot with the cooking and the oaths of the chef, one of the maids had had nervous hysterics and was being offered extra pay not to let the side down, while old Le Pape, lechery all over his face, was trying to persuade the landlord to get the girls to undo the buttons of their blouses and show a little more bouncing bosom in the best free and easy medieval style.

The tourists were already in position behind the tables. The sky was dark and the floodlights that had been erected and the torches flaring in their niches in the ancient walls gave the scene an air of unreality as the maids streamed out carrying the wine and the bread and the boar stew.

'But it's wonderful,' Ellen Briddon said as she arrived with Aimedieu. She was delighted to be there – if only as a spectator among the villagers and the noisy children – and delighted with his company. She had fed and watered him and was in a romantic mood and hoping to enjoy the evening.

She was excited as she pushed with him into the square. It was packed with people, the arcades crowded, the four entrances, one at each corner, jammed tight.

'It *looks* medieval,' she crowed.

It *did* look medieval, Aimedieu had to admit. The atmosphere was right and the ancient houses against the deep purple of the sky looked like a film set. But, he reminded himself, these were *real* houses, not wood and plasterboard constructions, and they were inhabited by modern people who were actually hanging out of their windows to watch the spectacle. The only artificial note, apart from the tourists at the tables armed with video cameras and flashlights, was the screen of canvas and wood in the doorway of the Mairie which, in addition to obscuring the modern furnishings inside, also hid the electronic gadgets and modern instruments of the group which was to play for dancing when the medieval entertainment finished.

The boar stew went down as well as Le Pape and Serge Vitiello, the artist and only other active member of the entertainments committee, had expected. Nobody questioned that it was cheap to produce, though it was costing them a small fortune, and the wine helped. A few pieces of bread were thrown and one of the older tourists tried to kiss one of the maids. Le Pape seemed to have had his way about the buttons and the girls had entered into the spirit of the thing and there now seemed to be acres of bouncing flesh on display.

As the plates were cleared, the tourists sat back expectantly and, as he pushed through the excited children, Aimedieu bumped into De Troq'. Aimedieu had already seen Didier Darras chasing Le Bernard's granddaughter and it seemed that all of that half of Pel's squad which wasn't deployed around Guinchay and Treffort was on hand.

'What are you doing here?' he asked.

'Following a hunch,' De Troq' said. He was with a girl Aimedieu recognised from the Palais de Justice and he seemed to be studying a young man near the bar.

'Following somebody?' he asked.

'Might be.'

'Gangster?'

De Troq' smiled. 'No. Just a carpenter.'

As Aimedieu found Ellen Briddon a seat, Mercédes Flichy climbed to the top of the boarded-up well. She was dressed in gaudy red and yellow, in a wimple, a spire-like head-dress and a long gown. Odile Daydé took up a position alongside her, in her hands not a guitar but what Aimedieu assumed was a lute. As she began to play, Mercédes Flichy started singing. She had no voice and she seemed to be flat all the time, but the song was a typically tuneless medieval ballad and the tourists, full of food and wine, didn't care anyway.

As the song finished, Remarque appeared, turning somersaults and walking on his hands in the manner of medieval tumblers. He was dressed as a jester. Béranger, dressed as the Devil, wandered along the fringe of the crowd, whirling two blazing torches made of tarred rope wound round pieces of broom handle, the flames sharp against the old stone. To the beating on a long drum played by Odile Daydé, Mercédes Flichy ran into the square again, now wearing a medieval mask with a long pointed nose, padded trousers and festoons of floating ribbons, and started to dance.

Like the song, which hadn't been much of a song, it wasn't much of a dance, and to Aimedieu the Flichy girl seemed to be making it up as she went along. It involved a little hip-wiggling and the pointing of toes, though there wasn't a lot of rhythm. But Odile Daydé knew how to play a lute and it made the dance seem better than it was, especially with Remarque and Béranger prancing round the fringes, whirling torches.

As the long tables of tourists broke into applause, Béranger began to ignite magnesium flashes which filled the square with bright light and rolling white smoke. In the glare, with the prancing figures in the middle, it all looked a little mad, and the excitement set the children screaming.

The bar was doing a roaring trade and the tourists and the campers started leaping about with flash cameras, taking pictures of the performance. Fireworks were being thrown and already the local police had picked up two pickpockets who had journeyed from Goillac specially for the performance.

Then Gus Blivet appeared, walking on high stilts, dressed in black and white, his hair jelled into a high coxcomb. A spotlight was directed on the third-floor window of the Mairie from which hung a long knotted rope, and Remarque began to climb out. With one leg over the sill, he lifted a bottle to his lips and blew a long jet of flame across the front of the old building. As he wiped his mouth, tucked his bottle of spirits into a pocket and continued his climb to the ground, Odile Daydé dropped her lute and began to skip with a burning rope. Béranger's Devil gave shouts of mad laughter and started to juggle with three burning torches.

The show went on for a good hour and was, everybody felt, well worth the money, though a few of the tourists had noticed by now that the square was full of townspeople who had got in for nothing to see something for which they had just paid through the nose. Nevertheless, everybody was happy. The tourists were sated with drink, food and medieval happenings and Ellen Briddon was trying hard to inveigle Aimedieu into her bed. He was pretending to be a bit dim and she wasn't making a lot of progress.

She had her camera with her and was taking photographs as if there were no tomorrow, snapping the Molière group, the buildings, even the unbosomed maids carrying away the dirty crockery and glasses – but always including Aimedieu in the corner. He suspected that whatever happened afterwards she would enjoy showing them to her friends in Surbiton and weaving a few spicy stories round them. It didn't worry Aimedieu. He'd had women admire him before and it didn't go to his head.

She was still taking pictures as the performance finished and the performers gathered in the corner by the bar and began thirstily to swallow beers. Aimedieu could understand their need. If he'd been filling his mouth with a mixture of paraffin and methylated spirits half the evening, he'd have needed something to take the taste away. As Ellen Briddon took another picture of him, he gently took the camera from her.

'Oughtn't I to take one of you?' he asked and she gave him a happy smile.

'Any special background?' he asked.

'Just the square and the people. Against the bar perhaps. Something real and French.'

He took the picture against the background of the bar where the Molière Company were drinking. They had stripped off their jesters' clothes, their masks and the Devil's costume, and wiped the make-up from their faces. He used the flash and she turned on a radiant smile for him.

'Shall I wind it on?' he asked.

'You can't. That's the last of the film. I can't wait to get them developed. How long do they take?'

'Here, five days. At the supermarket at Goillac three. If I handle them, one.'

'How?'

'Police photo lab. They're at it all the time. I can get them done tomorrow morning, printed and dried, and back here tomorrow evening. If they ask questions I'll tell them they're pictures I need as evidence.'

'Can you do that?'

'Easy.'

She beamed at him and kissed his cheek.

The noise in the square was extraordinary by now. People were shouting, a group singing. At one end a man with a guitar was playing '*Je suis fier d'être Bourguignon*'. At the other end half a dozen old men were singing 'Madelon' at the tops of their voices. A band that seemed to contain everybody in the town sober enough to play an instrument was hard at it under the arcades. Le Bernard was booming away on the trombone. Bernard Bis Bravo, his cheeks like balloons, was pumping away at a bassoon. Even Bernadette, his sister, was playing a flute. They were obviously a very musical family.

A few people were putting on an ad lib act of melodrama by the bar and a few stalls had been set up under the arcades by commercially-minded villagers eager not to miss the opportunity. Among them was Serge Vitiello. For fifty francs he was drawing the faces of anybody who would sit for him. He had done quite well and the two girls from the Molière Company were haggling with him over the price.

As the singing stopped, the drinking started. The bar disappeared in a haze of blue cigarette smoke and shouted orders. Among the crowd at the zinc, the Molière Company, their duty done, their pay in their pockets, were making heavy inroads into the stocks. Remarque was drinking brandy as if he were afraid of seeing the dawn and was already unsteady on his feet.

As the town band ground to a halt, everybody trooped to the battlements to watch the fireworks which had been set up in a field in the valley below. For the next half-hour the place echoed to the 'Oohs' and 'Aahs' as the black sky was filled with soaring lights, then they all trooped back to the square and the bar, where the staff had collected all the dirty glasses they could, drawn breath and were prepared for the next assault.

By this time the town band had been replaced by the rock group which had set up their instruments and microphones in the doorway of the Mairie, and people started dancing. Among them was Le Bernard clutching a stout lady Aimedieu assumed was Madame Le Bernard. Didier Darras was clutching Bernadette Buffel far more closely than modern dancing normally allowed. Aimedieu grinned. As a young man who, despite his angel face, had passed through the agonies of first love and beyond, he was pleased to see the tortured expression had gone from Didier's face.

He didn't realise it, but Didier had taken a chance by being there. He had left the city late, turning over the telephone at headquarters to the reluctant Misset and arriving flat out on his scooter. He knew he had to be on duty again at six the following morning and would probably be going to Treffort, but he had decided it was worth missing his sleep to be in Puyceldome this night with Bernadette Buffel. In fact, missing his sleep was something he was growing used to.

As he circled dreamily with her, she turned her head. 'That actor's coming,' she said.

'Don't worry,' Didier said, all protective police force. 'I can handle him.'

Remarque appeared alongside them and tried to separate Didier from the girl. She looked scared and clung tighter.

'Dance?' Remarque's voice was slurred. He'd drunk too much too fast.

'I'm dancing.'

'Why not with me?'

'Because – ' Bernadette nodded at Didier. 'Because I'm dancing with him.'

Bernard Bis Bravo had watched the exchange. 'That's my sister,' he said as Remarque drifted away.

'I know,' Didier said.

'You've met?'

'In the shop.'

Didier danced for a long time with Bernadette Buffel, then he took her down the alley to the ramparts and kissed her under the trees. He was beginning to feel more like his old self. As they returned, he saw Aimedieu still arm in arm with Mrs Briddon and, envying his confidence, wondered what he was up to. In fact, Aimedieu was growing more and more nervous. Ellen Briddon was still trying to get him into her bed but just didn't have the nerve to spell it out for him.

Then he saw Remarque appear from the bar once more. He seemed very drunk now and as if he were looking for trouble. He went straight up to Didier and Bernadette Buffel and tried again to push between them. There was a scuffle and Didier, who was far from small, shoved him away.

Aimedieu saw what happened and, gently putting Ellen Briddon aside, he excused himself quietly. She came to earth out of a pale pink romantic cloud with a bump to see him striding through the crowded couples in the square. As Remarque moved forward again he found Aimedieu in his way then, as Sous-Brigadier Lefêvre, stiff with authority and on the look-out for wrongdoers and mischief-makers, arrived, Remarque sat down abruptly, not because of Didier's push but because his feet no longer seemed to belong to him. A girl screamed and the dancers in the immediate vicinity of the incident drew back, halting their steps, the men protective, the women nervous. Round the edges of the square, a few people glanced over their shoulders but most went on dancing.

Aimedieu yanked Remarque to his feet. 'Come on,' he said. 'Shove off. Go and sleep it off. You've done your stuff – and very well too – but don't make a nuisance of yourself on the strength of it.'

Lefêvre moved forward importantly. 'Orders are, no arrests,' he said. 'Not tonight.'

'I'm well aware,' Aimedieu said coldly.

'All the same – ' Lefêvre liked to feel important. ' – let's have a note of it. This is my patch and I believe in doing things by the book.'

He fished in Remarque's back pocket and pulled out the actor's wallet. 'Let's have a look at your papers.'

Remarque scowled. 'Why?'

'Because it's usual.' Lefêvre looked up as he perused the documents. 'I thought your name was Remarque,' he said.

Remarque's words were slurred. 'Stage name,' he said. 'Who'd want to be called Pierre Dupont? Can you imagine it in lights? It's as exciting as a pile of sand. Parents don't think of what their children might become when they christen them. Mine thought I'd become a clerk or a lawyer or something and Pierre Dupont's not very memorable for an actor. It's not even memorable for a lawyer. Pierre Dupont. Who's he? I can just imagine Carlo Ponti saying that when I apply for a part in his next epic.'

'I'll get him home,' Aimedieu said. He gestured to Mrs Briddon. 'You go home. I'll join you.'

Lefêvre gave Remarque a little push. 'All right,' he said. 'Go and sleep it off and think yourself lucky that I haven't run you in.' He turned to Didier as Remarque slunk away. 'Remarque, indeed,' he said. 'His name's Dupont like any other Dupont.'

When Aimedieu returned to the square, he passed Vitiello sitting by his easel.

'Draw you?'

Since the proceeds were going to charity, Aimedieu submitted. The result was recognisable but not distinguished by much style.

'Getting much business?' Aimedieu asked.

'No.'

Frowning, Aimedieu studied two drawings on the easel. They were of Odile Daydé and Mercédes Flichy.

'Didn't they want them?'

Vitiello shrugged. 'They beat me down to twenty francs then said they were no good. Well, I suppose they're not all that good. I'm not Picasso. But they could have given me the twenty francs.'

He looked low in spirits and Aimedieu smiled. 'I'll give you twenty francs for them,' he said.

Vitiello looked up. 'You got a thing going for them?'

Aimedieu grinned. 'Not me. But it's for charity, isn't it?'

# 17

Kidnap was always the crime the police liked least. It was a growth industry these days and to a certain extent left the police helpless. There was no body, no blood – no splashes of red from which they might determine facts – no weapon.

It usually consisted of nothing more than a snatch into a car – leaving nothing to work on or with, and the relations of the victim more than willing to co-operate with the criminals. Invariably they were rich enough to go their own way – why otherwise a kidnap? – and were often willing to delude the police as to their intentions because they were afraid police intervention would prevent the return of the victim.

Pel often wished he had some of the skill of the great fictional detectives he read about. Private eye loners always seemed to do better than the police, as indeed did the elderly maiden ladies to whom the police were obliged to go for advice. Pel never knew how they produced their deductions without the facilities of police computers, the Lab, Photography, Fingerprints and the rest. Even the setting up of a central organisation to handle the statements was beyond them.

Inspector Goriot, who had once been senior to Pel, usually did the job of going through statements, analysing them and marking points in them for further enquiry. Pel never left it at hat, though, and always went through them again himself, looking for points that needed further action, further investigation. It kept him in the office more than he normally liked but somebody had to do it and, with two murders, a mummy and a kidnap, he had to leave the field work to his team.

Nothing had changed. Nosjean was still following up the N6

murder cases, De Troq' was continuing to keep an eye on the drugs on the side, and Aimedieu was pursuing his enquiries in Puyceldome. But his squad wasn't elastic. It couldn't be stretched indefinitely and Darcy had had to put aside the business of Alfred Fouché and the interesting involvement of Lorick Lupin for the time being.

He had been in contact with the Los Angeles police department and, promised unqualified support, was hoping for information before long. But the Atlantic was wide and so was America, and it meant possessing their souls in patience for a while. In the meantime a young girl was in danger and that was of far greater importance, and they had their men everywhere that Sybille Junot might possibly have been, enquiring of her friends and acquaintances and checking girls who were at school with her – not an easy job because a lot of them, in the manner of youth, had vanished into the blue after adventure, money or marriage. The Lycée at Guinchay had responded at once to their request for a list of pupils and had come up with the names of all who had passed through its doors during the last ten years. The Lycée at Vonnas was still hanging fire.

'The Director's away sick,' Darcy pointed out as they ended the day in Pel's office.

He pushed a packet of cigarettes across and, throwing caution to the wind in his weariness, Pel took one like a drowning man snatching at a straw. Lighting it, he drew the smoke down so far it seemed to be in danger of coming out through his trouser bottoms.

'We've been going steadily through the Guinchay list,' Darcy went on. 'Checking every single girl and boy. Those who aren't in the district are being traced and questioned. Some are easy. Some aren't. One girl's a doctor and she's in Angola. She'll take some finding. But we're progressing slowly because most of them are still in this area for the simple reason that they're not old enough to have moved very far away. One or two are at universities or technical colleges and they're traceable. One or two have taken jobs in Belgium, England, Italy and Spain, but their parents have been able to contact them for us. We'll do the same with the list from Vonnas when it arrives, but it seems they're also short of administrative staff. They've promised the list as soon as they can.'

He looked at Pel and turned a leaf of his notebook. 'That photograph of the girl they sent,' he said. 'It was a polaroid picture. Photography says it was one of the new cameras fitted with a flash. Just the thing for kidnappers. Snip, snap, and you've got evidence that you've done what you've said you've done. I've got Lagé asking round the photography and video shops to see if anyone bought one, and if so, who. Also if anyone interesting's been buying a tape recorder or tapes, because they used a tape to record that message they sent, and someone might have bought one.'

'I think they'll be cleverer than that, Daniel,' Pel said. 'Any word from Leguyader about the ransom note?'

'Not yet.'

Didier was typing out the details in the room he shared with Claudie Darel next door, and appeared at Pel's shout.

'Leguyader: did you tell him we were in a hurry for the report on the ransom note?'

'Yes, Patron.'

'What did he say?'

Leguyader, always eager to score off Pel, had been non-committal, but Didier didn't say so.

'He didn't say anything, Patron.'

'Go and see him. Tell him to hurry it up. We need it.'

It was late in the day and Didier had been hoping to get to Puyceldome. Feeling mutinous, he took his time. He still occasionally thought about Louise Bray's monstrous infidelity – she'd sworn undying devotion at the age of seven and had never swerved from it until he'd made the mistake of introducing her to former Cadet Martin. Mind you, he'd been aware that she'd noticed Martin's good looks some time before when they'd been involved in an enquiry and ended up in the Hôtel de Police with Martin writing the details down in his notebook.

Still dwelling on the circumstances of his vanished love life, he arrived at Leguyader's laboratory in low spirits. Immediately he noticed the ransom note he'd taken there, still in the plastic envelope on Leguyader's desk. He was studying it when Leguyader appeared.

'Well, what do you want?'

Automatically Didier noticed the difference between Pel and the Lab chief. Pel could be ironic, sarcastic, sharp and hurtful, but he wasn't normally downright rude, which was Leguyader's usual attitude towards lesser members of the staff of the Hôtel de Police.

Didier indicated the sheet. 'The Chief's asking for the report on that,' he said.

'It's not ready,' Leguyader snapped.

'He asked for it urgently. I told you.'

'What he considers urgent and what I consider urgent are two different things.'

'Shall I tell him that?'

Leguyader back-tracked quickly. He knew how far he could go. 'I'll get it finished and let you know.'

'What about the footprint on it?'

'Why?'

'The Chief will want to know. He was interested.'

'Tell him it's a footprint.'

'Whose?'

'We don't know. Nor are we likely to.'

'What about the paper?'

'It's paper-type paper.'

'Is that all?'

'If there's more, it'll be in my report.'

As Didier returned he bumped into Pel in the car-park as he left for home.

'What did Leguyader have to say?'

Didier toned down the replies he'd received. 'He's not quite finished, Patron,' he said.

Pel was on the point of climbing into his car when he stopped and turned. He eyed Didier sympathetically. He was going through a difficult period, he knew. His girl had transferred her affections elsewhere and that was always an awkward time. Pel had been through a few awkward times himself as a young man. In fact, every girl he met seemed to transfer her affections elsewhere as soon as possible. He was glad he'd married.

'I'll run you home,' he said. 'It's on my way.' He paused. 'Fancy a game of boules?'

The boy didn't answer and Pel wondered if it were because he was heavily indifferent or because he was finding it difficult to be friendly after his earlier sullenness. It wasn't easy for the young to change step.

'Thought I might try the Bar de la Frontière,' he said. 'My wife's still away and they do a good *blanquette de veau* there, and there's room for a dozen sets of boules.'

The boy didn't respond but he climbed into Pel's car without objecting. Didier knew the Bar de la Frontière. It was an old haunt of Pel's in the days before he had met his wife, and they'd visited it often in the days of Pel's bachelorhood. He didn't go there much now but if he were passing he still liked to call in for old time's sake. It was outside the city in an open space in the woods, with a huge sandy car-park which was used less for parking cars than for playing boules. It was an old building, with a fading advertisement for Byrrh painted on the gable end, and it smelled of Gauloises, cooking, wine and sausage. There were usually one or two old men playing dominoes and one or two more trying their hand at boules, often watched by a couple of small boys and an old woman with a long loaf sticking out of her shopping bag, who had dropped in to rest her aching feet.

The *blanquette de veau* was especially good and Pel ordered a *carafon* of red wine. 'How about you?' he asked. Previously the boy had always drunk Coca Cola but perhaps he was growing a little old for Coca Cola now.

'I'll have a beer, please,' he said.

As they ate, Pel looked at him. 'How are things?' he asked.

Didier shrugged.

Pel eyed him for a moment and came to the conclusion that the best thing to do, instead of fiddling about round the edges of the problem, was to dive in at the deep end.

'Losing your girl's always a nerve-shattering experience,' he said. 'I ought to know. When I was your age I lost mine on an average of once a month.'

Didier looked up, startled. It had never occurred to him that older men had been through the same experience.

'I was never very good with girls,' Pel said.

'Madame Pel's all right,' Didier said stoutly, and Pel knew it was meant as praise.

'Best thing that happened to me when she decided to marry me.'

'Didn't you ask her?'

Pel considered. He couldn't remember that he had. He supposed that Madame had organised it as efficiently as she organised everything else, slightly amused by him, even probably singing to herself one of the old songs she liked as she manoeuvred him. He could only imagine that she had grown tired of him wavering about, trying to pluck up courage, and had decided to take matters into her own capable hands so that, before he had known where he was, he was on the way to the altar. He shrugged. She had made a better job of it than he ever could have done.

'Do all men have problems with girls?' Didier asked.

'Some men', Pel said, 'have a lot of problems. I was one. It's part of growing up. My sister married a Rosbif, as you know. She's older than me and once when I was visiting her in England, she took me to see a musical show that was being put on in the town where she lived. Amateur. It was awful. The scenery wobbled. The leading tenor was too fat, the heroine looked like a barmaid and the chorus couldn't have made anything even of the "Marseillaise" – and anybody who can't make anything of *that* isn't very good. But it had a song in it I remembered. It went, "At seventeen he falls in love quite madly with eyes of tender blue. At twenty-one he's got it rather badly with eyes of a different hue."'

Pel translated for the boy. 'I remembered it because that's the way it goes, isn't it? But there are always other fish in the sea, you know. Or as they say in Paris, if you miss one bus, there's always another one coming along in a minute or two.'

Didier grinned unexpectedly. 'One has,' he said.

Pel looked up. 'Oh? Who?'

'Bernard Buffel Bis's sister. Bernadette.'

'It must be confusing with everybody in the family having the same name. What's her mother called. Bernadine?'

'No, that's the aunt. The mother's probably Bernadelle.' Didier gave another grin and Pel felt he was getting somewhere.

'Let's try our hand at boules,' he said. 'I'm feeling skilful tonight.'

When Pel arrived home, the telephone was ringing. It was his wife who had telephoned to make sure he hadn't dropped dead of neglect. He was so pleased to hear her voice he almost did a dance by the instrument.

'How's Madame Routy?' his wife asked. 'Is she behaving herself?'

'Yes.' Madame Routy at that moment didn't seem to have the spirit not to behave herself. 'When are you coming back?'

'It will be next week, I'm afraid. Do you miss me?'

'If I lost my legs, I'd miss *them*.'

'I tried to ring earlier. There was no reply.'

'I was out.'

'Police work?'

'Not exactly,' Pel said. 'A life-saving job.'

At Puyceldome, everybody was agreed that the medieval night had been a great success. There were more than a few thick heads about still and already they'd heard of people waking up in beds that weren't their own, one even, judging by his black eye, in the bed of someone else's wife. The barman at the hotel was in trouble too. Having locked up the bar and secured the doors at 4 a.m. after all the customers and the owner and his wife had gone home, he had fallen asleep in the cellar. It was unfortunate that he had had to be awakened by the police at 7.30 to unlock the door to let out a couple of German tourists who had hired the top bedroom and had come down to breakfast to find the bar and the dining-room still covered with the litter of the previous night's spree and no means of getting out.

'Suppose the place had caught fire,' one of them said indignantly.

Madame Plessis, the proprietor's wife, still had steam coming out of her ears with fury and Aimedieu could hear her screeches as he sat at a table in front of the hotel, a pencil in his hand, checking items in his notebook. Alongside him was a plastic carrier bag containing a few things he'd bought from a mini-supermarket situated just off the square. He had a feeling his work at Puyceldome was finished. He had seen no Maria Theresas and no napoleons or silver dollars floating around, and, after thirty years, didn't expect to. Instead of Ellen Briddon's excellent meals, from now on he would be cooking for himself and the plastic carrier bag – free with all orders over twenty francs at the supermarket – contained instant coffee, tinned meat, and frozen vegetables.

He had been present at the medieval night chiefly because Ellen Briddon had wanted to see it but hadn't wanted to be unescorted, and he had felt that he owed her a little politeness if nothing else. She had given him coffee and drinks without number and had even fed him once or twice. It was obvious she had gone out of her way to please him, too – which was what worried him because things the night before hadn't turned out quite as he had expected. Ellen Briddon had drunk more than she'd intended and had literally thrown herself at him. It had resulted in a session of very heavy breathing, but Aimedieu had had the sense to back off before they had gone too far and she had had so much to drink it didn't matter much, anyway, because she had promptly gone to sleep. She had wakened that morning feeling as if the side of her head was about to drop off.

He had taken his farewell of her early. He had delivered the photographs she had taken as he had promised but she had been feeling so hung over and miserable she hadn't been very interested. Her husband was due back in a few days' time and she had sadly accepted that, for both their sakes, it was wiser for Aimedieu to disappear from the scene. She had wept a little and clung to him, but she had seen the wisdom in the decision he had made and they had sorted things out with a degree of sense and determination.

As he toyed with his beer, thoughtfully wiping off the condensation from the glass with his finger end, he could see Remarque with Béranger and Gus Blivet propping up the bar. He'd noticed them packing and assumed that they, too, were about to move on. They weren't going to make a lot of money, he felt, the way they drank. He decided even that they were probably on drugs. It didn't surprise him. Nothing much did.

They didn't look like addicts, however, but, then, they were actors and could look like anything they wished. No wonder De Troq' had decided to pay a visit to Puyceldome the night before.

The two girls, Mercédes Flichy and Odile Daydé, were sitting at a table nearby drinking black coffee and smoking. As he watched, the Flichy girl picked up the glass ashtray she had been using and passed it across the table to the other girl. They looked as blurred and dazed as Remarque and he decided they were probably on drugs, too, and that the cigarettes they were smoking contained cannabis.

When he had taken Remarque home the night before, they had been there almost as if they were waiting to collect him. Béranger and Gus Blivet had looked scared but the two girls had looked angry, as if they had been having a tremendous row.

Aimedieu had ignored the scowls and laid Remarque down. Remarque had given no trouble. As Aimedieu had let go of him, he had crumpled like a sack of rubbish into the only decent chair the five of them possessed.

'The fool!' Odile Daydé said, staring at him with disgust. 'He was always a fool. He can't hold his liquor. He should lay off it.'

As he fished in his pocket for his cigarettes, Aimedieu's fingers came in contact with the two portraits of the girls he had bought from Serge Vitiello the night before. He took them out and unfolded them. They weren't particularly good. They were recognisable but, while Vitiello could capture features with an art teacher's precision, he didn't seem to have the flair of a true artist.

Without thinking, Aimedieu began to draw a moustache on one of the pictures and a pair of spectacles on the other. As he stared at them, he frowned, then sat up. Seeing Vitiello across the square, he took the pictures across to him.

'Got an indiarubber?' he asked.

'Artists always have a pencil, an indiarubber, a penknife and a sketch pad on them,' Vitiello grinned.

'I'd like to borrow the rubber.'

Sitting down, he rubbed out the moustache he'd drawn on the portrait of Odile Daydé. He looked up.

'Could you alter them?' he asked.

'Why?'

'They could be prettier.'

'You in love with them?'

They sat down together and Vitiello fished out a pencil and began to work to Aimedieu's orders. Aimedieu fetched him a beer. As he placed it on the table, Remarque and his friends left the bar. The two girls rose and followed them. Aimedieu glanced about him and, as they passed, he picked up the ashtray they had been using and transferred it to Vitiello's table.

'I don't smoke,' Vitiello said.

Aimedieu smiled and studied the ashtray. He emptied it on the ground then placed it carefully in his carrier bag.

'You nicking that?' Vitiello asked.

Aimedieu grinned. 'I'm short of an ashtray in my flat,' he said.

Vitiello grinned back. 'Once a cop, always a cop,' he said. 'You've had an eye on them for some time. I've noticed. You think they're smoking cannabis.'

Aimedieu smiled. 'Something like that,' he said.

When Vitiello had finished his alterations, Aimedieu studied the two drawings.

'I've hardly made them prettier,' Vitiello said.

'I didn't expect you to.'

'What's behind all this?'

Aimedieu shrugged. 'I always alter the pictures in the newspaper,' he said. 'It's a habit of mine. You can make the prettiest girl look like a grandmother with a few lines. You can make Robert Redford look like the Hunchback of Notre Dame.'

'Is that how you spend the evenings?'

'It's something to do when *Dallas* grows a bit dull.'

Vitiello decided they had some very odd cops these days. As he disappeared, Aimedieu sat studying the pictures for a while, then he jumped up, thrust the carrier bag into his car and set off for The Cat House.

# 18

Pel had just reached his office when Darcy burst in. He looked tired but his energy was undiminished. His face was a mixture of triumph and disappointment.

'You look as if you'd lost a franc and found a centime,' Pel said.

'I feel a bit like it.' Darcy shrugged. 'That money Goillac wants, Patron – the coins Fouché was after: they're not going to get it.'

'Oh?'

Darcy grinned. 'Unfortunately, neither are we.'

Pel sat back. Knowing Darcy, he was certain something important was on its way. 'Intorm me,' he said.

'I told you I contacted the Los Angeles police department. They found where Lupin went to.'

Pel sat up. His guess hadn't been wrong. 'They did?'

'I think we've got the whole story now, Patron. I've been in touch with his son. He was trying to contact me when I came in.'

'How?'

'By telephone.'

'What!' Pel jerked upright. 'That'll take some explaining to the Chief. He doesn't like long-distance calls to foreign parts.'

'He won't worry about this one. Lupin's son's wealthy. He paid for it. He heard about my enquiry and decided to get in touch. It was six o'clock in the morning where he is. He got up specially. It's cleared up the whole story.'

'You'd better pass it on.'

'It's a long one. I'd better start at the beginning.'

'I can think of no better place.'

Darcy pulled a chair forward. 'Caillas – or perhaps I'd better call him Luzeau – he and his boys stole those coins, Patron. Agents for the generals raised them but they weren't careful enough and it leaked out. Luzeau heard about them. That we know. But Luzeau was as clumsy as the generals and he and his boys left clues all over the place. Goillac police were on to them pretty smartly, and when they learned they'd been named as the thieves they decided they'd better get rid of the swag. There'd been no violence at the heist and I expect they thought the people who'd raised the coins, being dissidents and against the government, could hardly raise a fuss. In fact, *nobody* could make much of a charge stick. I reckon they thought that at the most they might be sent to prison for conspiracy and that would be all, and that when they came out the coins would still be there for them to pick up. This is pure speculation, of course, but I bet I'm right.'

'You're not doing badly so far.'

Darcy grinned. 'The Cat House, with the tower, was available at the time,' he went on. 'So they bought it. On a loan. Low deposit. Not much expenditure and not much expense. They called on Fouché, whom I expect one of them knew from prison, to put the stuff in the tower and seal it up for them.'

Darcy lit a cigarette and passed the packet. 'But soon afterwards,' he went on, 'there was an alarm. In the papers. I found it in *Le Bien Public*. Henriot told me of it. He owes us a few favours and he looked it up for me. The story was about the stolen coins being hidden at Puyceldome, but whoever wrote it got it wrong. It was a different collection and they weren't stolen, just mislaid.'

Darcy sat back. 'But Luzeau and his boys panicked,' he went on. 'They decided to remove the coins, so they called on Fouché again to get them out. Because he was strong and it had to be done quickly. Unfortunately for them, he had a heart attack and instead of getting the loot out, he fell inside on top of it. And while it was easy enough to deposit the box of coins inside, it was a different matter to get it out, because first they had to remove a heavy man. In addition, it was the period when they were holding the celebrations for the 700th anniversary of the founding of Puyceldome. *Son et lumière*. Same as now only more so. Dancing in the streets. Singing. Bands.

'The Prime Minister came with a descendant of the Ducs of Burgundy. Le Bernard's got a picture of it. You can see the Cat Tower in it – even a bit of scaffolding. Fouché's scaffolding, I reckon. It's surrounded by people. They wouldn't be able to do anything suspicious because of all the people around. I expect the local cops were there in full force, too. So, when Fouché died inside the tower they just had to leave him. The celebrations went on for a week and they'd have had to use something pretty clever to get at the coins because there's barely enough room in the tower for one man, let alone a second trying to get Fouché out. And they couldn't do it after dark because the place wasn't dark. Not ever. It was illuminated with floodlights and there was all-night dancing. They decided it was impossible and had to leave him. But they began to worry about the smell and perhaps people were growing curious about what they were up to. So they decided they'd better put things aside for a while until the fuss had died down. They sealed the tower and intended to return later. But they didn't and that's why the coins were never found.'

'But they were!' Pel said. 'They aren't there now!'

'No,' Darcy agreed. 'But Luzeau's lot didn't get them. They never returned because they were knocked off in Marseilles. The police thought it must have been some gang vendetta and still do, but I reckon it was someone connected with the conspirators who raised the coins – the guys who were against de Gaulle over Algeria.'

'I think', Pel said slowly, 'that after thirty years, we can safely forget *them*.'

'Yes. Anyway, Fouché had told his wife he was on a tricky job. That we know. But he didn't tell her what it was. He came home very pleased and she assumed everything had gone well. Then a few days later he was called out. He told his wife it was urgent and that something had gone wrong. He left and never came back. She worked out the date exactly because it was her daughter's birthday about that time and she thought he ought to have been there. That was the day the newspapers said the police were on the track of the coins. But when I checked I found it wasn't the coins *we're* interested in. It was another set that had only been left temporarily in Puyceldome and were thought to have been stolen.'

Darcy shifted the papers in front of him. 'It was enough, though,' he said, 'to send Luzeau and his friends bolting for safety. Unfortunately, they made the mistake of going back to Marseilles and Luzeau and Pulot were shot. Pirioux was killed in a car crash. Sammonix went to America where he died of cancer. That meant there was no one left who knew about the tower. Until later.'

'Later?'

'Lupin.'

'Lupin?'

'All this is speculation, as I say, Patron, but it's borne out by what I got from Los Angeles. Lupin got into the tower from the top – that again we know – but then he told Poulex he'd have to tackle the job from the bottom. So he bricked up the hole he'd made at the top and went away. Two or three days later he returned and opened the tower at the bottom and said he'd do what he could. He worked all through the night, you'll remember. Kept Poulex awake. Next day he said it couldn't be done and bricked up *that* hole, too. Then he disappeared. Poulex never saw him again. All this is fact.'

'And it was Lupin who took away the coins?'

'He must have, Patron. He told Poulex the tower was going to collapse, remember. But he had another go in spite of his warning, trying from the bottom. I think when he got in from the top he found the coins, grabbed one or two that he could reach and went off and had them valued. That was the day or two when he disappeared. Then he came back, all bright and smiling, and told Poulex he'd have one last go – from the bottom.'

Darcy grinned. 'He would, wouldn't he? He'd learned that the coins were valuable and there were a lot of them. So he made a hole and wriggled through. He'd got guts, because the tower might well have come down on top of him. But he was only a little guy so he didn't have to make a big hole, and I expect he made sure it wasn't big enough for Poulex to get inside. When he came out he said he felt ill.'

'Well, he would be, wouldn't he, fishing about under a corpse?'

'I don't think for a minute he was ill, Patron. By that time Fouché wasn't much better than a mummy.'

'Did the Los Angeles police provide all this?'

'No. But they did contact his son who told them that about that time his father went to Switzerland. He thinks he opened an account there. He often wondered where he got the money because Swiss accounts are big-time and Lupin was only a bricklayer.'

'And Swiss accounts are also usually dirty money that people don't want anybody to know about.'

'Exactly. Then suddenly the family all took off for America. The son was only young but he's got a good memory. I reckon Lupin scooped the box that contained the coins from under Fouché's body – leaving behind one he missed, which we found. He hid the box in his car or van or whatever he had, and bricked up the tower again without telling Poulex what he'd found. He disappeared back to Goillac, arranged to sell the coins, and having done so, bolted to America before he could be stopped.'

'What happened to him?'

Darcy's grin came again. 'He didn't make his fortune there as we heard,' he said. 'He took it with him.'

Pel sat back in his chair – extra comfortable for chief inspectors and above, to go with the carpet, and the picture on the wall. 'Have you proof?'

'Yes. Now: wherever Lupin obtained his money, he certainly invested it wisely and his family are rich.'

'Go on. And Lupin? Have the Los Angeles police spoken to him?'

'No. Lupin's dead. He died ten years ago. His wife soon after. That's why I talked to the son. He said they were living happily but very ordinarily at Goillac when suddenly, overnight, it seemed to him – he was only a boy at the time – they just packed up and went. He remembers there was no trouble about visas, so you can bet Father Lupin already had enough money in the bank to enable him to do without a work permit. The Americans are pretty fussy about that sort of thing. They just upped and went and when they got there they took an apartment. Soon afterwards they moved to a bigger one and started living in style. Unfortunately, it did for Lupin. He took to the booze.'

'Did the son ever find out where his father's money came from?'

'No. But he often asked. All he got for a reply was that it came from investments. He had a feeling though, that his father had won the national lottery or something and didn't like to admit it, preferring to let people think he'd made it by the sweat of his brow or by his own acuity as an investor. There are, in fact, two children, both now married to Americans and very well off, thank you. The son handles real estate. The daughter ended up as personal assistant to a lawyer whom she later married. They both have children but neither has the foggiest idea where Daddy obtained his money.'

Darcy gave a wry smile. 'We'll never get the money back now, Patron. It's thirty years ago and it was raised by a group of dissident generals to overthrow the government, so none of *them* is in a position to worry about it. The gangsters who stole it are all dead. So is the bricklayer who tried to get it from the tower for them – *and* the bricklayer who finally managed it. It seems his family's enjoying it and it's been put to better use than if the generals had had it. So we might as well forget it. At least it's sorted out and we can now concentrate on Sybille Junot.'

# 19

When Aimedieu appeared at her door, Mrs Briddon was still looking like death warmed up, her face pale enough to be almost green, her nose pink, her eyes hollow. She studied Aimedieu sadly as he entered.

'I thought it was finished,' she said.

Aimedieu gave her a chaste kiss on the forehead, standing well back so she couldn't clutch him. 'It is,' he said.

She turned away. There was a cup of black coffee on the table. 'You see what you've done to me,' she accused.

He tried to look anguished and guilty. 'You'll feel better tonight,' he said. 'Once you've had your first drink, it'll be all right.'

'I shan't feel all right *inside*,' she retorted. 'It won't be the same. In fact, I think I'll leave this place. I think I'll sell. I don't suppose my husband will argue. He never agreed with buying it, anyway.' She paused, took a sip of coffee, and looked reproachfully at Aimedieu. 'Anyway,' she said, 'why have you come back?'

Aimedieu gestured. 'I thought I'd like a photograph,' he said.

'Of me?'

'Just to remember you.'

She looked pleased and even seemed to recover a little. There was a portrait of her standing on a table by the window and she picked it up. It was a studio portrait and flattered her. She obviously thought it was a good one.

'You'd better have this,' she said.

'No.' Aimedieu shook his head. 'I'd prefer a less formal one.

The one I took of you last night at the end of the show, remember.'

She gave him a defeated look. 'I haven't even looked at them yet,' she admitted. 'I wasn't sure I'd be able to see them.'

She rummaged in her handbag and produced the envelope Aimedieu had brought her. Taking out the photographs, she spread them on the table and studied them.

'They're not bad,' Aimedieu said.

'That's the camera,' she said. 'Not me. I was never any good at working out lighting and distance and all the other rubbish so I bought a camera that does it all for you.'

Aimedieu picked up one of the photographs – the one he had taken outside the bar. It showed her beaming at him, bright in the light of the flash with the background dark and only one or two other people in the picture clearly illumined.

'It's not very good,' she said doubtfully. 'The wind's blowing my hair.'

'It's how I remember you,' Aimedieu said. 'It's how I'll always remember you.' It sounded tragic and romantic and she gave him a damp look.

'It needn't happen,' she said hopefully.

'It has to,' Aimedieu said. He had no intention of being involved in some sort of court action against George Briddon over her.

She picked up the other pictures. 'There are one or two good ones of you,' she said.

There should be, Aimedieu decided. She'd taken thirty-five of them and he'd been on almost every one.

As he left, he passed the newsagent's and stationer's under the arcades. Didier was in there talking to Bernard Buffel Bis's sister. He seemed to be considering buying a notebook.

'You seem to get through a lot of them,' she was saying.

'Oh, I don't want to buy one,' Didier said. 'I just wanted to look at a few. Have you sold many of them?'

'*I* haven't,' she said. 'Aunt Bernadine might have. I don't know.'

As Didier emerged, he saw Aimedieu. He stood looking at him for a while, deep in thought, then he started to life. 'Can I have a word with you?' he asked.

Aimedieu eyed the boy, wondering what he had in mind. 'Sure,' he said. 'Let's have a drink.'

As they sat down, Didier was nervous. 'I think I've found a clue,' he said.

'Oh?' Aimedieu regarded him with amusement. 'What about?'

Didier told him. Aimedieu listened carefully then he sat back. 'Told the Old Man?' he asked.

'No.'

'You should. It's your job.'

'My job lately's being a clerk.'

Aimedieu leaned forward, his elbows on the table. 'Your job's learning to be a good cop,' he said. 'And the Old Man, funny as he is, is the best man there is to learn from.'

Didier looked at him. 'Think he'll want to know?'

Aimedieu grinned. 'Well, I'll probably get my backside kicked for interfering,' he said. 'But I'd rather he kicked it for being too helpful than not helpful enough. Why don't we both go and see him?'

That night Pel's wife telephoned to say she was returning home. Madame Routy almost swooned with pleasure, and Pel appeared at the Hôtel de Police the following morning glowing with good humour.

About the time he reached the Hôtel de Police, Didier was calling in at the Lab. Leguyader greeted him unenthusiastically, gave him the plastic envelope containing the ransom note and a file containing two copies of his report on it.

'Inform your Chief', he said, 'that, thanks to his insistence on an immediate report, I was late picking up my family and taking them to the theatre last night.'

Didier couldn't imagine Leguyader at the theatre. He felt sure he would interrupt the play from time to time to put the players right on matters concerning acting, diction, the meaning of words, and the career of the author, all culled from *Encyclopaedia Larousse* the night before.

Leguyader gestured at the plastic envelope. 'The letters were cut from *Le Bien Public,*' he said. 'Local rag. Same paper. Same type. At least it shows somebody reads it. Can't think why. Stuck on with Gu, which is a product from Korea containing plastic. Very effective. I use it myself. There were no fingerprints. The sheet was torn from a notebook which was doubtless bought at the Nouvelles Galeries. Cheap. Easily obtained. Shops sell dozens a day – especially now, when the schools are due to reopen and the pupils are gathering their books, paper and pencils. Assure your Chief that it contains nothing that could possibly be of any use to him.'

'What about the footprint?' Didier asked. 'Doesn't that tell us anything?'

'Only that somebody put his large foot on it. Large shoe. Impossible to tell exactly what size. In fact, it was a sneaker. The sort of thing the young are wearing all the time these days, so it will be impossible to identify. Scruffy things. In my day it was black shoes, smart shirt, tie and hat. Take it to Chief Inspector Pel, give him my compliments and tell him I hope it chokes him.'

When Didier reached the office, Darcy was frowning at a list of names which had finally arrived from the Lycée at Vonnas. It wasn't complete and only included the names of those pupils who had attended the Lycée for the first three years of the period they wanted checking. There seemed to be hundreds and they were all written out in longhand.

'No wonder they took so long,' Darcy was complaining. 'All common or garden names and, at first glance, there doesn't seem to be anything significant about any of them.'

As Didier laid Leguyader's report on his desk, Pel bent to examine it. Didier coughed. Pel bent closer. Didier coughed again.

'Something stuck in your gullet, *mon brave*?' Pel asked. 'A bone, perhaps? It can happen. Didn't they have to rush the Queen Mother of England to hospital a year or so ago? Fish bone in her throat. Bolting her food, I suppose.'

'No, sir.' Didier coughed again. 'It's not that. But I saw that ransom note in the Lab. It was on the table and I got a chance to study it. I got a good look at it. I noticed something.'

'About the message?'

'Not about the message. About the paper.'

Pel eyed him shrewdly. 'Something Leguyader missed?'

'Yes, Patron.'

Pel sat up. He had been joking and hadn't been expecting 'yes' for an answer. This was one for the book. Next time Leguyader tried to tell him the police couldn't function without the Lab, he'd be able to retort with the information that the Lab couldn't function without the sharp eyes of the police – even those of the lowliest cadet. He hoped what was being offered was good.

'Inform me,' he said.

'It was on a page torn from a notebook, Patron.'

'That we know. So?'

'One edge of the paper was faded.'

'Yes?'

'Well, a little while ago I had to buy an extra notebook. Inspector Darcy gave me a dressing down for not having a spare, and I went across to the shop in the square at Puycel-dome and bought one.'

'And?'

Didier laid the notebook he'd acquired on the counter. Pel studied it. One edge was faded, the colour of the blue lines paler, the paper slightly browner.

'Tell me more,' he suggested.

'That's where I met Bernadette Buffel. The shopkeeper's her aunt.'

'Everybody there's related.'

'Yes, Patron. We got talking. She apologised because the notebook had faded a bit. They'd had it in stock a long time and it had been sitting on a shelf in the sun. They don't sell a lot of things. Most people go into Goillac to do their shopping at the supermarket there. I said it didn't matter because it was just important I had a notebook.'

'Because your senior officer had just given you a dressing down for not having a spare?'

'Yes, Patron. But I noticed that the ransom demand note's faded in exactly the same way. Along the same edge.'

'And what conclusion did you reach?'

'That it had come from the same shop, even the same pile.'

Pel was silent for a moment. 'I trust', he said eventually, 'that you made out a good case for yourself. Nasty-minded superior officer. Long-suffering cadet. And that the young lady was duly sympathetic and in the end agreed to take a walk with you.'

Didier was silent. Pel looked up at him.

'No matter,' he said. 'It happens to us all when we're young. If nothing else, it shows you can use your brain. When you've learned to be patient and suffer the knocks fortune gives you in the shape of boring jobs, inconstant young women and unpleasant elderly inspectors, you have the makings of a policeman. You'd be wasted as a clerk in a railway station. In the meantime, we'll say nothing of the fact that you were in Puyceldome when you probably weren't supposed to be.'

As Pel was enjoying himself at Didier's expense, the troops were gathering.

During the course of all enquiries there had to be times when everybody was brought together to discuss what had happened. It was the time when the superior officers were able to lay down the general direction of their thoughts, and when the junior officers, those who did the leg work, had an opportunity to produce any thoughts *they* might have had. Pel believed firmly in his conferences and so did the Chief, who held his own regularly, and this was an emergency one called hurriedly because of the circumstances. Pel's brain was ticking away like clockwork and Didier's disclosure had set things in motion. The local cops had been given instructions to keep their eyes open and report on movements while Pel's men were brought in at a rush to see what they had to contribute. Among Pel's team were one or two bright boys who occasionally did a bit of thinking and on more than one occasion they had changed the direction of an enquiry. As Brisard had said, it was team spirit, but not quite as Brisard visualised it. *He* liked to see himself directing and everybody else jumping to attention.

Pel's conferences were always free and easy affairs but this one concerned two vicious murders and a kidnapping – never a formula for calm. The demise of Alfred Fouché had been removed from the list, of course. They were never going to get any further with that now, and the police at Goillac had been informed of what had happened and, what was more, that the credit for sorting the affair out would go into Pel's statistics not theirs.

Darcy gave them the latest on the affair at Puyceldome, then they turned to the other cases.

'We've got names,' Nosjean said. 'One of them's called Gabrielle and the other's Sonia.'

'Not much to go on,' the Chief observed. 'No surnames?'

'Nothing definite, sir. The names they gave at the hostel at St Just were false and the hostel didn't know what their real ones were. But one of the staff, a girl called Jeannette Rebichon, came forward. She's employed in the office. She heard about our enquiry and she realised the names they'd given were wrong. Apparently the older of the two girls dropped her shoulder bag in the hall as they were leaving and her belongings spilled out. The Rebichon girl helped her pick them up and she got a glimpse of her identity card. Her surname appeared to be Dufort or Durand or Dunois. She wasn't sure which but when she heard of our enquiry and the names that had been passed on to us, she felt she had to contact us.'

'Have you checked?' Pel asked.

'As far as we can, Patron. But there are a lot of names begining with "Du" – Durand, Dufort, Dugast, Ducret, Dubois. There are hundreds of them.'

Pel said nothing and Nosjean became silent. He was still at a bit of a loss. He had the names and he had the movements of the owners up to and just after the murders of Vienne and Burges. After that they had lost them and he could only assume they had gone to ground somewhere and were lying low. They had questioned every contact of Vienne in the hope that his murderers might have been known to him. In Burges' case he had obviously simply been doing his duty and couldn't possibly have had any personal connections with his killers. But they had studied Vienne's papers and his diary, and checked every single telephone number they had found. Most of them turned out to be business contacts but one or two seemed to be thinly disguised names of girls. One number alongside the name 'Jacques', turned out to belong to a girl by the name of

Jacqueline. Another girl was listed as the name of a firm. It had become clear that Vienne had had an eye for the main chance sexually, and they had turned up a number of female contacts who clearly existed for him for no other reason but for overnight stops when he was away from his wife. He had them all over the west and south of France.

'But we put out a request for information,' Nosjean explained. 'Asking if anyone knew a girl – Christian name Gabrielle, surname beginning with "Du" – aged about nineteen, who'd been involved with the police. We found one who called herself Gabrielle Dufort. Her papers are believed to be false though. She was known to be strong-willed. She had a sister and two brothers but she was able to reduce all of them and her mother to tears – separately or all together. She was known to have tried hard drugs while still very young and liked watching violent and porno videos and films and reading books about violence and sex. She worked for a time as a hairdresser but it didn't last. Even before she entered her teens the family was unable to exercise any control over her. Finally, she ran away. She was placed in a home for delinquents and it was there she met another girl – name Sonia Gaum – and they joined forces and became a formidable team, too much even for the authorities. I think they're the girls we want.'

Nosjean turned a sheet of his notebook. 'Both – either accidentally or deliberately as a means of escaping – somehow contracted venereal disease and were transferred to hospital for treatment. From there they escaped – three months before two girls answering their description were seen in Beaune purchasing butchers' knives. They'd taken with them money they'd stolen or bullied from other prisoners. They were good at that sort of thing. But the money they took wasn't much and they were in need of more and they obviously decided it was worth murdering to obtain it. All we have to do now is find them.'

They discussed the Vienne and Burges cases as far as they could then turned to the kidnapping of Sybille Junot. Dunoisse, from Treffort, and his deputy were present and Darcy had a pile of papers in front of him containing the names from the Lycées at Guinchay and Vonnas. He wasn't looking forward to the job of sorting them out, and the belief that the kidnapping was somehow connected to the murder cases was still only a hunch rather than a fact.

It was about this time that Aimedieu produced the drawings he'd bought from Serge Vitiello, doctored a little here and there by himself and the artist.

'Where did you get these?' Nosjean asked sharply.

'Puyceldome. Artist there drew them.'

'He copied the Photofits?'

Aimedieu shook his head. 'He drew them from life.' His smile grew more self-satisfied as he laid the photograph he'd taken of Ellen Briddon on the table. He'd had Photography blow it up.

Pel stared at it. 'Pretty,' he said. 'So?'

'Look at it carefully, Patron.'

Pel did. 'I see a woman,' he said. 'A pretty woman. Madame Briddon, I believe. You've been paying her a lot of attention, I hear.'

The bugger had eyes in the back of his head, Aimedieu decided. 'Only as far as the job permitted, Patron,' he said. 'I got a lot of information from her.'

'Nothing else?'

'No, Patron.'

'So, why the photograph?'

'Look at the background, Patron. It's Puyceldome. It shows members of the Molière Company who gave the medieval show there. Quite clearly.'

'Sinking beers.'

'Without their make-up, Patron.'

'What's that supposed to mean?'

'Look at the girls, Patron.' Aimedieu's finger fell on one of the faces. 'She's not wearing glasses. She took them off because they didn't wear specs in the Middle Ages. She has thin eyebrows and the other one, you'll notice, has thin lips. Their appearance around Puyceldome was always assisted by make-up. But in the photograph they've wiped that make-up off with the make-up they put on for the show and, because they thought nobody was looking at them and it was dark, perhaps because they'd had a drink or two, they haven't replaced what was underneath. It was taken with Madame Briddon's camera. By flash.'

'Did she take it?'

'No, I did.'

'Deliberately?'

'Chiefly to please Madame Briddon, Patron. I didn't realise its importance at first.' Aimedieu's finger jabbed again. 'This one always wore glasses round Puyceldome. Here she isn't wearing them.'

'Go on.'

Aimedieu gestured at the picture. 'Those glasses she wore didn't magnify,' he said. 'They're just property glasses. The sort people wear on stage. I've seen her reading without them and I once saw them on the table resting on a newspaper. They did nothing for the print. She didn't need them. They were just a disguise, Patron. I think they're the girls Nosjean's after.'

Pel studied Aimedieu. He didn't like praising the younger members of his team too much in case it went to their heads and they started demanding extra pay, promotion or just time off, but this time he felt Aimedieu deserved a word. He hadn't just stumbled on something. He'd used his eyes and his head.

'I think that was very perceptive of you, *mon brave*,' he said. 'You may well be right.'

Praise from Pel was praise indeed. Aimedieu felt two metres tall.

'Well, you know the descriptions, Patron,' he went on. 'The tall one was blonde. Well, now she's dark. And the smaller one who was dark is now gingerish. They were also said to have been well developed – '

'So how do we account for girls with big boobs now being a different shape?' Darcy asked.

'Binding.' Aimedieu had looked it up. 'From time to time women appear on the stage as boys or men. They flatten themselves.'

'Does this Remarque character climb into bed with them?'

'Not with the Daydé girl. I once talked to him about his family. I asked him how he came to be an actor. He mentioned he had two sisters, and a brother who went to Canada. One sister married, the other had a row with the family and walked out. Isn't that what Nosjean's Gabrielle Dufort did? She had a sister and two brothers. Same family as Remarque. It came together when Remarque picked a quarrel with young Didier over Bernard Buffel's granddaughter. Remarque isn't his name. His name's Pierre Dupont.'

Darcy looked up quickly. 'Dupont? You're sure?'

'I saw his papers. The local cop demanded to see them. They were made out in the name of Pierre Dupont. He calls himself Remarque for the stage. His real name's Dupont and, I reckon, so is hers.'

There was a long silence as Aimedieu became silent.

'She's his sister, Patron, I bet,' he went on. 'When they murdered Vienne they moved back north for safety and Burges bumped into them and they did for him with Vienne's gun. So what then? They had to go out of circulation for a bit. They'd been on drugs and probably still were, so the obvious place to head for was where they could be certain of safety – Big Brother's. They took the place of two girls who left. Since I'd never seen the first two I assumed they were the same girls. Especially as they used the same names and turned up with a third girl as if they were all together. The other girl left – probably because Remarque tried to get into her bed, probably because she suspected something fishy was going on and decided she was best out of it. It was sheer chance they all arrived together and I didn't associate them with Nosjean's case.'

Pel said nothing and Aimedieu went on. 'They could even fit into the acting lark. Dupont, or whatever she's called, knew how to play a guitar and sing and do tricks. She could even do a bit of juggling. She did it with her brother when they were young. He said so. The only one without any experience was the Flichy girl – Sonia Gaum – and she didn't have much to do but sing and dance. It was awful. But it didn't look awful because it was medieval and, if you ask me, everything medieval's awful.'

There was a ripple of laughter then De Troq' spoke.

'I think Aimedieu's right,' he said firmly. 'I think this type, Remarque, follows Speedy Sam and Philippe Douanet, known as Gorgeous. Douanet told me he was a carpenter and that he'd done a course in design at the Technical College, but when I enquired, it turned out to be stage design. He'd built stage sets and it seems he knew Marceau because Marceau painted the flats he'd built. And they were both at the Théâtre des Beaux Arts at the same time as this Remarque type. I let Douanet out and followed him to see where he went. He went to Puyceldome the night of the show. Marceau was there, too – fixing some sort of screen he'd painted to hide the band. They went into the bar and this Remarque type joined them.' De Troq' gestured. 'Who better for the job, Patron? Dupont gets around, arranging his little shows.'

Pel lit a cigarette and drew on it slowly, almost as though he were trying to make it last all day. 'Could one of these two girls have been the old school friend Sybille Junot said she met?' he asked quietly.

They all became silent again as they were suddenly presented with a whole new can of worms. Darcy furiously began to rummage through the lists of names from Guinchay and Vonnas.

'If only the buggers would put them in alphabetical order,' he said. Then he slapped the sheets. 'There's one here!' he said. 'Gabrielle Dupont! Same town. Same school, too, Patron.'

'They probably *did* know the girl,' Pel said. 'And they were surprised when they met her in the Chemin des Marguerites at Treffort.'

'They probably weren't thinking of kidnap then, though, Patron,' Darcy said. 'Not at first. Probably just thinking of lying low at Puyceldome under Big Brother's wing. All they probably thought was envy at Sybille Junot having come into money. But then – or soon afterwards – it dawned on them what she was worth.'

'What do you think, Nosjean?'

'Girls don't usually go in for kidnapping, Patron.'

'They don't usually go in for murder,' Darcy said sharply. 'But these two did. Twice.'

'They're certainly known to be vicious,' Nosjean agreed. 'They're also known to be tough.'

'If they're vicious enough to murder,' Pel said, 'they'd be vicious enough to kidnap someone. Especially Sybille Junot, who's small and slight. She must have bumped into them on the bridle-path as they were making their way back north. They'd probably taken it after they shot Burges to get away from the main roads where we were looking for them. She mentioned meeting an old school friend.'

Darcy took up the story. 'And the old school friend had a friend with her. They exchanged the time of day, probably even tried to borrow money off her. She might even have given them some, except that she never carried any. But as she rode off, they started thinking. She'd doubtless told them why she was there and the following day they waited for her, dragged her from the saddle, bundled her into a car and drove her away.'

'Only one thing wrong with that idea, Patron,' Nosjean said drily. 'They couldn't drive. They'd been in institutions since they were old enough to drive, so they never learned.'

'The Dupont girl's learning now,' Aimedieu pointed out. 'Fast, too, I dare bet. She'll be hell on wheels when she can. Literally.'

Pel was still mulling things over. 'You can't kidnap a girl on your own,' he pointed out. 'Not even a child. An adult would require three or even four. One to drive, two to bundle the victim into the car. Another to be ready with a blanket to throw over her.'

'If the Dupont girl knew her brother was on drugs,' De Troq' said, 'she could easily blackmail him into helping.'

'*Did* they blackmail him into helping? Or was *he* the force behind it?'

'Not on your life, Patron,' Nosjean said firmly. 'That would be the Dupont girl.'

'She's only nineteen!'

'She's a tough nineteen,' Aimedieu said. 'I think her brother's scared stiff of her.'

'Can we be certain it's her?'

'I have their fingerprints,' Aimedieu said. 'I lifted a glass ashtray they'd been using.'

'Somebody round here,' Pel observed drily, 'has been using a lot of brains and initiative. So they took her and hid her. Where?'

Didier, who had been taking notes, sat bolt upright. 'She's the ghost!' he said.

They all looked at him.

'What ghost?'

'Bernadette Buffel told me her grandfather had heard noises. He said it sounded like wailing. Perhaps it was Sybille Junot shouting for help.'

'Patron – ' Aimedieu leaned forward. 'Le Bernard told me he saw Remarque – Dupont, if you like – and his pals arrive home one night carrying a heavy property basket. I bet Sybille Junot was inside. That was the night the third girl was away so the coast would be clear.' His eyes were gleaming. 'There's another thing, Patron. I once saw seven plates of food at their place. There were six of them at the time. They said the extra one was for a dog. I never saw a dog there.'

Pel rose. 'I think', he said slowly, pushing a packet of cigarettes into his pocket, 'that it's time we went to see our friend. Remarque, or whatever he's called. Alfred Fouché's body was in the Cat Tower for thirty years without being discovered. So why shouldn't Sybille Junot be concealed somewhere there, too?'

# 20

Puyceldome seemed empty as the two car loads of men roared in.

Stuffing the vehicles hard up against the arcades, they moved in ones and twos into the Rue Nobel where they paused outside the door of the narrow-gutted little house rented by the Molière Company.

'That's a thick door,' Pel said, eyeing it. 'Let's make sure that once they open it, they don't get a chance to close it. We don't want a hostage situation.'

'Shove your foot in, Aimedieu,' Darcy said. 'It's big enough.'

As Pel nodded, Darcy hammered on the door. There was a long pause then they heard a key being turned. As the door opened a fraction, Darcy got his shoulder to it and it swung open, sending Remarque flying. As he rolled over, Aimedieu barged in.

The single room was as untidy as usual and contained Béranger, Gus Blivet and the Flichy girl. De Troq' pushed Remarque in to join them. The girl Puyceldome had known as Mercédes Flichy was at the table writing on a theatre programme with a pen – in violet ink. The glasses she normally wore lay on the table. Alongside them was a riding whip.

Darcy snatched the sheet from under her hand. 'Violet ink,' he said. 'Same as the underlining on the ransom note.'

Remarque/Dupont and his friends seemed frozen, but the girl gave a cry that was almost a snarl and reached for a drawer in the table. As she straightened up, she had a pistol in her hand. As she turned, Darcy sent her reeling with a backhand swipe and the gun went flying. Aimedieu wrenched her to her feet and Darcy picked up the gun.

'Vienne's?' Pel asked.

'Same number, Patron,' Darcy said. 'I expect we'll find it's the one that did for Burges. We'll probably find a few other things belonging to him here, too.'

'Where's the other girl?' Pel said, rounding on Dupont. 'Gabrielle Dupont. Where is she?'

'She's not here.'

'She's your sister, isn't she?'

Dupont paused, then he nodded.

'I told you not to let the bitches hide here!' Gus Blivet yelled.

'Where is she?' Pel persisted as Aimedieu pushed them apart.

'She's not here. She went out.'

'Where's Sybille Junot?'

'Who?'

Darcy grabbed Dupont by his shirt and half lifted him to his toes. 'We know you've got her somewhere – '

'Patron!' It was Didier who had been poking around in the shadows. 'There's a door behind this screen!'

'Right.' Pel gestured to Aimedieu. 'Open up, Aimedieu. Didier, stand back.'

But Didier didn't wait for Aimedieu and wrenched at the door. It was locked but there was a huge iron key on a hook in the wall. Grabbing it and inserting it in the lock, he started twisting. As he did so, they heard a cry from somewhere beyond. Heaving the door open, Didier stepped forward into a passage that lay behind.

There was a long corridor and, pressed on by Aimedieu, through another door he found himself in a small bare chamber. Then, in the light from the living-room that filtered down the passage, diffused by the old stonework, he became aware of someone crouching in the shadows.

'Don't.' The voice was a girl's. 'Don't hit me!'

'It's the police,' Aimedieu said.

The next thing Didier knew, the figure had thrown itself at him and, to his startled amazement, he found himself holding a totally naked girl who clutched him, sobbing and half out of her mind with terror.

'We've found her, Patron,' Aimedieu called.

In the few moments before Pel arrived, Didier realised that the girl's flesh was icy cold and that she was filthy dirty. One eye was swollen and her hair hung over her face in damp rats' tails. Her body was covered with bruises and her buttocks and the backs of her thighs had livid weals on them as if she'd been whipped.

'Surely to God – ' The voice was Pel's, brisk, no-nonsense and imperative. ' – one of you idiots can find something to put round her.'

Aimedieu snatched up a dirty blanket from a scruffy bed Didier could see in a corner and with Didier's help wrapped it round the sobbing girl.

'She kept hitting me,' she said.

'Who did?'

'The big one.'

Darcy fished out a flask – trust Darcy to have a flask, Pel thought – and persuaded the girl to take a sip from it. Instead she took a swallow and started coughing. As she almost collapsed, Didier clung to her, suddenly feeling like a knight in shining armour. His arm round her, he helped her along the corridor to the living-room where Nosjean and De Troq' had the others lined up against the wall. Darcy glared at them and, without thinking, he took a swing at Dupont and sent him reeling.

'You bastards!' he snapped. 'The magistrates can only send you to gaol for life. That's not enough for what you've done. I'd happily see you guillotined. I'd even pull the lever myself.'

'Cut it out!' Pel snapped.

'I'd like to do it to the lot of them, Patron,' Darcy growled. 'Someone's tortured her. I'd enjoy doing it. They never intended to free her. We'd have found her eventually in a ditch. She'll remember this to the end of her days. An ordeal of this sort doesn't finish when she's rescued.' He stopped and gestured speechlessly at the sobbing girl.

Pel stared coldly at the four lined up against the wall. Without her spectacles, the Flichy girl might almost have been described as pretty, apart from the bitter expression on her face. No wonder she hadn't been recognised. None of the men who had picked her up had been able to give a good description of her or her companion. Only Vienne and Burges had probably been able to take a good look at the two girls, and neither of them had lived long enough to pass on a description.

'Not difficult to disguise themselves,' Aimedieu said. 'They had the contents of the property and make-up box to go at.'

'Gabrielle Dupont had worked as a hairdresser,' Nosjean added.

'And her brother was a make-up man.'

As they talked, they heard a step outside and the heavy street door was flung open. Framed in the opening was Gabrielle Dupont and in that instant they saw the similarity in her features and those of her brother. For a second the tableau was frozen. Didier felt the girl he was holding cringe in his arms then he saw the startled expression of Gabrielle Dupont's face dissolve in a flash into one of fury and, with a swing of her arm, she flung the door to. Aimedieu was just springing forward to grab her and it hit him in the face and sent him reeling back to knock Darcy flying into Nosjean and De Troq'. As they wrenched the door open again and started running, Didier heard a car door slam and an engine scream as it revved up.

The policemen bursting out into the alleyway saw the white Peugeot brake start away with spinning wheels and protesting tyres. Reaching the square, they saw it head into the Rue Goillac which led down the hill, then they were racing for the police cars to set off in pursuit.

The white brake spun away, its rear end swinging, and as it disappeared down the Rue Goillac, Le Bernard, who was just coming out of his house, stepped back in such a hurry he tripped over the lintel and fell flat on his back, his feet in the air. A wooden-framed stall, a relic of the medieval night, was knocked into flying pieces of timber as the wing of the brake hit it. A woman snatched a couple of children back into an alley.

Gabrielle Dupont had managed to learn how to drive a car but it was clear her experience didn't stretch to handling a big vehicle at speed. The Peugeot was disappearing down the Rue Goillac in a snaking route and several times they saw dust and sparks leap from the stone of the ancient walls as the swinging rear end hit them. Then it vanished round the corner with shrieking tyres and began the swift descent down the winding road to the plain.

The police car was close behind. De Troq' was handling the wheel, but he was a good driver and despite his speed he was careful to watch what he was doing. The brake, driven by an inexperienced girl, was hurtling towards the plain at a tremendous rate, even gaining on the men in the police car. Then as it reached The Cat's Jump, the wing hit the wall again and the brake went into a series of uncontrolled swerves.

'She's going over,' Darcy yelled.

The brake swung back to the centre of the road and they could see Gabrielle Dupont, her hair flying, heaving desperately at the wheel. The brake hit the wall again, sent stones and pieces of fence whirring away, then it shot out into space, shedding parts in an incredible leap. As De Troq' jammed on the brakes and the police car screamed to a halt, they saw the brake smash on to the rocky slopes below. Pieces of metal whipped through the air, a wheel detached itself from the rolling bundle and went bounding down the hillside as if it were alive, then, looking as if some giant hand had folded it in two, the brake stopped rolling and burst into flames.

As they climbed out of the police car and ran to the wall, a second car containing Nosjean and Aimedieu slid to a halt behind them. Darcy stared into the valley at the rolling black cloud of rubber smoke beginning to spiral into the air.

'It's yours, Nosjean,' he said. 'I think you and De Troq' can handle it. She was your case, anyway. Turn your car round, Aimedieu. Take me back. I think two will be enough and I suspect the Chief will need the rest of us up there.'

When Darcy returned, Sybille Junot had stopped sobbing but she still had Didier's arm round her as if, recognising him as of her own age and generation, she had refused to leave his side. Dr Mercier from across the square was with her and an ambulance had arrived at the end of the Rue Nobel. Dupont and the others had vanished. Mercier had insisted they went first. 'I'm thinking of her sanity,' he explained.

He looked at the girl clinging to Didier. 'She'll be all right in a while,' he said. 'But you were the first person she saw. She'll let you go eventually.'

'It doesn't matter,' Didier said, willing to hold the girl until Doomsday if necessary.

'I always knew when they were all going out,' she was whispering. 'Because they always tied my hands and feet. I tried to shout for help. But they always said nobody would ever hear me.'

'We're going to take you to hospital,' Mercier said. 'And then we'll send for your parents. You're safe now.'

They got her on her feet and, with the blanket still wrapped round her, helped her down the alleyway to the ambulance.

'Get hold of Claudie,' Pel said quietly to Aimedieu. 'I want her at the hospital. It's a woman she wants, not a great hairy policeman.'

As they walked, the girl stumbled and Didier instinctively swept her up into his arms. She was only slight and her cheek rested against his.

He put her down as they reached the ambulance but as she stood upright she turned and looked beseechingly at him. She was still clutching his hand as if she intended never to let it go. Mercier recognised the symptoms.

'I think he'd better go with her,' he said to Pel. 'She's still confused and frightened. She's been pretty badly treated and she must have been frozen and terrified in that cellar in the dark. He's the one she associates with security. Let him stay near her until her parents arrive and a policewoman turns up.'

Pel gestured. Didier climbed into the back of the ambulance. Even then, the girl refused to lie down and, instead, sat upright, still in the dirty blanket, still clinging to Didier as the vehicle drew away.

A few days later Pel headed from the Hôtel de Police to his car. It was over. Not one case but two. Paperwork, as Didier had been informed in no uncertain terms on several occasions, took time, but it was done now.

They'd even got the name of the big boy who had been

supplying Dupont, Speedy Sam and the boy called Gorgeous, and the Marseilles police had picked up a nice little crop of criminals and a haul of cocaine. They had thought the Cat Tower case was the complicated one but it had turned out instead to be the murder on the N6.

It was all a bit of luck really. But then there was always an element of luck in police work. If the body in the tower hadn't turned up, they'd never have been at Puyceldome and therefore would never have found the two murderous girls. A bit of luck, a lot of hard work, some inspiration and, above all, team spirit. Team spirit – plus party spirit, because if Ellen Briddon hadn't wanted to join in the celebrations in the ancient *bastide*, she'd never have wanted to put out a flag. And if she hadn't, there'd have been no need for a flagstaff, and in the end no hole in the Cat Tower and no collapse. The Chief was pleased at the teamwork, and so was Pel because it was *his* team.

He arrived home early, set up a chair in the garden, then went indoors to pour himself a whisky, full of the thought that his wife was due home the following day. As he reappeared he was surprised to see Didier in the drive talking to Yves Pasquier, the small boy from next door.

'Hello, *mon brave*,' he said. 'Come to see Aunt Routy?'

'Sort of,' Didier said.

'It's over now,' Pel said. 'Even the paperwork.'

'Yes.' Didier blushed. 'I'm sorry about that.' He paused. 'I went to Treffort to see Sybille Junot,' he added.

'Oh?'

Didier was offhand. 'Just to see how she was getting on.'

'Your concern becomes you. Police officers should always show as much interest in the victim as in the criminal. She's also a pretty girl. Interested?'

Didier shrugged. 'Not really. I also called at Puyceldome to see Bernard Buffel Bis. His sister was there.'

'Ah!'

Didier grinned. 'There's also a new girl in the typing pool in the Palais de Justice. Blonde.' He held out his hand. 'About this tall.'

Pel gave him a sharp look, aware that his leg was being

pulled. But if nothing else, Didier seemed to have got over his problems.

'Then,' the boy went on, 'I thought I'd come round here to see Madame Pel.'

'She's not here till tomorrow.'

Didier grinned. 'In that case, Patron, I'll have to make do with you.'

Pel looked at him gravely. If he hadn't been Pel he might even have smiled. 'Fancy a game of boules?' he asked.

Didier shrugged. 'Wouldn't mind.'

'We'll play a three-hander.' Pel gestured at the small boy from next door. 'This is Yves,' he said. 'He's no mean hand with boules. Yves, this is Didier Darras. We used to play boules a lot. He's a policeman.'

Yves' eyes glowed. 'Honest?' He looked at Didier. 'I'm going to be a policeman when I grow up,' he announced. 'What's it like?'

Pel waited, his breath stilled in his throat. Then Didier replied.

'It's all right,' he said.

As he spoke he glanced at Pel. Pel knew exactly what the look meant. All was well again.